Love to the Rescue

Acclaim for Radclyffe's Fiction

"***Dangerous Waters*** is a bumpy ride through a devastating time with powerful events and resolute characters. Radclyffe gives us the strong, dedicated women we love to read in a story that keeps us turning pages until the end."—*Lambda Literary Review*

"Radclyffe's ***Dangerous Waters*** has the feel of a tense television drama, as the narrative interchanges between hurricane trackers and first responders. Sawyer and Dara butt heads in the beginning as each moves for some level of control during the storm's approach, and the interference of a lovely television reporter adds an engaging love triangle threat to the sexual tension brewing between them."—*RT Book Reviews*

"***Love After Hours***, the fourth in Radclyffe's Rivers Community series, evokes the sense of a continuing drama as Gina and Carrie's slow-burning romance intertwines with details of other Rivers residents. They become part of a greater picture where friends and family support each other in personal and recreational endeavors. Vivid settings and characters draw in the reader…"—*RT Book Reviews*

Secret Hearts "delivers exactly what it says on the tin: poignant story, sweet romance, great characters, chemistry and hot sex scenes. Radclyffe knows how to pen a good lesbian romance."—*LezReviewBooks Blog*

Wild Shores "will hook you early. Radclyffe weaves a chance encounter into all-out steamy romance. These strong, dynamic women have great conversations, and fantastic chemistry."—*The Romantic Reader Blog*

In **2016 RWA/OCC Book Buyers Best award winner for suspense and mystery with romantic elements *Price of Honor*** "Radclyffe is master of the action-thriller series…The old familiar characters are there, but enough new blood is introduced to give it a fresh feel and open new avenues for intrigue."—*Curve Magazine*

In ***Prescription for Love*** "Radclyffe populates her small town with colorful characters, among the most memorable being Flann's little sister, Margie, and Abby's 15-year-old trans son, Blake…This romantic drama has plenty of heart and soul."—*Publishers Weekly*

2013 RWA/New England Bean Pot award winner for contemporary romance *Crossroads* "will draw the reader in and make her heart ache, willing the two main characters to find love and a life together. It's a story that lingers long after coming to 'the end.'"—*Lambda Literary*

In **2012 RWA/FTHRW Lories and RWA HODRW Aspen Gold award winner *Firestorm*** "Radclyffe brings another hot lesbian romance for her readers."—*The Lesbrary*

Foreword Review Book of the Year finalist and IPPY silver medalist *Trauma Alert* "is hard to put down and it will sizzle in the reader's hands. The characters are hot, the sex scenes explicit and explosive, and the book is moved along by an interesting plot with well drawn secondary characters. The real star of this show is the attraction between the two characters, both of whom resist and then fall head over heels."
—*Lambda Literary Reviews*

Lambda Literary Award Finalist *Best Lesbian Romance 2010* features "stories [that] are diverse in tone, style, and subject, making for more variety than in many, similar anthologies…well written, each containing a satisfying, surprising twist. Best Lesbian Romance series editor Radclyffe has assembled a respectable crop of 17 authors for this year's offering."—*Curve Magazine*

2010 Prism award winner and ForeWord Review Book of the Year Award finalist *Secrets in the Stone* is "so powerfully [written] that the worlds of these three women shimmer between reality and dreams…A strong, must read novel that will linger in the minds of readers long after the last page is turned."—*Just About Write*

In **Benjamin Franklin Award finalist *Desire by Starlight*** "Radclyffe writes romance with such heart and her down-to-earth characters not only come to life but leap off the page until you feel like you know them. What Jenna and Gard feel for each other is not only a spark but an inferno and, as a reader, you will be washed away in this tumultuous romance until you can do nothing but succumb to it."—*Queer Magazine Online*

Lambda Literary Award winner *Stolen Moments* "is a collection of steamy stories about women who just couldn't wait. It's sex when desire overrides reason, and it's incredibly hot!"—*On Our Backs*

Lambda Literary Award winner *Distant Shores, Silent Thunder* "weaves an intricate tapestry about passion and commitment between lovers. The story explores the fragile nature of trust and the sanctuary provided by loving relationships."—*Sapphic Reader*

Lambda Literary Award Finalist *Justice Served* delivers a "crisply written, fast-paced story with twists and turns and keeps us guessing until the final explosive ending."—*Independent Gay Writer*

Lambda Literary Award finalist *Turn Back Time* "is filled with wonderful love scenes, which are both tender and hot."—*MegaScene*

Applause for L.L. Raand's Midnight Hunters Series

The Midnight Hunt
RWA 2012 VCRW Laurel Wreath winner *Blood Hunt*
Night Hunt
The Lone Hunt

"Raand has built a complex world inhabited by werewolves, vampires, and other paranormal beings…Raand has given her readers a complex plot filled with wonderful characters as well as insight into the hierarchy of Sylvan's pack and vampire clans. There are many plot twists and turns, as well as erotic sex scenes in this riveting novel that keep the pages flying until its satisfying conclusion."—*Just About Write*

"Once again, I am amazed at the storytelling ability of L.L. Raand aka Radclyffe. In *Blood Hunt*, she mixes high levels of sheer eroticism that will leave you squirming in your seat with an impeccable multi-character storyline all streaming together to form one great read." —*Queer Magazine Online*

"*The Midnight Hunt* has a gripping story to tell, and while there are also some truly erotic sex scenes, the story always takes precedence. This is a great read which is not easily put down nor easily forgotten."—*Just About Write*

"Are you sick of the same old hetero vampire/werewolf story plastered in every bookstore and at every movie theater? Well, I've got the cure to your werewolf fever. *The Midnight Hunt* is first in, what I hope is, a long-running series of fantasy erotica for L.L. Raand (aka Radclyffe)."—*Queer Magazine Online*

"Any reader familiar with Radclyffe's writing will recognize the author's style within *The Midnight Hunt*, yet at the same time it is most definitely a new direction. The author delivers an excellent story here, one that is engrossing from the very beginning. Raand has pieced together an intricate world, and provided just enough details for the reader to become enmeshed in the new world. The action moves quickly throughout the book and it's hard to put down."—*Three Dollar Bill Reviews*

By Radclyffe

The Provincetown Tales

Safe Harbor
Beyond the Breakwater
Distant Shores, Silent Thunder
Storms of Change
Winds of Fortune
Returning Tides
Sheltering Dunes

PMC Hospitals Romances

Passion's Bright Fury (prequel)
Fated Love
Night Call
Crossroads
Passionate Rivals

Rivers Community Romances

Against Doctor's Orders
Prescription for Love
Love on Call
Love After Hours
Love to the Rescue

Honor Series

Above All, Honor
Honor Bound
Love & Honor
Honor Guards
Honor Reclaimed
Honor Under Siege
Word of Honor
Oath of Honor
(First Responders)
Code of Honor
Price of Honor

Justice Series

A Matter of Trust (prequel)
Shield of Justice
In Pursuit of Justice
Justice in the Shadows
Justice Served
Justice for All

First Responders Novels

Trauma Alert
Firestorm
Taking Fire
Wild Shores
Heart Stop
Dangerous Waters

Romances

Innocent Hearts
Promising Hearts
Love's Melody Lost
Love's Tender Warriors
Tomorrow's Promise
Love's Masquerade
shadowland
Turn Back Time
When Dreams Tremble
The Lonely Hearts Club
Secrets in the Stone
Desire by Starlight
Homestead
The Color of Love
Secret Hearts

Short Fiction

Collected Stories by Radclyffe
Erotic Interludes: *Change Of Pace*
Radical Encounters

Stacia Seaman and Radclyffe, eds.:
Erotic Interludes Vol. 2–5
Romantic Interludes Vol. 1–2
Breathless: *Tales of Celebration*
Women of the Dark Streets
Amor and More: Love Everafter
Myth & Magic: Queer Fairy Tales

Writing As L.L. Raand

Midnight Hunters

The Midnight Hunt
Blood Hunt
Night Hunt
The Lone Hunt
The Magic Hunt
Shadow Hunt

Love to the Rescue

by

RADCLYfFE

2019

LOVE TO THE RESCUE

ISBN 13: 978-1-62639-973-0

This Trade Paperback Original Is Published By
Bold Strokes Books, Inc.
P.O. Box 249
Valley Falls, NY 12185

First Edition: April 2019

Credits
Editors: Ruth Sternglantz and Stacia Seaman
Production Design: Stacia Seaman
Cover Design by Sheri (hindsightgraphics@gmail.com)

Acknowledgments

Quite a long time ago I started a series where a place was as much a character as any of the people in the stories. Sometimes the community, the land, the spirit of a place affects how we live and see the world. That first series turned out to be the Provincetown Tales, and sixty books later I have added a new novel to a new series also defined by place as well as people. The Rivers Community novels follow friends, new and old, as they come home, find love, and find themselves. I don't think I could tell these stories in any other setting, and I hope you feel at home here, too.

Many thanks go to: senior editor Sandy Lowe for her advice, insights, and supreme publishing skills; editor Ruth Sternglantz for understanding what I mean to say on every page; editor Stacia Seaman for treating every book like the only project she has going on her busy schedule; and my first readers Paula and Eva for feedback, suggestions, and critiques.

And as always, thanks to Lee for home. *Amo te.*

Radclyffe, 2018

Acknowledgments

To Lee, where the roads lead

Chapter One

At a quarter to seven in the morning, Brody sat in her pickup truck staring at the Rivers. She'd pulled into the guest lot around the east side and had the place mostly to herself. Too early for regular visiting hours. The smattering of dusty vehicles parked here and there probably belonged to the families of patients in the ICUs. The cup of takeout coffee from the café that now occupied the old bank building on a corner in the center of town sat growing cold beside her. Almost as cold as the stone lodged in the pit of her stomach. Her mouth was dry and so were her eyes. She blinked and rubbed at the grit behind her closed lids. Too many hours on the road in the last week and not enough sleep. The trailer had been hot and stuffy, and she'd tossed and turned all night. Even with the window cracked above the almost-double platform bed, the breeze had been mostly hot air laced with a hefty helping of dust.

The hospital looked exactly as she remembered it, as unchanging, it seemed, as the rolling hills and distant mountains that stretched north to Canada and east into New England. The two-story central brick building with its arching wings and white colonnades stood as regally as it had for over a hundred years. The gardens that bordered the road circling the front and branching off to secluded parking areas were lush with flowering hydrangeas, roses of Sharon, and late-blooming perennials. Ivy climbed the cut stone foundation and trailed over trellis-covered walkways. An ache settled in her chest, an unbidden and unwelcome reminder of just how much she had not forgotten.

Damn Matt. Damn her too for not asking where to, when he'd offered her a promotion with more pay and more responsibility if she was willing to move. And why wouldn't she have said yes? She didn't have any ties in Ohio, and she hated the place. Not the people and, to be fair, not even the countryside so much. It was just that everything was so flat, and so…yellow. She'd never gotten past missing the countless variations of green in the hills and valleys of upstate New York, with the surprising stretches of pastureland punctuated by orchards and streams and the sweep of mountains appearing unexpectedly around a bend in the road. Maybe the Midwest flatlands just reminded her too much of the desert, another endless dry, hot yellow place. So of course she'd said yes to the offer—a bump to senior flight medic and shift supervisor with a nice jump in pay. Besides, Jane had signed on already, and Brody didn't have enough good friends that she could afford to lose one. Then, when Matt'd told them where they were going, she'd been stunned speechless. He had to be joking. But he wasn't, and then it was too late.

She watched out her rolled-down window as a stream of vehicles came steadily up the winding road from the village, climbing toward the hospital that sat on a hilltop overlooking the town nestled below and still dominated everything around. Ten years, and the changes hardly amounted to anything. Maybe that was just her memory, though. She hadn't actually walked around in town yet. She'd managed to convince herself staying holed up in her trailer wasn't cowardice. She had a good reason, after all. After nine hundred miles and twenty hours on the road, the used, eighteen-foot Gulf Stream she'd hauled her worldly goods across half the country in was in need of an overhaul.

She hated to think she was hiding. Wanted to think she'd come a lot further than that, and it was terrifying to even think that time could roll back so easily just by returning to a place she'd never expected to see again.

She sucked in a deep breath and reached for her coffee. Well, she wasn't who she had been, and she wouldn't *let* herself be pulled back to a place she'd escaped. She had a job to do, and the job mattered more than whatever ghosts beckoned when she wasn't on guard. She had every right to be here. More than that, she had an obligation to her team.

Resolved, she set the cold coffee aside. It was good, nothing like the diner coffee she remembered getting from the only place that had been open in town back then. She just didn't have any taste for it. Maybe that's why the chill had spread into her bones. She couldn't blame the temperature outside for the way she was feeling. Mid-August, the dog days of summer, hot and oppressively humid. Nothing like the heat of the Midwest, either. Funny, she hadn't realized she'd missed those seemingly endless days of languid heat and hazy afternoons until now. Probably the only thing she'd come to discover she missed.

A Pathfinder, as out of place for its mud-free shining white exterior as for its Ohio plates, pulled in and parked beside her black Dodge. Matt climbed out and sketched her a wave, and a little of the weight lifted off Brody's shoulders. After rolling up her window, she got out, locked the truck, and squared her shoulders.

"Morning," she said.

"Morning," Matt said briskly. His graying hair was neatly trimmed and cut close on top and around his ears in the military style he still wore twenty years after retiring. His body was still army-trim too, even with the little bit of thickening in the middle that came with being in his fifties. He put his hands on his hips and pivoted slowly, shaking his head. "Still can't get over the view from up here. Sure is pretty."

"Yeah." Brody resisted the urge to tell him he might change his mind come winter, when the trees were bare and the snow was three feet deep down the slopes and the air froze with every breath. He didn't know she had history here—none of them did. And she didn't plan on telling them.

"Well," Matt said, "where's Montgomery?" He looked at his watch. "Don't want to keep the CEO waiting."

Five minutes to seven. Brody looked down the twisting road and couldn't see anything through the pines on either side, but the rumble of a motorcycle climbing toward them was hard to miss. She lifted a shoulder. "My guess is that's her."

Matt's lips thinned, and he shook his head. "Wish she'd give up that thing."

Brody laughed. "She trailered it all the way from Ohio. I don't think that's likely."

A leather-jacketed figure in a smoke black helmet, a grayed-out visor, and blond hair streaming below her shoulders pulled in beside them. Jane put her long legs down on either side of the bike, cut the engine, and pulled off her helmet with a shake of her head and a big smile. "Hey. Great day, isn't it?"

Matt grunted and Brody nodded.

Shedding her jacket, Jane climbed off her Yamaha Sport Heritage and locked her helmet to her bike. "You would not believe the roads around here. It's amazing. No traffic, awesome curves, and the air smells so…alive."

Her voice vibrated with her usual enthusiasm and good humor. Brody couldn't recall her ever being down and wondered how they ever ended up friends.

"Just don't be taking those curves too fast," Matt muttered. "And that's cow…poop…you're smelling."

"Yes, Chief." Jane rolled her eyes. "You're just grumpy because you're staying in…what's the name of that place? The Bluebird Inn?"

"More like the Pigeon Coop," Matt said. "My room is the size of a broom closet."

The three of them started toward the hospital, and Jane teased, "You could always rent a trailer and come join us out at Shady Acres."

"I've got an appointment with a Realtor later this week. I want a house like a grown-up person," Matt said. "Besides, I thought you were renting a place in town."

"I am," Jane said. "But there's been some delay. Something with the plumbing. It's going to be a month or so."

"What about you, Clark?" Matt held open the door at the side entrance to the hospital and waited for Brody and Jane to enter.

Brody hesitated, picturing the long walk through the outpatient wing, deserted at that hour, to the central foyer with its sweeping columns rising two stories to the vaulted ceiling and the walls lined with portraits of Rivers doctors going back a hundred years. She imagined the faces of the people she might see, and those she hoped she wouldn't. Not yet, at least. Not until she'd worked out what she was going to say.

"Clark?" Matt asked again, still holding the door.

"Oh." Brody stepped over the threshold, putting the past aside. She'd approach this day and every day going forward the way she would a callout in the field. No thoughts other than the job that had to be done. Back then there'd been troops who needed her service, and now civilians, who weren't all that much different. Her pledge to do the best she could for them came first. She wore a different uniform now, but for her, duty was duty.

"I'm staying where I am," Brody said. "And it's the Riverside

Green, not Shady Acres." She shot Jane a look. Jane smirked back. One of them was happy to be here, at least.

"I didn't think you'd be giving up that trailer, not after you dragged it all the way here," Matt said.

"Yeah, I'm kinda used to it." Mentally, Brody grinned at the irony. Growing up all she'd wanted was to get away from the trailer park, and for a while she had. But maybe it was in her blood. Some people had a word for that. *Trailer trash.* She knew better and most other people did too, but when you were ten, you didn't. "It's a quick run to the hospital, and so far it's been pretty quiet. Honcho likes it. Not much traffic to worry about."

"You got the run finished already, I noticed," Jane said. "Honch good with the new digs?"

"She seems to be settling in okay. The quiet suits her too. Not much to spook her."

"Mm. Good. She's earned an easy retirement." Jane craned her neck for her first look at the hospital. "Wow. This place is…nice."

"Yeah, it is," Brody said quietly.

"So after we do this introduction thing," Matt said in his start-of-shift briefing voice, "we'll set up our duty roster. Ought to be simple at first. Twelve on, twelve off. We'll split shifts with one of the local crews until Air Star recruits more teams for here."

"So we really work for this place now, huh?" Jane said, still scanning the wood-paneled walls and polished floors.

"Technically we still work for Air Star, but SunView Health Consortium just bought up Air Star, and this place is part of that." Matt shook his head. "Most of that is above our pay grade anyhow."

"But you're still in charge, right?" Jane sounded as uneasy as Brody felt.

"When we fly, it's all our call," Matt said, "just like always. They tell us where, we go."

"How soon will the helipad here be ready?" Brody wanted to keep the conversation and her thoughts headed away from the personal. The job was safe terrain, even if the whole picture of how things were going to work wasn't clear yet.

"According to the update I got last week, the inspectors have cleared the pad, but they haven't finished our quarters or the ready room yet."

"They must have on-call rooms or something," Jane said. "It'd be a hell of a lot easier for us to bunk here than at a temporary airfield."

"That's what I plan to talk to them about today. I don't like the idea of being stationed twenty-five miles away either." Matt slowed as they reached the atrium in the center of the building. The vast vaulted ceiling was painted in swirling patterns of dusky rose, periwinkle, and pale cream. A line of brass chandeliers with candelabra bulbs lit the upper recesses, and floor-to-ceiling windows on either side of the massive entrance let sunlight in to dance across the highly polished marble floors. "So, we're looking for the Rivers conference room." He shook his head. "I guess everything around this place is owned by the Riverses."

"Not owned, and not anymore," Brody said before she could stop herself. So much for keeping her past and her personal life to herself. She would've liked to have kicked her own ass, but neither Matt nor Jane seemed to think it odd she knew anything about the hospital. "I… understand the place was founded by a couple of doctors in the Rivers family along with other businessmen in the area a hundred years ago or so. There have always been Rivers doctors here."

"No kidding," Jane said, gesturing to the portraits along the side walls, each illuminated by small lights mounted above the frames. "Look at all the past hospital presidents. Sounds like some old-fashioned dynasty."

"I suppose," Brody said. More a legacy, but she had no reason to defend them.

Matt slowed before the huge walnut desk opposite the main doors and the sprightly gray-haired woman, her close-cropped curls shimmering above a smooth unlined face, who commanded it.

She smiled at them. "Good morning. You're all right on time. You want to take the corridor behind me to your left to the administration wing. Just before you reach the first turn you'll find the conference room."

Brody kept her chin down. Mrs. Brundidge hadn't changed a bit.

"Do you have to be a mind reader for your job?" Jane asked with a laugh.

Mrs. Brundidge laughed. "No, but your uniforms are kind of a dead giveaway."

Brody and the others wore their standard navy blue shirts and pants, Air Star patches on the sleeves depicting yellow helo blades in a red star, name tags, and short serviceable boots. They all laughed as they passed by.

"Thanks for the directions," Matt said.

"Of course. Welcome to the Rivers. We are all so happy you're here."

"This place is amazing," Jane murmured as they followed the wide hallway at the far end of the lobby and turned left as directed. "I didn't even think there *were* any places like this anymore."

"Yeah, it sure is a far cry from Ohio," Matt said.

"Sure is," Brody said, too quietly for anyone else to hear.

Val parked across the street from the café and grimaced as she climbed out of her Subaru. A streak of mud slanted down the leg of her Paige jeans from knee to ankle where she'd just brushed the door as she slid out—*brushed* as in barely touched the damn thing. Of course, look at her charcoal SUV. Six weeks old and it looked like every other vehicle on the street. Smudged and smattered with grime, its windows pocked with the corpses of innumerable bugs. She sighed. She hated dirt. Manhattan was anything but clean, but as long as she hadn't trekked through the gutters or traversed questionable alleyways, she'd managed to keep herself clean. Out here, that was a losing battle. By noon she'd be dusty and sweaty and her clothes would look like she'd been sleeping in them for a month. Just another fact of life she couldn't control. Seemed to be an awful lot of them these days.

A pickup slowed, waiting for her to cross, and she waved her thanks as she jogged across the two lane to the Breadbasket Café. A man called out from the rolled-down window, "Morning, Doc," as the truck passed.

"Morning," Val called automatically for the first of what would probably be two dozen times that day. That was another thing, the absence of anonymity. She suspected she hadn't been back long, probably no more than a couple of days, before everyone knew the prodigal daughter had returned. Not that there was anything all that dramatic in her past, of course, just the usual high school rebellions and an urge to leave small-town life behind. Dogs and cats and exotic birds, that was going to be her life. Not cows and horses and goats and sheep and God knew what all. And dirt. Lots of dirt among other gifts from nature's bounty.

What was that saying, Man plans and God laughs? Something like that. Well, whoever was designing her life was laughing.

"Morning, Doc Valentine," the fresh-faced teenage boy behind the café counter said as she got into line behind an octogenarian couple in matching khaki pants and sweaters over their cotton shirts who were just collecting their plates of eggs and bacon and toast to carry to one of the tables in front of the big front windows. She saw them every time she came in for coffee at this time of day. Some small—very small—part of her envied them. She hadn't fallen into the romance trap when she was sixteen, and she certainly wouldn't now at practically twice that age.

Converting the old bank into a café had been inspired. The setting was actually beautiful, with gorgeous walnut wainscoting, high beaten tin ceilings with an honest to goodness still-working brass chandelier, and huge two-story-tall windows all around that took advantage of the corner location. She had to admit, there was something to be said for the craftsmanship evident in the two-hundred-year-old buildings lining Main Street that seemed to have disappeared with the need to build taller and bigger buildings faster and faster. The nondescript establishments geared for the pace of modern living so often ended up bland and soulless. Starbucks made a heavenly mocha, but she wouldn't want to spend much time in one. She laughed to herself. Listen to her. Starting to catch whatever romantic nostalgia kept people around this place. Well, she wasn't going to convert. She'd give it a year until she could find someone, train them, and convince Joe they'd be as good as her. A year. She could handle that.

"Black eye," she said to the boy in the neat plaid shirt.

His brows drew together. "Um. That's…ah…coffee with…um…" His face reddened and he shrugged helplessly.

Nope, definitely not Manhattan anymore. "A large coffee with two shots of espresso added."

His deep cornflower blue eyes brightened. "Right. I knew that. It's the red eye with just one shot, right?"

She laughed. "That's right. But you can forget that one. Why bother if you're only getting one shot."

He smiled again as if he wanted nothing more in the world than to make her coffee, and suddenly the dirt on her thigh didn't bother her half that much. She smacked it away, collected her coffee and left him a five—keep the change—and turned to head out to the Subaru for morning farm call.

"Oh, sorry!" Val jerked to a stop before barreling into the woman who'd just stepped up to the counter behind her. The face a foot away came into focus, and she froze in mid-sidestep. Had to happen sometime, of course. What was surprising was it hadn't happened already.

"Hi, Court," Val said quietly.

"I heard you were back." Her cousin's chocolate brown eyes, the family trait that seemed to mark all the Valentines, were flat and cold. "I can't believe you deigned to return to the backwater. Whatever could have drawn the princess away from the glitter and glitz?"

"How's your internship going?" Val asked, ignoring the bait. "I hear the new merger has really increased the volume at the Rivers."

"What's it to you? Still sniffing around the Rivers? Maybe you haven't heard Flann's a newlywed."

Val sighed. That was not a newsflash. "Look, Court…"

"You might have been gone for the better part of ten years, *Sin*," Court said, disdainfully emphasizing the nickname Val'd acquired in high school and left behind along with the reputation, "but nothing's going to change the fact that you're just like the rest of your disloyal, back-stabbing family."

"Right," Val said softly. "Well then. Have a nice day."

She skirted around her cousin, aware that the few patrons in the café probably heard the entire conversation and before long the entire town would be privy to it. But then, the feud between the two sides of the Valentine family was practically town lore at this point. All the same, she had no intention of adding fuel to the story.

She settled behind the wheel and closed her eyes for a second. She was going to be late picking up Margie and Blake, but they'd probably gotten used to her habitually being five to ten minutes behind schedule. No matter how she tried, she just couldn't quite get all her morning routine finished when she intended to.

At least she wasn't likely to run into Flann out at the homestead. Small favors, but she'd take it. She'd had enough of the past come back to bite her in the ass for one day.

Chapter Two

The tight feeling between Brody's shoulder blades, the ever-present subconscious expectation of a bullet striking she'd learned to live with out in the field, eased when they headed in the opposite direction from the emergency room. She hadn't even noticed the feeling until it was gone. Probably not a good start to the new job, feeling like she was back in the line of fire again. As she walked along with Matt and Jane, she noticed that some things *did* change. A new wing hadn't been visible from where she'd been parked, and a sign indicating *ER* pointed down a corridor that was clearly a modern addition still under construction. Portions of the hallway were barricaded with construction tarp—probably hiding unfinished treatment rooms—and a fine layer of dust covered the ubiquitous gray and tan speckled tile floors. Bright lights shone at the far end of the corridor, and the low hum of voices drifted out. The renovations—expansion, more accurately—weren't yet complete, but clearly no one was waiting for that. Business as usual was under way.

"Looks like they're not wasting any time getting the new ER functioning," Brody said.

"I understand the CEO likes everything done yesterday," Matt said. "Which explains how they got a helipad built and approved so fast. Course the Air Star takeover was likely in the works for a while."

"Probably good to have a big boss who can get things done," Brody said. "At least if it means we'll get our quarters pretty soon."

"Well, you know what the suits are like," Jane put in. "They always have their priorities, and they're usually the ones that affect the bottom line." She snorted. "Where we sleep probably isn't one of them."

Brody grinned. "I suppose that could be good too."

Jane smirked and rolled her eyes. "Since when are you worried about that?"

Since never, seeing as how I usually don't have any reason to be. Brody just shook her head.

"This looks like it," Matt said, checking his watch. "And we're right on time. Come on."

He pushed open the door with a brass plaque announcing the *Rivers Conference Room* and stepped inside. Brody followed with Jane beside her and blinked as she crossed the threshold. The conference room was more like a mini auditorium, and it was full. Not exactly what she'd been expecting. She'd hoped for more time. Heat rose up her spine and tingled the back of her neck. Her body's signal for danger. She sucked in a breath as Matt started down the center aisle between a dozen rows of seats, all of which were occupied with people in scrubs, casual business clothes, and the occasional white coat. Medical staff and administration, it looked like. A blonde in a sharp navy suit with a white shirt and low heels stood by a simple lectern at the front of the room. She beckoned to them to join her.

Presley Worth, the CEO.

Younger than Brody had anticipated. She didn't look much beyond midthirties, if that. But then, age really was no good index of competence. She'd learned that pretty quickly in the Army. She kept her eyes front as she followed Matt. She wasn't quite ready to pick out the familiar faces she knew had to be there. Dr. Rivers for certain, and Harper and Flann almost certainly as well. She didn't know about them for sure, but she couldn't imagine it any other way. They'd both planned to be doctors since they could walk and talk. Not for the first time, she wondered if their influence had been what prompted her to tell the recruiter she wanted to be a medic.

"Good morning, everyone," Presley said as the three of them stepped up onto the low stage to join her.

Brody put on her combat face—expressionless, in control.

Worth went on, "As I'm sure you all know, Air Star has joined the SunView Corporation nationwide, and as of this morning—or as soon as we get these three settled in—we will be the only hospital in the lower half of the county and all of neighboring southern Vermont to have medevac capability." She waited out what sounded like genuine applause. She smiled as the noise subsided. "We will be both receiving patients directly from point of injury and, if necessary, transferring by helicopter from here to other regional centers." She turned to Matt. "We are fortunate to have an experienced medevac flight team joining us as part of the Rivers emergency medical system of care. Matt Hobson will direct Air Star operations here at the Rivers. I'll let him introduce his colleagues."

Matt cleared his throat and squared his shoulders.

Brody had never served with him, but she didn't have any trouble imagining him at morning briefing. When his command voice rolled out, the heat in her spine slowly melted away. Whatever the mission, she was up for it because her team was up for it.

"Thank you, Ms. Worth." Matt slowly scanned the room. "I guess I should start out by apologizing for getting you all here when you were either ready to go home or just starting your day. So thank you."

Quite a few people chuckled.

"It goes without saying, we are honored to be here. My first team is here with me and we're ready to go to work. Between the three of us, we have logged 20,000 hours flying for Air Star, and before that, all of us logged time in the military."

He glanced toward Brody and Jane. "You'll get to know all of us pretty quick, I wager, since Air Star prefers to have its teams hospital based. That makes for quicker and clearer lines of communication and, in our experience, faster dust-off and evac times. Something we all want." He waited a beat to let that sink in. "To jump-start all of us getting to know one another a little bit, I'll give you a thumbnail on these two. On my far right, Jane Montgomery. She's our pilot, and before Air Star, she flew Seahawk medevacs for the Navy, two tours. Jane?"

"Thanks, Chief," Jane said. "I suspect some of you will be flying with us, and I look forward to meeting you all."

"And our senior flight medic is Brody Clark," Matt indicated Brody, "who flew SAR—search and rescue—and medevac for the Army during three Mideast deployments."

Brody's throat was suddenly dry and she swallowed. Her gaze was drawn inexorably and unavoidably to a face in the front row. Flann's eyes bored into hers, hot and angry. Flann Rivers hadn't changed all that much. She wore surgical scrubs and a green OR cover gown. Her sandy-blond, collar-length hair was wavier than Brody remembered. Even from thirty feet away she could make out the fierce intensity in her deep brown eyes. Harper sat on Flann's left, her deep blue eyes as intense as Flann's, and Brody figured she'd find their father Edward close by but she stopped searching. She already felt as if she'd been fragged by the heat coming from the two younger Riverses' expressions. She didn't need to see Edward staring at her with the same surprise and anger.

Brody dragged her eyes away from Flann and Harper and focused on a spot at the far back of the room where no one was pinning her in place with a look. "Our team has one goal here—to make sure the injured reach you in the fastest, most secure way possible so you can do what you do best, give them the best care anywhere. You can depend on us to do that. Thank you."

Presley took half a step forward and Brody slowly let out her breath as the CEO took control again.

"I'll be sending around general guidelines detailing how Air Star will interface with our trauma team and our mobile emergency medical partners. For now, please direct your questions to your department head. Thank you all for your attention."

Brody waited with Matt and Jane while the attendees stood, talked amongst themselves, and slowly moved out of the room. Flann and Harper walked out without a backward glance and the tightness in her chest eased a fraction. She just needed some air. Just a little space to breathe.

"So, Ms. Worth," Matt said, "I'd love to hear some of those details you mentioned."

Presley laughed. "No doubt. Let's go to my office."

"Sure. Just one thing—when do we start officially?"

"If your team is ready, twenty-four hours."

Matt snorted. "Hell, we're ready now."

"Well then, let's take care of those details."

Matt pointed a finger at Jane. "I'll catch up to the two of you later. You—keep your damn phone on you so I can reach you."

"Yes, Chief." Jane smiled an indulgent smile that usually indicated she'd heard and might or might not follow through. Striding up the aisle with Brody, she said, "Had breakfast yet?"

"Uh—no," Brody said.

"Good, 'cause I'm starving. Any idea if there's someplace to eat close by?"

"A couple maybe. Feel like walking?"

Jane nudged her shoulder into Brody's. "What, scared to get on the back of my bike? Or you just don't want to ride in the bitch seat?"

"Well, I'm not scared," Brody said.

Jane smiled. "Knew it. Not studly enough for you to ride behind the girl."

"Never said that."

Jane looked her up and down. "You didn't need to."

Jane's teasing helped dispel the burn left over from Flann's glare. Harper had just looked surprised, but then she'd always been slower to heat up than Flann. Flann was fire, through and through. Brody pushed the door to the hall open and held it for Jane.

As she stepped into the corridor, Flann's voice hit her like a torch. "Brody."

Jane must've picked up something in Flann's voice because she moved closer to Brody until their shoulders touched.

"Hello, Flann," Brody said.

Flann's smoldering gaze skimmed over Jane and lasered in on Brody. "What the hell? You show up here, just like that?"

"It happened pretty fast."

"*Fuck* that," Flann said, low and hard. "You had more than ten years."

"I've been in touch."

"You call a card to my mother once a year keeping in touch?"

"Look, Flann…"

Flann edged in on her, her face inches away, their bodies almost touching. From anyone else, Brody would have pushed back. She kept her hands at her sides, fists loose, not planning to defend herself. Not now, not here. Not in Flann's territory.

"You make it right with her, you hear?" Flann poked her finger into the center of Brody's chest. "You do it or you don't work here."

"Hey!" Jane wedged herself into Flann's space. "Who the fuck do you think you are?"

"This is personal," Flann said, still not looking at Jane, her gaze riveted to Brody's.

"It's okay, Jane," Brody said quietly.

"The hell it is." Jane raised a hand, about to shove at Flann.

Brody caught her wrist and tugged it down lightly. "Let it go."

Jane gave her a look. "Why?"

"This is Flannery Rivers." Brody grimaced. "I imagine she's somebody important by now. Best not to get off on the wrong foot."

"I don't care if she is the reincarnation of Apollo, she doesn't have any right to hassle you and throw her weight around."

Flann raised a brow.

"God of healing," Brody muttered, and for a second, Flann almost smiled. Then the hard glint eclipsed the fleeting glimpse of the old Flann. "Chief of staff yet?"

"That'll be Harper's job when Dad decides to retire," Flann said. "I'm chief of surgery, and that has nothing to do with this."

"I know," Brody said. "I know what needs to be done."

"Then do it, and then stay out of my way."

Flann spun on her heel and stalked away.

"You want to tell me what that was about?" Jane said quietly.

"No," Brody said. "I really don't."

"Okay then," Jane said agreeably. "Let's go find breakfast."

Halfway down the winding road into the village, Brody let out a long sigh. Jane hadn't said anything since they'd left the hospital. Jane was her best friend. Let's face it, her *only* real friend. She'd had friends in the military, but that was different. They were men and women she depended on to keep her alive on the battlefield, for sure, but also through the long hours of waiting that bore down on the body and the soul. And so much more—the uncertainty of what was to come, the doubts that crept in about what she was doing and why she was there. The camaraderie, the unity, the unbreakable bonds with her fellow troops had provided a shelter and a shield against the dark and the fear and the silent, lonely hours. They'd been bound by common experience, and most of them rarely talked about their life beyond the world they inhabited. She'd never talked about her past because her past wasn't important. Not there, not since the day she'd signed up and taken the bus into a new world and a new life.

Jane wasn't part of that life either, although they had the shared bond of both having served. Jane was the friend she had made almost by accident when she'd started at Air Star. Jane was the extrovert, the one who sat down with a cup of coffee and introduced herself to all the new guys. And with Brody, she was the one who talked about…everything. The weather, the news, the job, and her first love—her motorcycle. And bit by bit, Brody had opened up enough for the threads of connection to form. Those threads were stretched tight now, but much stronger than at the beginning.

"Ropes," she muttered.

Jane strolled along as if she had nowhere to be and nothing pressing to do. Jane was the rare person who actually *did* live in the moment. Brody would give a lot to have that skill.

"What kind of ropes?" Jane asked.

"Thick ones."

"You want to elaborate on that, or are you going to chew on it a while longer?"

"I used to live here," Brody said.

"No kidding. When did you leave?" Jane never broke stride, but then, she never did. Nothing fazed her. Maybe that's what it took to be a pilot, to wrestle the aircraft through storm and fire with the lives of her crew and everyone else aboard on her shoulders. She was pretty much unflappable.

"When I was eighteen."

"That's when you went in?"

Brody nodded. "Yeah."

"First time back?"

Brody cut her a look. "I figured that might've been obvious."

Jane flashed a crooked grin. "Little bit. So Flann Rivers—friend or foe?"

"Funny question."

Jane shrugged. "Not really. Just because someone chews your butt out, just because they're pissed as hell at you, doesn't make them an enemy. Sometimes they're the closest people to you."

Her voice had taken on a pensive tone, and Brody allowed that they all had secrets.

"We used to be friends," Brody said quietly. "A lot more than that. Now, I don't know."

❖

Val drove down the curving dirt lane to the sprawling, three-story brick house and parked her Subaru under the porte cochere. Only ten minutes late. Well within her margin of timeliness. The Rivers homestead dominated a knoll above the Batten Kill as it ran along the county line. Fields of corn as high as her shoulder bounded the homestead on three sides. A rolling slope of green cascaded from the back porch down to the river, spreading out to apple orchards and stands of towering maples and locust trees on either side.

Val hurried around to the rear of the house, quickly scanning the pastures and the turnaround by the barn. No one was about. Edward would have already started his day at the hospital, and most of the Rivers clan—Harper and Flann and Carson—had moved out. Just Margie was still at home now.

When she mounted the steps to the wide wood porch, the scent of fresh baked bread wafted out the screen door. That nostalgic feeling hit her in the pit of her stomach again, and she gritted her teeth. Really. Enough already. She rapped on the door. "Hello?"

Ida Rivers appeared in the doorway, wiping her hands on a snowy white dish towel with red stripes. She wore a blue-checked apron over a short-sleeved pale yellow shirt and comfortable-looking blue jeans. Ida's smile was warm and welcoming. In her midfifties, she was nearly as trim and toned as all her children. Ida pushed the door open. "Well, good morning, Val. It's nice to see you."

Val flushed with unexpected pleasure. After Court's vitriolic greeting that morning, she appreciated the feeling that someone besides her mother and Joe were happy to see her back. Funny, she hadn't realized she needed that until just now. "Thank you. You too."

"Well"—Ida gestured her in—"I've got biscuits and fresh coffee if you've a moment."

Val laughed. "For your biscuits? I've always got plenty of time."

"Sit then. I imagine these two have room for more." Ida glanced affectionately at the teens at the table and pulled a tray of biscuits from the oven.

"Hey, Val," Margie called from the far end of the table. Somewhere between sixteen and seventeen, Margie Rivers was just on the brink of turning into another gorgeous Rivers sibling. Her strawberry-blond curls framed a lightly freckled bold face and her blue eyes verged on turquoise, just like Harper's. Her lankiness was starting to verge on willowy, saved from being delicate by her naturally athletic build. Best of all, she was bright and daring and filled with joy. Val envied her.

"Hey, Margie, hi, Blake," Val said.

Blake Remy grinned, his sparkling blue eyes sending a greeting. His dark brown hair was side-parted and long on top. She hadn't seen him since his surgery, and he looked…great. Happy and sure in a way she hadn't noticed before. He sat on Margie's right, where he seemed to be at any time Val saw them together, even when they were in a crowd of their friends. She marveled at the ease of their friendship, and how differently boys and girls seemed to interact from when she'd been their age. Even though she sometimes felt ancient around their youthful enthusiasm and refreshing innocence, she wasn't all *that* much older. But when she'd been their age, she hadn't had any friends who were boys. Come to think of it, she hadn't had any girls who were friends either. Of course, she'd had a hard time deciding exactly what she wanted with any of them, which hadn't helped, but the boys mostly looked at girls with sex on their minds. And all the girls that Val knew, with the exception of Flannery Rivers, looked back the same way. She shook her head. Maybe things were easier now that kids had more permission to explore who they were and what they wanted without censure—at least in a lot of places. She hoped they were, and she hoped this was one of those places. Especially for Blake and every other kid who wasn't exactly like everyone else.

"You two ready to work?" Val asked.

"Oh yeah," Margie said. "I love farm call."

"Of course you do." Val rolled her eyes. "I thought you were the one who decided after a week in the ER to be a people doc. Are you finally coming over to the light?"

Margie smirked. "Nope. I already saw the light. Blake is still set on being the vet. But I still love farm call."

"Me too," Blake murmured.

"Well, give me five minutes and I'll make your dreams come true." Val took the coffee Ida offered her in a big blue ceramic mug. "Thank you, Mrs. Rivers."

Ida chuckled. "I believe you can call me Ida, Val."

"Old habits."

"How are you enjoying being back?" Ida asked casually as she placed a tray of biscuits on the table. Blake and Margie reached for them immediately, and Val managed to wait an appropriate five seconds before doing the same. A slab of butter appeared in the center of the table on a cut glass plate like the kind her grandmother always used.

"I imagine it's a change from New York City," Ida said.

"A little bit," Val said, keeping her tone light. She glanced at Ida and caught the twinkle in her eye. She laughed and shook her head. "A lot. I'm adjusting. And the practice is really busy, so that's been good. And…" She shook her head. "I've discovered a few things that I missed while I was away."

"I think that's in the nature of coming home." Ida squeezed Val's shoulder as she sat at the table with her own coffee. "How's Joe doing?"

"His hip's still bothering him. He's healing up really well, but the heavy stuff…well, he's got me for that."

"It was good of you to come home to help him out," Ida said. "I imagine it was a sacrifice."

"No," Val said quietly. "Joe is the reason…he's pretty much responsible for me being where I am in life. If I'd known how hard things had gotten for him, I'd have been here sooner."

"Well, you're here now, and that's what matters." Ida frowned at the sound of a car approaching down the drive and went to the window. "Too early for the mailman. I…" She gripped the counter and went very still.

"Mom?" Margie said.

"It's fine," Ida said quietly, still looking out the window. "Just an unexpected visitor."

Chapter Three

Brody sat with the engine running behind the Subaru parked under the porte cochere. Maybe this was a bad idea. This was for sure a bad time to second-guess the impulse that had her deserting Jane in the middle of the sidewalk, jogging back to the hospital, and hopping into her truck to drive over here.

Jane hadn't even looked surprised when she'd stopped outside the diner and said, "There's something I have to do," as if she'd been expecting something like that all along.

"This have to do with what Lord Rivers was talking about?" Jane slid one hand into her back pocket and shot out her hip. A couple of guys walking by gave her a long look. She ignored them. She was used to getting looks.

"Yeah. I need to go talk to Flann's mother."

"Let me guess, she's another Rivers doctor and owns half the town."

Brody smiled. "Not exactly. She's—well, she's the heart of the family, the rock at the center that holds everything together. And she's a pretty popular person in town too."

"The matriarch, huh?"

"Good a word as any."

"When were you planning on telling me what you've done to get on her bad side?"

"Maybe once I've made it right. Or tried to."

"I'm going to eat alone, aren't I?"

"I'm sorry."

Jane waved her off. "I can handle a solo breakfast. Come find me when you're done. If Matt hasn't caught us first, we'll go for a ride in the country. But you'll have to sit in the bitch seat."

"You never give up, do you."

Jane smiled. "Nope."

"I'll find you. And thanks."

"Don't beat yourself up too much, hear? Whatever it is, you would have had a reason."

"Not sure they'll hold much water now, but…thanks." Brody was damn glad Jane was Jane—she might not be making any more friends anytime soon.

"You said that, and it wasn't necessary the first time." Jane squeezed her arm. "See you soon."

A shadow moved across the window over the kitchen sink—someone looking out. Brody's stomach clenched. Flann was right. This had to be done, and she was dragging her feet. She'd never been slow about facing the hard stuff. She winced. Not exactly true. It had taken her the better part of a year to face up to her only real choice before she'd left. But since then, she'd tried a lot harder not to lie to herself. Besides, she wasn't doing this for Flann or Harper or even her job. She was doing it for herself, and Ida.

She switched off the ignition, pocketed her keys, and strode around to the back of the house without glancing at the window. She stopped at the foot of the three short steps to the back porch. The kitchen beyond the screen door was dark—a trick of the light, sun reflecting off the fine metal mesh of the screen. She didn't need to see inside to picture the big room with the porcelain country sink, the long wood counters beneath windows that gave a view to the adjacent fields, the big white refrigerator, the massive stove with cast-iron grill top, double ovens, and warming drawer, the oversized oak dining table, and the fluted lampshade hanging high above everything in the center of the exposed beam ceiling. She'd gone through that screen door a thousand times before, the slap of it closing behind her as natural as the sound of roosters in the morning and the lowing of cattle at night. She'd entered hesitantly at first, eventually with ease, and finally with barely any notice, the way you do when you come home.

Home. She guessed that didn't apply to her anymore. Sadness settled in her depths, making the scant few feet to the door seem like miles.

Ida appeared behind the screen, the light shifted again, and her face was framed in the bright morning sun. Their eyes met.

Brody's heart thundered and her throat was dry. If Ida told her to go, she'd get back in her truck and drive into town and give Matt her resignation. She'd go…somewhere. She'd leave town a lot the way she had before, heading into a future she couldn't quite see. At least she'd had the Army then. Now she wouldn't even have that. She watched Ida, waited for judgment.

Ida opened the door and held it with one arm. "You've almost missed breakfast, Brody. You'd best get in here."

"Yes, ma'am." Brody climbed the steps, seventeen again and late to breakfast because she'd gone out on her bike at dawn after a restless night. She wiped her feet carefully on the mat in front of the door even though her boots were clean. Another habit. She smelled the biscuits, figured there was ham somewhere, and coffee. What she hadn't figured on were the people at the table. She halted just inside the door, felt heat rise to her face. "Sorry, I'm interrupting."

"You're not," Ida said on her way to the stove. "We've empty chairs at the table. Take one. Coffee?"

"I could use some. Thanks." Brody waited, taking stock.

A girl and a boy sat at the far end of the long, narrow oak table. The same eight chairs still surrounded it—one at each end and three a side. She was certain she didn't know the boy, and she hadn't seen Margie Rivers since Margie was six years old, but she knew her. Couldn't be anyone else. Margie had the Rivers boldness, studying her now without embarrassment, without judgment or censure or anything other than open interest. She recalled Margie having golden blond hair, and now the blond was shot through with red. She was also nearly a grown woman, and Brody knew nothing about her. She'd be a stranger now to Margie too.

She was a stranger in this house.

The boy next to her looked like every other teenage boy. Slim, from what she could see of his shoulders and chest beneath the navy T-shirt, just waiting for that imminent growth spurt to hit when he'd thicken a little in the body and his face would broaden and his beard would start to come in. That wild time when boys became men in body, if not spirit and soul.

She recognized the woman on Margie's left and her chest tightened.

Val. The last time she'd seen her, Val had been a teenager, as Margie was now, on the cusp of going from pretty to beautiful. Val had become a woman even more striking than Brody'd imagined. Her straight blond hair fell to her shoulders, cut in layers around her face. Her brown eyes seemed larger, more serious than Brody remembered, even a little cautious. Val studied her as she might any stranger at the door, with polite but distant curiosity. Brody wasn't surprised. Val'd never really seen her, not where she'd stood in Flann's shadow, not the poor kid, the abandoned kid, the charity case. The trailer trash.

Brody sucked in a breath. She'd promised herself this place would not take her back there, and neither would Val's dismissal. She'd weathered it when she'd been a lot softer, when she'd wished for something she'd known even then was impossible. Girls like Val did not notice girls like her, and the women they became never changed. But she had, and she was well past hopeless dreams.

"Hi, Margie," Brody said as she walked to the table.

"Hey, Brody," Margie said flatly.

Brody held out her hand to Val. "Brody Clark. Sorry to interrupt your breakfast."

"You didn't. I'm Val." Smiling, her gaze still assessing, Val half rose and shook Brody's hand, her grip warm and firm. "We were just about ready to leave." Val paused, cocked her head. Her eyes narrowed. "I know you, don't I?"

"Not really," Brody said. "We went to school together, but there's no reason you would remember that."

"Of course I remember." Val glanced at Ida, obviously putting the pieces together. She colored faintly. "Sorry. I haven't thought about high school in a long time. I didn't recognize you."

"No need to apologize," Brody said. "We weren't friends, after all. Hardly acquaintances."

Val seemed startled, as if she was just trying to decide if the observation was rude or merely dismissive. "I guess we've all changed."

"I guess so."

"Are you back here for a while?" Val asked.

Brody recognized the social nicety for what it was and shrugged. "I'm not sure just yet."

"Well, I hope you enjoy your…stay." Val smiled again and leaned over to say something to Margie.

Brody turned to Ida. "This is a bad time. I should have called. I'll come back anoth—"

"No, really, we have to get going." Val rose hastily and gestured to Margie and the boy with her. "Let's go, you two. The animals are calling."

"Take these." Ida held out three paper bags. "You'll all be hungry in two hours."

Val took the bags and rolled her eyes. "If you keep feeding me, I'm going to get terribly spoiled."

Ida smiled. "Consider it my thanks for keeping Margie occupied this summer."

"Not necessary," Val said, "but I won't say no." She paused, met Brody's gaze. "Good to see you again, Brody."

"You too." Brody suddenly wanted to say something, anything, to dispel the cool distance between them and didn't have any better idea how to do it now than she had when she was seventeen. Then Val walked out and it didn't matter any longer.

Margie slowed as she passed by and said quietly, "You should've said good-bye."

"I know." Brody wasn't sure Margie heard her. Margie was out the door without another look.

The boy with her, after one curious and mildly reproachful gaze, followed after her. A friend, then. He might not know what Brody had done, but he was on Margie's side all the same. The screen door closed with its signature bang and a moment later a car started up and stones crunched under tires.

Brody met Ida's even gaze and let out a breath. "Well, my timing sucks."

"There's never a bad time to come back." Ida smiled. "You've gotten taller. Still too skinny, though. How are you?"

"Good, I guess." Brody laughed. "And I'm not skinny. I prefer lean."

"Lean is just a fancy word for it." Ida pointed at the table. "Take your chair. We'll feed you all the same."

Brody sat while Ida fixed her plate and set it down in front of her. She'd been right. Biscuits and ham and a steaming cup of coffee. Her stomach grumbled. Last night's dinner had been a slice of pizza in the microwave. "I don't know where to start."

"You eat first, Brody." Ida sat at her usual place at the end of the table with her cup of coffee. "Whatever you want to say will keep a few minutes longer."

Brody angled in her chair to face her. "I'm sorry."

Ida sighed. "Stubborn as ever. Not that I expected you to change."

"People don't," Brody said. She'd learned that lesson the hard way a long time ago.

"Maybe, maybe not." Ida sipped her coffee and reached for a biscuit. "But here's the thing." Ida gently pried the flaking halves apart and spread them with butter that instantly melted. "You never left me to worry if you were lying in a ditch somewhere, dead or worse. You weren't very good at keeping in touch, but you did, and you did it regularly. Once a year I got the letter. Almost to the day every year. When I did, I knew you were all right for at least another year."

"Hardly seems enough," Brody murmured. Flann sure didn't think so. But what could she have said? If there'd been anything else to say, she would have done that already. "Flann and Harper, probably Carson too, aren't going to forgive me."

Ida sighed. "Every one of them is as hardheaded as you. Which means time is needed. You were eighteen when you left, which made you an adult and capable of making your own choices. I don't agree with them all, but you had the right. So you don't owe me—or them—an apology."

The biscuits, the most delicious Brody'd ever known in her life, were sawdust in her throat. She washed them down with the coffee, aware it was still too hot to drink and that she'd forgotten to put cream in it. She didn't care. The pain helped clear her head. She rested her hands on either side of the big ivory ceramic plate, one she'd probably eaten off hundreds of times. She didn't look away—she wasn't that big a coward—and she couldn't miss the sorrow in Ida's eyes. She'd hurt her, and the ache of knowing that was worse than any physical pain she'd ever experienced.

"I've got no excuses," Brody said.

"Reasons?"

"Yes, or so I thought at the time."

"But none you wanted to share."

"None I thought I could."

"Now that," Ida said quietly, pointing a finger at her, "hurts worse than you leaving with just a note on the table."

Brody looked away for the first time. "I know, and I'm sorry. It wasn't because I didn't trust you. Never that."

"That might take a little explaining at some point. When you're ready."

"I just…I'm sorry."

"You're going to need to tell one of us one of these days, Brody."

"Before you'll forgive me," Brody said around the stone in her throat.

"Of course not. There was never anything to forgive. But for you." Ida reached across and covered Brody's fist with her warm fingers. "Right now all that matters is that you're home. You're staying for a while, aren't you?"

"I wish I knew." Brody gripped Ida's fingers and held on, trying to find her way in the dark, the way she followed the roar of the engines and the whir of the rotors when the dust was so deep and the night was so dark she couldn't see her own body. Her eyes watered the way they did in the smoke and the clouds of grit dusted with blood and metal shards. The tears ran on her cheeks, but not from the heat and agony of war and death, but from a sensation she hadn't experienced since she'd walked out that back door so long ago. Safety.

Chapter Four

Margie chewed on her lip and looked out the passenger window, not really paying attention to what was out there. She'd seen everything there was to see a million times already, but almost every time she looked, she saw something new or something to make her smile. Who ever got tired of seeing baby deer, after all? And she had a special liking for groundhogs, even though they were pests and ate the crops. They were just always so busy looking, and cute. Even they probably wouldn't help right now.

Right now nothing made her feel much like smiling. She didn't feel like talking either. Her stomach twisted around, and she didn't have to work too hard to figure out what was wrong. Brody showing up like that was weird. Why didn't she tell someone she was coming? Margie sighed. Course Brody never said she was leaving, either, so why expect any different. Or maybe she didn't want to see the rest of them. Maybe she'd leave again, scattering questions behind like the last time. That made the twist in her middle spread a little higher and ache in her chest.

"You okay, Margie?" Val asked.

"Yep. Just thinking."

"Mm." Val nodded and drove on silently, quieter than usual.

Maybe she'd been surprised by Brody popping up out of the blue too.

Margie didn't know Val all that well, not like she knew her sisters—with them, she could read their moods by the way they walked, the set of their shoulders, the faint variations in the color of their eyes. The things you noticed about people who had been there your whole life—the people who once had *been* your whole world. Brody had almost been one of those people.

That might be why she couldn't decide if she was more mad or surprised or, if she really thought about it, happy that Brody was back. Combination of all of that, probably. She remembered Brody, and most of the memories were good ones, but it seemed like an awfully long time ago, and the Brody she remembered didn't seem a lot like the Brody who showed up this morning. For one thing, she was grown up and looked different. Older, sure, and still sort of quiet, in a kind of thinking inside her head way, not a shy way. But the wary way Brody had taken in every corner of the kitchen and the people in it before stepping past the threshold, like she was expecting trouble or danger or *something*, seemed new.

Margie couldn't really be sure what had changed. Maybe it was her and not Brody. She'd been pretty little when Brody came to stay. She only vaguely remembered the very beginning, she was maybe three. Brody was just another one of the older kids, one of her sisters who paid attention to her but lived in a different world than she did. They all had their places and she was just the little one. Margie grinned. Like all that had changed so much. Yeah, right. Not that she *really* minded…for sisters they were all pretty cool.

Harper had always been the leader—the one everyone checked in with, the one who always seemed to know the answer, and the one who stepped in to defend them when it looked like they might be getting in trouble. Flann organized everything—the games, the adventures, the exploits—and more often than not was the reason Harper had to come to their defense. Carson was more like Mom, checking to make sure Margie was included, when the adventures weren't too grown up, and to see if she was keeping up, even though she *always* was. Brody had always been part of the group but never quite took a place like the others.

But she could have remembered wrong. She was little, after all. She remembered when Brody left, though, and how quiet Harper had been and how Flann had seemed angry and Carson sad. Margie'd missed her for a while but she had the others and she'd forgotten.

Blake leaned forward from the back seat. "Who was that?"

Margie shot a look at Val, who didn't seem to be listening, or at least was pretending she wasn't. "Her name is Brody Clark. She used to live with us. For a long time, I thought she was my sister. Until she left."

"Wow." Blake's expression was thoughtful and curious. "Like, months?"

Margie shook her head. "No, years."

"So she's related, like a cousin or something."

"I don't know, I don't think so. I was just a little kid." She might have sounded cranky without meaning to. Blake flushed and ducked his head.

"Sorry," Blake murmured. "You don't have to tell me stuff if you don't want to."

"It's not like it's a secret." Margie rolled her eyes. "Like nothing around here is a secret."

"Tell me about it," Blake said, and the edge of pain in his voice made Margie realize her long-ago unhappiness was nothing compared to what Blake faced every day.

Of course he knew there were no secrets—not anywhere, really, but even less, it seemed, in a place like this where everyone knew everybody else like…forever. Everybody had to know his story, right down to the fact he'd just had top surgery, and Blake knew that too. How much more personal could you get? Everywhere he went, he was practically naked.

Not all the talk was bad. People liked to talk, sometimes in a mean way but mostly just in an interested way. What was going on with your neighbors was practically bigger news than anything else that happened anywhere else, especially when the next closest town was twenty miles away and cities an hour drive or more. Big-city problems weren't the same as theirs, and what mattered there wasn't always the same as what mattered out here. The local politics were a whole lot more important than decisions made hundreds of miles away that didn't have that much impact on day-to-day life. Out here, the most important things were the weather, if it delayed the planting or stunted the crops or made for an especially bountiful season, and if the roads got fixed and the school taxes went up and the sports teams had enough money to buy equipment. Those things dominated the daily conversation, not like people were ignorant or didn't know about what was happening in the rest of the world, but most of the time the things closer to home affected people a lot more personally.

Blake's mom had brought him here from the city for a fresh start—at least that's what Blake said. Coming from New York City, Abby might not have realized that he'd be just as exposed here, probably more, as anywhere else in the world.

Margie couldn't hide anything in her life either, and she didn't want to with Blake. "I don't know why Brody's back. I don't know how I feel about it."

"Your mom seemed okay," Blake said cautiously.

A little of the gloom lifted and Margie laughed. "True. That counts for a lot at our house."

Blake shrugged. "I guess maybe it won't matter so much if she's not staying."

"Yeah." Margie poked at the spot like a bruise. The idea hurt. "But if she isn't, why is she here then?"

"People come home for lots of reasons, I guess." Blake nudged Margie's arm. "Just like they make new ones."

"True." Margie grinned and settled back in the seat. She'd find out soon enough. After all, nothing stayed private very long around here.

When Val sensed the conversation winding down, she said, "So, let's talk about gestation in cattle."

Blake sat up straight, practically quivering with anticipation. He had the bug, that's for sure. For a city kid, he seemed to have taken to country living as if he was born to it. Margie was planning to live her legacy, another Rivers to the core. Oh, she'd toyed with the idea of being a vet for about two minutes, probably because Blake did, and good friends often made plans to do great things together, but she'd come back around to being a physician like two of her older sisters and her father and forefathers.

Val hadn't had a friend like Blake, one she counted on so much she'd wanted to change her future for them. Maybe she wouldn't have been quite as wild or quite as angry, if she had. Thank goodness for Joe. What had started as a summer job as his receptionist had changed her life. He'd seen more in her than her spoiled entitlement projected. Now it was time to pay a little back, and gladly. She eyed her apprentices. "For starters—some of these cows are going to be pregnant with late-season calves. In addition to our routine health checks, what do we need to do for them?"

As they walked toward the line of long, open-sided barns on the Ramseys' dairy farm, each holding hundreds of cows, Blake and Margie alternated giving her the answers. Nice to see them not trying to one-up each other. She listened with half a mind, nodding when they got everything right, while the other half was still puzzling over the mystery of Brody Clark.

She'd heard Margie and Blake's conversation about Brody in the car, of course, but tried to give them the illusion of privacy. She was as curious as Blake, though, about the meaning of Brody's apparently unannounced return. When they'd all been growing up together, she'd never really given Brody Clark very much thought or wondered why she was living with the Rivers family. They'd all gone to the same schools since they were children—her, Harper, Flann, and Brody—but even with the relatively small classes, she and Brody hadn't moved in the same circles. Val had lived right on the border between two school districts, and if she'd lived just a tiny bit farther down the road, she would've been able to go to one of the bigger schools—the better schools—the schools with more money and more opportunities and more…everything. She'd resented for a long time, well, really the entire time, being stuck in the smaller school district with fewer kids, a lot more of whom were farm kids, whose biggest expectations were joining the 4-H and running their family farm when they graduated from high school. She had nothing in common with them. Her father was a successful architect and her mother one of the Saratoga horse set who belonged to the right clubs and the right circles. If not for her father's insistence that she attend a public school to learn a little about her roots—ha, as if that had mattered so much to him when he'd moved up the social ladder—she would have been able to go to a private school with other children of the privileged.

Of course she'd refused to embrace her so-called roots. She'd gravitated to the Rivers kids, particularly Flann, who was a bad girl back then. Val had been a bad girl in her own way, resentful and, looking back on it now, something of an obnoxious princess. She glanced at Margie and Blake. They were so different than she'd been, or the classmates she barely remembered now. But then, maybe not. Maybe if they'd been among her peers in high school, she wouldn't have noticed them either. That thought didn't exactly fill her with pride.

For some reason she pictured Brody Clark, someone else she hadn't bothered to notice. She wondered why. Brody was certainly nice to look at. An inch or two taller than her, which she always liked in a woman, well-built and confident in her serviceable blue uniform, and eye-catching with her jet-black hair and midnight eyes. Who knew—Val might have noticed her more if she hadn't been so busy trying to get Flann Rivers to show a little interest. But then, probably not. Flann was a Rivers, and Brody was—not.

"God," she muttered. "Shallow much?"

"Sorry?" Blake said, looking confused. "Did we miss something?"

"Nope," Val said briskly, putting on a smile and extinguishing the uncomfortable recollections. "You both got everything right. Come on. Let's go see about some cows."

❖

Flann rounded the corner to the short hallway leading to Presley's office, barely slowing as she passed Carrie Longmire's desk.

"Whoa," Carrie called, "she's with someone."

For about ten seconds, Flann stared at the paneled walnut door and debated going in anyhow. "With Matt Hobson, right? The Air Star manager?"

"That's right. She shouldn't be much longer." Carrie frowned. "Is there anything I can help you with?"

Carrie was a lot more than an administrative assistant. She handled the bulk of the day-to-day business of running the hospital and everyone knew it. The way Flann heard it, Carrie somehow managed to defuse 80 percent of the problems before they ever crossed the threshold to Presley's office. That's what made the two of them such a powerhouse team. They got things done faster and more efficiently than anyone at the Rivers had ever thought possible. Presley was a steamroller when she wanted something done—a brilliant, highly capable steamroller—and Carrie was her pit boss.

Flann shook her head. "This is one of those rare instances when I don't think you can help."

"You want to try me?" Carrie's tone was that of a concerned friend as well as a colleague.

Crap. None of this was Presley's fault, but she *was* the boss. Who else was responsible? Flann sighed. "I think I better take it to her first."

"Okay." Carrie tilted her head. "Aren't you supposed to be in the OR now?"

Flann grimaced. "What, do you know everybody's schedule by heart?"

Looking smug, Carrie lifted a computer printout and waved it in the air. "We get a copy every day, just like every other department. I always look at it, and"—she shrugged—"I have a very good memory."

"Yeah, I think I knew that."

Flann leaned against the wall opposite Carrie's desk. "I told them I might be a few minutes late, but it's covered. Glenn is opening for me."

At the mention of the physician assistant who'd just recently been appointed to head the developing PA training program, Carrie grinned. "You know, you really shouldn't tempt Glenn away from her job in the ER. Your wife will be mad at you."

"Ha. My wife is the one who stole my personal PA right out from under me."

Carrie laughed. "Look, if it's really important, I'll interrupt—"

Presley's office opened, solving the problem. Presley and Matt stepped out as Presley said, "I'll see about those arrangements and let you know by noon today."

"I appreciate it," Matt said heartily. He nodded to Carrie and Flann and strode out, looking like a happy man.

"Carrie—can you get Abby for me?" Presley said before turning to Flann. "Flann? You need me?"

"If you've got a minute."

"Whatever you need. Come on in." Presley gave Carrie a look. "Hold on Abby until I'm clear. Better yet, let her know we need to house the new air crew down there until the addition upstairs is done."

"I've got it."

"Thanks," Presley said.

"Sorry to interrupt your morning," Flann said as she closed the door behind her. She wouldn't ordinarily have done that, knowing damn well Carrie knew everything of importance at the hospital, but this…this was personal.

"Of course. Anytime." Presley gestured to the small seating area in one corner of her office and took one of the chairs flanking the coffee table. Flann made herself sit on the small sofa although she felt like pacing.

Presley said, "So I take it there's some kind of problem."

"These new hires from Air Star," Flann said. "I don't know what kind of vetting you do, but Brody Clark has no business working at the Rivers."

Presley's brows rose and her blue eyes sharpened. "You want to tell me why, and before you do, every employee fills out standard personnel forms, and we run basic security checks. We're not the Pentagon, Flann, but we're also diligent about identifying potential problems in new hires before they sign on. You might want to elaborate."

Presley was Flann's sister-in-law, but she was also the CEO of the hospital and she called the shots. Flann knew it and figured Presley wouldn't be very happy with her challenging a decision Presley had made. She really didn't give a damn. "Brody grew up here, and she's got a past."

"All right," Presley said slowly, crossing her legs and looking as relaxed as ever. Flann knew better. She could drop the ax in the blink of an eye. "Is there criminal history that for some reason wouldn't have shown up on a standard security sweep?"

"Not that I'm aware of," Flann said.

"You do realize she's a decorated vet, honorably discharged, with three tours overseas. She was awarded at least one medal for valor under fire."

"I didn't know that." Flann gritted her teeth. She wasn't surprised. Brody had never been afraid of much, just another reason why her leaving the way she did made no sense. But that was done, and Flann didn't care what her explanation was now. Whatever it was, it was too little, too late.

Presley continued in her casual tone, every word glinting like the honed edge of a knife blade. "And her record at Air Star is exemplary. She received a recent promotion based on merit, she has advanced certification as a flight paramedic—exactly the kind of experience we need, *and* she has teaching experience. That will work well with our PA program here."

"Look, Presley, it's a family thing."

Presley stiffened. "I see. Well then, whatever it is affects me too."

Flann closed her eyes. She was sinking fast. "Okay, maybe I'm not going about this the right way."

"Maybe if you led with the facts instead of letting your temper do the talking, we could get to the bottom of this a lot faster."

Presley was still smiling, and the knife slid a little closer. Yep, she was getting pissed. Flann tried the grin that had worked for her her entire life, and sure enough, there for a teeny tiny second was an itty-bitty smile.

"I'm really glad you married Harper," Flann said, "because the cool voice of reason would drive me crazy in about a week."

Presley laughed. "Well, I'm rather glad I married her too, for a lot of reasons besides the fact I adore her. Not the least of which, Abby's my best friend, and *she* wanted you—sometimes I wonder why."

Flann rubbed her face and chuckled. "Okay. Brody used to live with us. From the time she was fifteen until she was eighteen."

Presley blinked. That was a first. "She's related?"

"Might as well be, but no, she was fostered. We were all pretty much the same age—Brody and I were the same year in school—and she was one of us."

She was family. The rage rose again and Flann swallowed it down. That was done. Done and over.

"Why haven't I ever heard of her? Harper never mentioned her. Why hasn't she been at any of our weddings or the holidays?"

"Because she walked away one day, like we'd never even existed. Like we never mattered."

"I see," Presley said softly, only how could she. She hadn't been there. She sighed. "I wish I'd known. I could have told Harper and the rest of you. At least you would have been prepared." She paused, leaned forward, looked Flann in the eye. "Brody Clark is an integral part of the Air Star team, and she's done nothing wrong—professionally. You and the others will have to leave the personal out of the hospital."

Chapter Five

Brody pulled the truck into a free space a few spots down from the diner and sat with the engine off. With her window open, a bit of a breeze snuck in, but the cool stream did nothing to relieve the heat prickling her skin. She knew this feeling—had experienced it every time she'd returned from a mission and the adrenaline seeped away, leaving her muscles trembling and her mind blank. Nothing about her visit with Ida was anything like the terror of flying into possible death, praying that the troops she'd been sent to aid were still alive, and that she could reach them in time and somehow keep them alive until she could get them to safety. Today was nothing like that, but her body hadn't caught up to her brain just yet.

She didn't fear Ida, but she'd dreaded what she'd see in her eyes, and she'd been right to. The pain she'd seen there had been more wrenching, more piercing, than the anger in Flann's or the disappointment in Harper's. She'd never wanted to hurt any of them, and she'd tried as best she could to avoid it, but today her failure had been clear. At eighteen she thought she'd had no other choice. Maybe she'd been wrong, maybe not, but there was no way to go back and undo the past. She took a long breath. The last thing Ida had said to her was make sure she came back soon—the rest of the family would want to see her.

Brody chuckled. Ida hadn't talked to Flann yet, obviously. Flann definitely did not want to see her again, and probably none of the others did either. She missed them all, but Flann most of all. They were the same age, and at sixteen they'd shared the same undercurrent of discontent, maybe a little insecurity even, that they hid from everyone else. Countless times Brody and Flann had been on the same side of an argument while Harper took the rational, often more conventional position. Still, when some plan went awry, Flann was often the one held accountable—Brody always seemed to disappear a little into the background. The same way she faded from view when Flann joined a group or struck up a conversation with someone.

Funny she should see Val at the homestead. Val had always circled in Flann's orbit—or maybe the other way around—and she'd never looked beyond Flann and Harper, at least as far as the Rivers teens were concerned. Even Carson had never held any interest for her, but Val had plenty of other people interested in her. She could pick and choose, and she did. Someone new every week or so it seemed, but she always came back to Flann and Harper's crowd. Brody had been there too, but as she'd said that morning, Val had had no reason to notice her. She wasn't…anybody.

Brody closed her eyes and leaned her head back. This was getting her nowhere. All of that was in the past.

"Hey!"

Brody jumped at a sharp rap on the passenger window. Jane looked in at her.

"Door's open," Brody said.

Jane slid in, rolled the window down partway, and leaned back against the door. She raised a brow when Brody said nothing. "Well?"

"Well." Brody shook her head. "Looks like I'll probably have a job for a while."

Jane sat up straighter. "You're serious, aren't you."

Brody nodded. "Flann wasn't kidding. I think if Ida—that's Flann's mother—had been against me coming back and working here, I probably would've had to leave."

"That's crazy," Jane snapped. "Unless…is there something—dammit, Brody—I don't want to pry into your business…but is there something they're holding over your head?"

Brody smiled. "Only my own doings. I'm not in trouble with the law, and I don't have a shady past. Well, maybe it's a little dark and twisty, but I wasn't a drug addict or a thief or anything like that."

"Oh, good to know." Jane rolled her eyes. "Like I thought that. So my point is, private citizens can't dictate who gets hired for a job. And if they're not holding something over your head…"

"They're not, really. It's a…thing…from a long time ago."

"A thing. So where does Flann come off threatening your job."

"Flann is…the Flann I remember…" Brody amended. After all, she didn't really know Flann, any of them, any longer. "Is a little quick on the draw, but she's someone with influence at the hospital."

"Because she's a Rivers," Jane muttered. "Back to that again."

"Not *just* because she's a Rivers. Presley Worth is Harper Rivers's wife. And Abby Remy, the head of the emergency room? She's Flann's wife."

"Oh my God," Jane said, groaning. "You have got to be kidding me."

Brody smiled wryly. "And Edward Rivers? He's the medical chief of staff and I understand Harper will eventually have that job."

"You're *not* kidding. Are there any more of them?"

"Carson—the other older sister, there's one younger than those three—is a vice president in the management end of things."

"And you knew all this coming back and didn't say anything?"

"Not all of it. I've kind of followed what's been happening here since I left, but I didn't know until I'd already signed on where we were going to end up. I didn't in a million years think it would be here. If I had…" If she had known sooner, would she have been such a coward that she'd have said no to the job, to Matt and Jane? "I don't know what I would have done."

"Wow. Is it all nepotism, or are they actually any good?"

"I guess I can't say from actual experience, but knowing Harper and Flann? They're going to be the best at whatever they do."

Jane pursed her lips. "So were you ever planning to tell me any of this—like how exactly you know them, for starters?"

"I would have, eventually. I just need a little time to sort things out first." Brody rubbed her face with both hands. "For now, can I just say I used to be close to the family. Hell, I lived with them for almost four years."

Jane caught her breath. "Holy hell, Brode. That complicates this whole thing a little."

"Yeah, you think?"

Brody must have sounded desperate. Jane's expression softened and she leaned over and squeezed Brody's arm. "Nothing to do till we get to work and see what happens. But we'll handle it—okay?"

"Okay. Thanks for the backup."

"Don't be a jerk. We're a team, right." Jane slapped Brody's leg. "Come on. Let's go get my bike and we'll head out—" Jane's phone rang and a second later Brody's followed.

Brody checked the message and sighed.

"Oh, great," Jane said. "Matt summons."

Brody started the truck. "Maybe there's some good news for a change."

When they got to the Rivers, Matt waited for them in the parking lot, leaning against his truck. Brody pulled in beside Jane's bike, and she and Jane joined him.

"Good news first," Matt said with a big smile. "SunView has deep pockets—we are going to have our very own helo based right here. A brand-spanking-new, state-of-the-art EC145."

Jane made a moaning sound. "Where? Where is my baby?"

Matt laughed. "Delivery today. Airvan is sending a field rep so we can all get a once-over of the equipment. They're big on tech support, so they might ride along the first few times."

"Presley Worth is going all out to put this place on the map," Brody said.

"I think SunView is using this place as a model for their expansion program. But hey—it works for us."

"I'll say," Jane said. "So what's the bad news?"

"Just more good news," Matt said. "We're *also* going to have our very own on-call rooms. Well, two temporary ones. I get mine, and the two of you have to share."

Jane put her hands on her hips. "What, we don't even get a vote?"

"One of you want to bunk with me, then?" Matt's tone was innocent but he was holding back a grin.

"Not me," Brody and Jane said simultaneously.

"Then I guess it's settled." Matt laughed. "We'll billet temporarily down in the ER and use their on-call rooms. That means some of the ER staff are gonna have to double up, and they'll probably grumble for a while, but it's just until our own quarters are finished on the upper level adjacent to the helipad. Hopefully that won't be too long."

"Works for me," Jane said.

Matt cocked his head. "Brody—you good?"

"Yeah. Sure. I can handle Jane talking in her sleep." Brody made light and they laughed but she wasn't in love with the idea. Temporary quarters in the ER meant they'd be spending a lot of time down there—not just transporting injured, when everyone was so focused on the medical care there wasn't time for personal BS, but downtime when there was nothing *but* personal stuff to focus on. The itchy sensation in her skin was back.

"At least I don't snore," Jane said. "So when do we get the bad news? There's got to be bad news."

"Not exactly." Matt grimaced. "In case you haven't noticed, this hospital is a little bit different than what we're used to. It's a big part of the community."

Jane glanced at Brody. "We noticed."

Matt frowned. "I miss something?"

"Nope," Brody said quickly. "So what's the story?"

Matt got a faintly sheepish look. "I kind of signed you two on for a community thing the hospital's doing."

Brody and Jane looked at each other.

"A *thing*?" Jane echoed. "Lot of that going around."

"What does that mean exactly?" Brody said suspiciously.

"You're going to be representing Air Star at a booth—or tent—or something, at the fair."

"The fair?" Jane's voice rose. "You mean out in a field with cows and horses and screaming children?"

Matt nodded. "Yeah. The hospital will have paramedics out there to take care of emergencies and also for informational purposes. Air Star is now part of the hospital system, and we're the new and shiny right now. I'm guessing Presley Worth wants to make an impression with the community. She volunteered us."

"For how long?" Brody knew what the fair was like. She'd spent plenty of time there when she was a kid. A week, nonstop, morning till night with farmers showing stock, 4-H kids exhibiting animals and crafts, entertainment, food, amusements. All of it in the broiling sun or thunderstorms. Heat stroke. Accidents. Sick and lost children. A potential medical madhouse.

"Ah." Matt rubbed the back of his neck. "This is a county thing—"

"I'm starting to hate that word," Jane muttered.

"And we're the only air evac team in the county, and…new and shiny, remember."

"Chief," Brody said slowly, "the fair is open from, like, nine in the morning until eleven o'clock at night. We can't cover all of that."

"You can switch off with some of the ER people from here. They'll be getting volunteered too."

"When exactly does this volunteer duty start?" Jane said.

"Ah, tomorrow."

"Great," Brody muttered. "Any more good news?"

"Just that the three of us have a meeting with the ER chief and her staff this afternoon at four. Right after we take command of our helo at three."

Brody said, "I'm going home to check on Honcho, then. Jane—you want to tag along?"

"Right behind you."

As Jane headed to her bike and Brody hurried to her truck, Matt called, "Three o'clock on the helipad. Don't be late."

Brody started her engine. A few hours, then. A few hours before she'd have to make a place for herself at the Rivers, unless Flann or someone else stood in her way.

❖

"Just to be clear," Val said, "we're not going to make a habit out of this. If we do, I'll have to double my morning run—no, triple it—by the time you guys are ready to go back to school."

Margie grinned as the teen in the band T-shirt behind the take-out window handed her an enormous ice cream cone. After she swiped a bite off the side, she said, "Come on, it was right on the way. And we worked hard, right?"

Blake took the sundae that arrived in a dish the size of a soup tureen. "Just get a small."

"Right. Like that one." Val accepted her cone. "Come on, let's take these out back before we head over to the office. We've got clinic this afternoon, remember."

"And pizza for dinner, right?" Margie said.

"You're killing me." Laughing, Val turned the corner toward the pine-shaded area behind the ice cream stand where picnic tables were set out for people to enjoy their takeout.

Brody Clark sat at a table with a blonde Val had never seen before.

Somehow the blonde managed to look effortlessly sexy even in the blue uniform pants and shirt, and any other time Val would have taken a lot more notice. Right now, though, she was much more interested in Brody and the gorgeous brown and black Belgian Malinois pressed close to Brody's knee. Brody held down a vanilla ice cream cone, and the dog delicately licked it. The two of them made a very enticing picture.

In the next second the dog alerted to their presence and tensed, shifting to keep the three of them in view. Brody looked over and zeroed in on Val. Val slowed, feeling as if a spotlight had suddenly been focused on her. She could practically feel the heat on her face as Brody's gaze traveled over her.

If someone had told her before that morning that she knew this woman, she would've denied it. She would've sworn she'd never seen Brody Clark before in her life. How was that possible when they'd practically grown up in the same town? True, she hadn't lived in the village, but she'd gone to school with everyone who lived there. But she didn't know this dark-haired woman with the intense, wary gaze and the still, coiled-spring body poised to *move*. Everything about Brody radiated controlled tension, as if she expected danger to come from any direction at any second. Brody and the dog at her side shared an unwavering intensity that pulled Val in, unexpectedly captivated by the image of the two beautiful animals.

Margie broke the tension. "Hey, Brody."

"Margie," Brody said, her gaze still focused on Val.

The blonde straightened, her expression curious and a little surprised. Val gave her another look. A little taller than average, slender in a muscular kind of way, strong bold features, and even sitting down, something confident in her carriage. Val wondered if they were a couple. They looked it, the way they lounged close together, their shoulders nearly touching. Irritation and something else not quite identifiable buzzed beneath her skin. What was the matter with her? She shook it off and smiled at Brody. "Hello again. That's a beautiful animal."

"Thanks," Brody said.

Maybe the reason Val had never noticed Brody way back when was because Brody was a master of understatement. *Tall, dark, and silent* flashed through Val's mind and she gave herself a mental kick. When was the last time she'd found a woman so interesting? Ever since she'd left New York City, she'd been reverting to some previous version of herself she'd been all too happy to leave behind. She did not fall under another woman's spell, even when she *was* interested. She held the reins of whatever trip the two of them were about to take.

Blake put his sundae down on a nearby table and took a step forward. "Is he friendly?"

"She. And yes, when she knows you." Brody dropped her hand onto the back of the Malinois's neck. "That usually takes a while."

"Okay." Blake stopped six feet away and crouched down, his arms resting loosely on his thighs. The dog tracked his movements, tilted her head, and regarded him steadily. "Hey, I'm Blake."

"Blake has never met an animal he doesn't love," Val said quietly.

"This is Honcho," Brody said. "Why don't you come over here, Blake. Honcho will either ignore you or give you a go-ahead sign."

"So," Blake said as he walked carefully toward the dog, his voice soft and warm, "I don't have a dog, but I've always wanted one. I used to live in the city and most dogs aren't too keen on city living." He crouched a few feet away, within easy petting distance. "Plus, my mom is a cat person. Both my parents, really." Blake laughed and held out his hand "Well, Flann isn't really a cat person either, but I think she pretends to be to make my mom happy. I've been working on the whole dog thing, though."

Val picked up on the sudden stiffening of Brody's shoulders and the quick, assessing look she gave Blake. Brody didn't know about Blake, so she probably didn't know about Flann and Abby. Everyone who knew Flann knew about her whirlwind romance with the new doctor in town and her son. Strange, considering Brody's history with the Riverses. But then, she had been away a decade. More mystery added to the tantalizing reappearance of Brody Clark.

The dog sniffed Blake's hand, and Brody grunted in surprise.

"Here." Brody handed Blake the ice cream cone. "She's a sucker for this."

"I get that. Me too." Blake's smile blazed as he held it and Honcho's ears perked up.

"Go ahead, Honch," Brody murmured.

Honcho's tail lifted and she wagged it once as her tongue snaked out and slurped the side of the cone where the ice cream had run down.

"Honcho," Blake said, turning the cone so the dog could continue her careful attack on the ice cream. "That's a very cool name." He looked up at Brody. "Why is she afraid?"

Brody's expression softened, and for an instant, Val saw a different woman behind the wariness and the expectation of danger. The tenderness that turned the chiseled edges of her face into a gorgeous canvas of sweeping planes and soaring angles surprised her. Brody clearly adored that dog.

"She's not afraid," Brody said. "Honcho is probably the bravest animal you'll ever meet. She's a warrior, a veteran. But the war taught her that everything isn't always the way it seems." As she spoke, her gaze drifted from Blake up to Val.

The shadows swirling in her eyes were a punch to Val's solar plexus. Brody was a cipher, but one thing she couldn't hide was the undercurrent of pain in her eyes.

"What work did she do?" Blake said, now softly stroking Honcho's flank.

"She was mainly SAR—search and rescue. She'd help find injured troops during a firefight and did a lot of forward action work too, scouting out terrain ahead of troop movement. She could sniff out the enemy…" Brody trailed off and her expression cooled. "She earned her retirement."

Val sat down at the end of an adjacent picnic table with Margie and held out her hand to the blonde. "Hi. I'm Val."

"Jane," the blonde said, smiling for the first time.

Her smile was nice and the friendly appraisal in her eyes was nice too.

Val smiled back, but she was drawn back to Brody. "So you adopted her."

"Yes. We mustered out together." As she spoke, Brody petted the dog, who was now eagerly devouring the last of the cone.

"It's not easy for those dogs to make the transition all the time," Val said.

"She's steady," Brody said. "Except she doesn't like really loud noises. Sometimes she has trouble sleeping. I think she thinks she's still on patrol."

Val nodded. "Have you tried medication with her? Sometimes that helps with the anxiety, and they're actually more comfortable."

"We tried Xanax, but she didn't react well."

"That can happen, but there are alternatives." Val hesitated. "Totally up to you, but if you bring her by the clinic sometime, I'd be happy to take a look at her and talk it over with you."

Jane said, "So you're a vet?"

Val nodded. "Yes."

Jane gestured to Blake and Margie. "Vet students to be?"

Margie grinned. "Apprentices. Blake wants to be a vet, but I'm planning on being a neurosurgeon." She held out her hand to Jane. "Margie Rivers."

Jane's eyebrows shot up as she shook hands. "Let me guess—a lot of your family are doctors at the Rivers, right?"

"Most everybody. My sister Carson isn't, but she works there."

"Yes, I heard that."

"But it's animals for you, right?" Jane said to Blake.

He nodded. "Yep. My parents work at the Rivers too. My mom's the head of the emergency room and Flann is chief of surgery."

Jane laughed. "Is everyone around here part of the Rivers?"

"You'd be surprised," Val said. "That hospital isn't just the main employer in this part of the county. Almost every single one of us has been there for one reason or another in our lifetime—births, broken bones when we were kids, accidents, and emergencies when we were sick. The place is the beating heart of this community."

"Huh." Jane smiled wryly. "Well, we're part of it too now."

"I gathered you were medical." Val indicated the patches on their shirts and glanced at Brody. "Everyone knows about the construction of the new helipad at the hospital. Are you part of that?"

Brody nodded. "We're part of the new aero-medevac program. Jane's the flyboy. I'm a flight medic."

"Really. So that's what brought you back," Val said to Brody.

"That's right," Brody said.

From the tone of Brody's voice, Val got the feeling Brody wasn't very happy to be back. But then, she had disappeared leaving a trail of questions and gossip as to what provoked her sudden departure. All that would probably be resurrected once word got around she'd returned. If she'd wanted to leave her past behind, coming back was the last thing she should have done.

Chapter Six

Honcho finished off the cone in one careful bite and eased back against Brody's thigh. Blake stood, a broad grin on his face. So this was Flann's kid, Brody thought. Maybe he'd had an easier time settling into a new family than she had, but then maybe not. Parents and kids came with all kinds of history, she ought to know. He looked pretty happy right that minute, but then all he seemed to see was Honcho. One thing she could tell for sure, this kid was a natural with animals. "Honcho considers you a friend or she wouldn't have taken that from you."

Blake flushed. "She's amazing. Does she still do any SAR work?"

"Not officially. I take her out and let her track to keep her from getting bored, but like I said—mostly retired."

"Were you her handler in the service?" Val said.

"No," Brody said abruptly and eyed the two kids. They weren't children, and probably were ten times as knowledgeable about the world than she had been at their ages. She had a childhood spent with a drug-addicted teenage mother with very little in the way of support to thank for that. Still, some things she didn't talk about with civilians. "When Honcho was ready for retirement, I got lucky. I was stationed at the same FOB as her and was leaving at the same time. I knew a couple of people who managed the paperwork, and here we are."

"FOB?" Margie asked.

"Forward operating base. We were in Afghanistan at the time."

"Huh." Margie looked thoughtful. "You know, I've kind of been thinking I might get some experience in the military I'd never get a chance to have again. Maybe I could talk to you sometime about that. My brother-in-law served, but on the command side, not medical."

Brody swallowed. She could just see Flann's face if she found out her little sister was getting career advice from her. Especially when she could end up somewhere she might get killed. Margie regarded her steadily. Yep, she was a Rivers. She knew what she wanted. "Sure."

Margie grinned. "Awesome."

"Hey," Blake cut in, "do you think I could watch you train Honcho someday? I could walk her, even, sometimes, if you needed someone. I mean, not right away, but…"

He broke off when he saw what must have looked like incredulity on Brody's face. Flann's sister and now her kid? Could the day get any weirder?

"Let's see how she settles in for a bit, and I'll let you know." Brody didn't have the heart to say no, and Honcho could do with some company. "But I wouldn't trust her with just anyone, so if I need someone, you'd be the guy."

"Okay, great!" Blake stuffed his hands in his back pockets and looked satisfied.

Val put a hand on Margie's and Blake's shoulders. "Okay, you two. We have work to do and Brody probably needs a chance to get settled before you two show up on her doorstep."

"It's no problem," Brody said, knowing that was almost certainly not true. Val smiled and Brody took a hit to the midsection. That might be the first time Val had ever looked at her long enough to even smile.

"Well, good luck with the new program at the Rivers," Val said.

"Thanks," Brody said.

Jane called good-bye as Val and the two kids left the picnic area, leaned back with her elbows on the picnic-table top, and regarded Brody with a raised brow. "Seemed like you knew all of them."

"Mm-hmm." Brody watched them disappear around the corner, still thinking about Val. She'd never pictured her as a country vet, but back in high school she wouldn't have figured Val for any kind of vet. Or anything else where she'd have to get dirty. Val had been one of those girls who always wore the newest fashion and the right makeup, and who drove the nicest car. A Mazda roadster, red of course. The few girls who were anywhere close to her social status were the same. Perfect princesses.

Sexy as hell and untouchable for someone like her, or so she'd thought. When she'd lived with the Riverses she sure hadn't looked like a bum, but the past trailed along behind her all the same. Her clothes might make her look like everyone else, but she wasn't. She knew and so did they. Brody laughed at the memory. Now women like Val barely rated a second glance—all the trappings of money and status had long ago lost their shine. Six years of war would do that to you.

Funny, though, if she'd just met Val, she wouldn't have put her in that privileged, elitist category. Val might not have been countrified, but she'd had a hefty streak of mud on her jeans, a smudge of…something on her chin, and a casual friendliness that was at odds with the aloof disdain she'd worn like a mantle in high school. She figured Val would end up going to some private Ivy League place, maybe Bryn Mawr or Brown. She wondered what happened to her to change her path. That didn't happen all that often—of course, look at her. She'd been set to go to the community college once she graduated, even though Ida and Edward had urged her to go four year and offered to help her out. She hadn't wanted to take any more of their help, even though she'd appreciated it. She never figured she'd end up as a flight medic, either. Funny how a decade could make strangers of everyone.

Brody shrugged. "I knew Val and Margie from when I lived here, but that was a long time ago. I don't really know them now. I just met Blake."

"And he's Flann Rivers's kid," Jane said.

"Apparently."

"You would've known that, right? He's gotta be in his midteens."

Brody shook her head. "There weren't any kids on the horizon when I was here, but I guess—who knows."

"Seems like a nice kid, both of them were."

"Margie was practically a baby last time I saw her. She's got the Rivers spark, though. And I guess she's got the Rivers genes too." She laughed. "Neurosurgery."

Jane grinned. "Never hurts to dream big."

"I guess not," Brody said quietly, although she knew better.

"Maybe the bird has arrived." Jane practically bounced on her toes. "Let's drop Honcho off and go see. I might have time to play with her before we have yet another meeting."

"Sure," Brody said, more than happy to get moving. Motion was the only thing that kept her from getting lost replaying every minute of the past few hours with Ida, Flann, and most of all, Val.

❖

"It's really cool we're getting mobile air transport." Margie leaned forward from the back seat. She'd switched off with Blake, only fair after all. "Maybe we can get them to take us out on a run."

"Yeah." Blake turned to Margie. "Maybe you can talk to Flann."

"Wait a minute," Margie said, "your mom is the head of the ER. *You* talk to her."

"I don't like to take advantage of my position," Blake said very seriously.

Margie cracked up. "That's such bull. What are you scared of?"

Blake grinned sheepishly. "I'm saving my ammunition to work on the dog thing."

"I can't believe they don't want to get one," Margie said.

"Oh, you know. No one's home enough, the place is too small, wait until we move into the new place and see what it's like." Blake sighed. "Can't argue about the space thing."

"Well, that's going to be soon, right? I thought you guys were moving even if the renovations aren't done."

"Hopefully. My mom has been really busy with the ER expansion and this new mobile air thing."

"Yeah, so cool!" Margie said. "We'll figure out a way to get in on it. Oh, hey, did you get the text about the fair meet-up tomorrow?"

"Yeah. I'll be there. Did you…"

Val listened to the two of them chatting as she drove, trying to remember when her life had been filled with simple plans, rather than complications. The two of them seemed so comfortable with their families and each other. She was pretty sure she'd never felt that way. She'd loved her parents, and she and her mother still managed to communicate as long as they weren't living in the same house, but she'd grown up in a family at war with the rest of their family. Her parents had tried to keep her out of those fireworks, but like all kids, she'd heard things and seen things, and when she'd gotten old enough to start school, she'd felt things. Courtney had been raised to hate her, and it was pretty clear she still did. Val sighed. Just bumping into more of her past that couldn't be changed.

She caught her reflection as she glanced up before turning into the clinic, and horror washed through her. What was all over her face? It looked like—no, no—it could not be chicken poop. Absolutely not. Had she just stood there talking to Brody Clark with poop on her face? Nope, she hadn't. She couldn't entertain any other possibility.

Val stopped the car, pulled a crumpled napkin from the compartment on the door, and swiped at her chin. Good thing she hadn't wanted to impress her. Damn it.

❖

Brody crouched in the belly of the bird while Jane played up front in the cockpit making crooning noises as she worked over the controls. The Airvan rep, a Latinx wearing casual tan pants, flats, and a short-sleeved cotton shirt, was just about finished with her introductory spiel, a practiced litany of all the modern medical equipment that would be available for Brody in flight. Brody was duly impressed. She'd thought the Black Hawks she'd flown in had been state of the art, but this was something else. For one thing, the body was bigger and so efficiently designed the place could substitute for a hospital operating room. The Black Hawks had been well equipped, but they were still war birds. This thing was a trauma unit with wings.

"As you can see," the rep, who'd introduced herself as Devi Lopez, finished up with a smile, "you've got room back here for two medics and multiple patients. Dual life support systems allow you both to work independently if necessary."

"It's amazing," Brody said.

Devi beamed. "I'll ride along the first few callouts just to make sure you're comfortable with the layout."

"You have medical training?" Brody didn't mind being observed—she just wanted to make sure she wouldn't have a civilian aboard who couldn't handle a major trauma up close. And she wasn't above taking suggestions, especially when some of the equipment was new. All she cared about was getting the job done.

"No, I'm an engineer," Devi said. "I helped design some of the upgrades. I spent three months with a trauma team in Texas while this version was on the drawing board so I'd know what you needed."

"I'm impressed. Any reason they're sending so much talent out with this one? I wouldn't think you'd be doing fieldwork now."

Devi smiled. "Ordinarily, I wouldn't, but SunView is a big client, and we're expecting to field a considerable fleet for you over the next six months across all fifty states. I wanted to get a sense of your needs."

"Hand-holding. Got it." Brody laughed. "Well, my needs extend about as far as the bay door over there. But I'm sure the hospital CEO will be more than happy to fill you in on what she wants."

"Oh, I've met Ms. Worth. The higher-ups from Airvan have met with her several times, but I'm more interested in ground-level requirements. That's the fun part of the job."

"Tell me that in a couple of days when you've been sleeping in the emergency room." Brody frowned. "You'll probably be roughing it a bit."

"Not a problem. And don't worry, I'm not going to get in your way."

"Wasn't worried about it. Thanks for the tour."

"My pleasure," Devi said, her gaze holding fast on Brody's.

Brody wasn't sure what to read into the gaze, if anything, but she smiled and turned toward the cockpit. "Jane, time to stop playing, we've got to meet the chief down in the ER."

Matt had left them after the initial introductions to meet with the ER chief, PAs, and residents. He'd be coordinating flights and organizational details most of the time while Jane and Brody took the callouts. Anything else he needed to know he could get from them when the time came. Brody jumped down to the rooftop, turned back to give Devi a hand, and Jane finally followed.

"What a beauty," Jane murmured, giving one last longing glance at the bird.

"You are easy to please," Brody said.

Jane lifted a brow. "Au contraire."

Laughing, Brody shook her head. As they neared the elevator, her good humor dissipated. Chances were good at least one of the Riverses would be at the meeting, but she'd gotten through a lot of things in her life that she'd wished she could avoid. At least the new ER wouldn't bring back the kind of memories she'd prefer not to have resurface.

Jane looked as if she wanted to ask her something, but Devi's presence made anything more than casual chatter impossible. Even though she'd thought she was prepared, Brody's chest tightened as they headed down the hall to the central receiving area. The closer they got to the heart of things, the more the noise level picked up and the lights grew brighter. She needed a better handle on herself than this. Physically the place was different, but she recognized a few familiar faces right away. Fortunately, no one recognized her, which was exactly the way she wanted it.

"Hey," Matt said when he saw them, "you're right on time. We're down this way."

Brody and the others followed him down the hallway and left the hustle and bustle of the receiving area behind. Unlike this morning, only a handful of people were present in the conference room when they arrived. The handful, however, probably represented 60 percent of the power that ran the place.

Flann was there with a green-eyed blonde in a white lab coat that identified her as Abigail Remy, MD, Chief of Emergency Services. She was also Blake's mother—he had her eyes, although his were more blue than green, and he still shared a certain classic facial elegance with her that hadn't yet been blunted by the typical late teen male growth spurt. A sandy-haired, rangy woman and a midtwenties Latinx in scrubs completed the group. The sandy-haired one had a stance that was distinctly military—some things just never went away—but her appraising gaze seemed pretty even.

Flann, on the other hand, gave her a hard, hot look.

Remy held a hand out to Brody and introduced herself, then did the same with Jane and Devi. Brody couldn't read much in Abigail Remy's expression. Either Flann hadn't told her anything, or she was a lot better at putting on a professional face than Flann. Not really surprising. One thing about Flann, you never had to guess what she was thinking. She either couldn't or didn't bother to hide her feelings.

"This is Glenn Archer," Remy-call-me-Abby went on, pointing to the rangy one, "the head of our PA training program, and Mari Mateo, one of our clinical teaching PAs. We're hoping once you get into gear, you'll work them in to your rotation."

"Planning on instituting a flight medic training program?" Matt said amiably.

Abby smiled. "Something to think about for the future."

Matt laughed. "SunView moves fast."

"We have a CEO with vision."

"Glad to hear it."

They all sat down around the conference table, and Abby and Matt for the most part talked protocol, scheduling, and other things Brody didn't really care about. Her job was to get to the injured as fast as possible, extract them, and get them back to where they could be stabilized safely and efficiently. All the rest of it was administration and didn't interest her. The entire time the others talked, Flann watched her.

At length the briefing wound up and Abby rose. "Glenn will show you the temporary on-call rooms we've assigned you. Devi, I'm afraid you'll have to share with one of our ER residents. Our construction is still under way."

"Absolutely not a problem," Devi said. "I appreciate you accommodating me."

"Fine, let me introduce you to the ER residents."

Jane followed them out with Matt and Glenn, leaving Brody behind with Flann.

"Something you want to say?" Brody asked when Flann made no move toward the door.

"My mother called me," Flann said.

"Okay."

"She's got a soft heart, but I don't."

Brody laughed. "If you say so. Anything I *don't* know you want to tell me?"

"You fucked up, and now you're back, but there's no going back. You know that, right?"

Brody's stomach clenched. "What's your point?"

"We can work together because that's the job, and I understand you're good at it."

"Exactly how do you know that?"

Flann smiled thinly. "You think Presley Worth would bring on a first team without review?"

"Hard to tell. Everybody around here seems to think she can walk on water."

Flann snorted. "I think only Harper believes that, but I'm not so sure it isn't true."

Brody's stomach twisted. For a second, Flann sounded like the old Flann. The look in her eyes when she mentioned Harper was familiar too. A little bit of hero worship, and a fondness that ran deep. Once upon a time, the fondness, at least, had shone on her. Flann was like that, a comet illuminating everything in her orbit—ever so briefly, but unforgettably.

"I am not here for any other reason than the job," Brody said flatly. "I'll steer clear of your family."

"I'm not sure my mother will allow that." Flann's jaw clenched. "She wants to see you again. All I'm saying is, you might sit at the table, but it was your choice to walk away the way you did."

Brody nodded. Maybe circumstances had changed, but her actions had not. She was responsible for what she had done and the decisions she'd made. Flann walked out without giving her a chance to reply, but what was there to say? Flann was right. She'd closed the door behind her, and she couldn't walk through it again. That was the nature of life. There were no do-overs.

Chapter Seven

Abby caught up to Flann just as the elevator doors slid open, and for a heartbeat, Flann considered jumping in. Ordinarily she'd take any excuse to see her wife, but the conversation with Brody lingered like a slow burn on the surface of her brain and she needed a minute to walk it off.

"Flann," Abby said. "See you for a sec?"

"Sure." Flann waved off the people in the elevator, followed Abby into her office, and closed the door. She had a feeling they'd need privacy for this conversation. Course, she could get lucky and maybe Abby just needed a quick curbside consult.

"Do you have a case right now?"

"Nope. I'm waiting on a CT before I drain a subdiaphragmatic abscess on the guy who flipped his tractor last weekend."

"Good. I just need a minute." Abby leaned with her hips against the front of her desk, a quizzical look on her face and a frown between her eyebrows. "Something going on?"

Well, so much for keeping anything from her. Like she ever could, even if she'd wanted to, which she didn't. She hadn't said anything to Abby about Brody yet. Hell, she hadn't even had a summit meeting with Harper—and she needed to—about the best way to handle the whole deal, because she was still getting her balance back after being blindsided when Brody'd shown up out of the blue.

"Not really." Flann shrugged, figuring she could give it a try and maybe she'd buy herself a little more time to sort out her feelings before she'd fill Abby in.

A little smile tugged at the corner of Abby's mouth. "Want to try that again?"

Guess not. Flann sighed and ran a hand through her hair. "Yeah. How much time do you have?"

The little smile went away and Abby took her hands, kissed her gently. It was an I-love-you kiss, not a I-want-you-right-now kiss, but Flann still felt the zip, knew she always would. She wrapped her arms around Abby's waist and held her. The familiar scent of her hair, the warm curve of her body, the brief touch of her lips to Flann's collarbone nudged her world back into order. The heat simmering beneath her skin cooled. Flann kissed her temple and let her go. "So, did you know who was coming from Air Star?"

Abby frowned. "You mean who exactly, or that a team was coming?"

"Who exactly."

"No, why?"

"Not that it would've mattered, I guess," Flann muttered. What could Abby have done, hell, what could she have done? Brody wasn't a criminal, and just because she'd committed the cardinal sin of betraying the family, because that was exactly what she had done by walking out on them when she had to know they all loved her, God damn it, she hadn't done anything that would prevent her from taking the position with Air Star. "Even if you'd gotten names, you wouldn't have known anyhow, and then it wouldn't have made any difference. Never mind. It's not important."

"Are we going to need a translator? As it seems whatever you're trying to work out is, in fact, important."

Flann dropped into a chair in front of Abby's desk, and Abby took the one next to it. That was about all the room there was in her small office in addition to her piled-high desk. She never spent much time in there anyhow, just using it to do paperwork. She was a hands-on ER doc.

"Brody Clark—the flight medic—I know her," Flann said. "We all know her."

"Who's we?"

"My family, and a lot of other people around here too. She grew up here. In town with all of us."

"Really? That's a coincidence."

"Yeah, it sure is."

"And what about that has gotten you into a twist?" Abby's tone was gently probing.

Somehow she banked Flann's fire when she needed to think coolly and could amp her up again just as fast. Right now just having her listen, knowing she would understand, was enough. Hell, it was everything.

Flann considered where to start. Suddenly going through the whole thing all over again left her exhausted, and for an instant, she wondered if Brody was as tired as she was of it all. Probably. But that wasn't her fault, was it.

"I'll give you the short version for now."

When she'd finished, Abby shook her head. "Okay, really a coincidence, but, I don't know…I don't exactly believe in fate, I'm a doctor after all, and I know how random life can be. But I wouldn't have thought I would be up here, or that Blake would be my son and not my daughter and that would feel so right, or that I'd find the love I have. But here I am, and I have you, and Blake is Blake and he fits as if he'd always been here, so maybe Brody's back for a reason."

"She could've said no," Flann muttered. "She could have said no and left it all where it belongs. Over and done with. Spared us all."

Abby reached for Flann's hand. "It doesn't feel like it's done with for you. Maybe not for her either."

"We would have talked her out of leaving, if she'd told us. We could have fixed…whatever the hell was the problem. But there was no chance. She'd already enlisted." Flann stared at Abby. "She didn't trust us."

"I'm sorry," Abby said softly. "That must have hurt you…all of you. There must've been a reason, and maybe when you find out what it is—"

Flann got to her feet. "No reason could've been big enough, important enough, to just walk out on your family."

Abby took her hand on the way to the door. "Are you going to be able to work with her? It won't be one-on-one most of the time, but we're making a big push to establish the regional trauma center, and the air mobile unit is a major part of it."

"It'll be fine." Flann kissed her quickly. "No problem at all."

❖

Brody begged off dinner with Jane and Matt and picked up a take-out pizza at Clark's. The last time she'd been in there, the place had a different name and a different girl behind the counter. That girl had flirted with her a little bit. She smiled to herself. The boy behind the counter back then had too. Nice to have an enjoyable memory for a change. If she'd let herself, she'd probably discover more, but locking everything away had been easier—then she couldn't be ambushed by an unwanted recollection. Ever since she'd pulled off the interstate and headed out into the country, that lockbox was getting leaky. More and more bits of the past were surfacing.

"Here you go," the teen said, passing the box across the counter with barely a glance.

"Thanks." Brody paid, brought the pizza back to the trailer, and ate it sitting in a lawn chair from Kmart out behind the trailer with Honcho beside her. She fed Honcho the crusts. The look she got suggested that ice cream would've been more welcome.

"You have to have more than one food group," she muttered.

Honcho tilted her head, then dropped down beside her with a huff and rested her muzzle on her paws. Even in repose, she watched everything within her sphere. Honcho needed to work to be happy, maybe like her. Maybe working chased the bad memories away for her too.

Brody ruffled the fur behind Honcho's ears. "We'll get up early tomorrow and find you something to track."

Honcho's ears twitched and Brody was pretty sure Honcho understood. Bringing her home rated right up there as one of the smartest moves she'd ever made. Right beside joining Air Star and letting Jane talk her into being friends. She'd made some questionable decisions in her life, but Honcho wasn't one of them.

Brody stretched out her legs and finished the last of her beer as the sun went down. Sundown came a little earlier every night. In another few weeks the temperatures would drop and the leaves would follow. She'd missed the look of the mountains in fall. Missed a lot, if she thought about it. Which she didn't plan on doing. The day had been as exhausting as a twenty-five-mile march under full pack. Her body ached and her mind was bruised. The past bludgeoned her more than she'd thought it would.

Maybe if she hadn't started the day with a run-in with Flann before she'd mustered up the guts to go visit Ida, she could have avoided some of the beating. Walking in on Val in Ida's kitchen had thrown her too. Of all the people she'd managed not to think about over the years, Val had never been one of them. Maybe because there'd never been anything between them, thinking about her had been safe. Funny, thinking about her now didn't feel safe at all. All she felt was confusion, especially considering the way Val had looked at her out behind the ice cream stand. Curiously, as if she'd never seen her before.

The Val she remembered but had never really known was gone, and the one she'd just met haunted her like an afterimage dancing on the edges of her awareness when she'd stared too long into the simmering desert. Elusive, mysterious, and more than a little dangerous.

With the sun barely up, Val parked in the small gravel lot beside the river a few miles outside town. The running path snaking along through the pines and fields adjacent to the water had once been a local rail line transporting produce and goods between neighboring towns. Some article she'd read described people who needed a full eight hours and couldn't be rushed in the morning as bears—or maybe it was wolves. Whichever, she identified. She'd almost rolled over and stayed in bed when the alarm rang, but some sadistic part of her brain conjured up an image of the ice cream cone she'd had the afternoon before, and here she was. But then, thinking about it, she'd be able to replace that image with an actual ice cream, as reward for her torture.

Laughing to herself, she started off down the trail. She passed a woman running in the direction of the parking lot, but otherwise she was alone. After a quarter mile, her protesting muscles began to stretch out, the endorphins started to kick in, and she decided she wasn't going to die. At the mile mark, with the still-cool morning air whispering over her bare arms and legs, the sunlight a warm glow that teased rather than parched, and the brilliant blue sky overhead, she decided she was glad to be awake. When she hit the two-mile mark, she stopped for a drink of water from one of the spigots along the route provided by the county, splashed a little on her face, and turned around to a familiar face. Her heart did a funny jump in her chest, and for a second, she wondered what was wrong with her.

"Val," Brody said.

"Brody! Hi." Flustered, Val swiped at her messy hair, tried to ignore the fact she was sweaty and not wearing her best running outfit, and held out a hand to Honcho to cover up her nerves. "Good morning, beautiful."

Honcho allowed a little pat on her head and panted with obvious happiness.

"Well, she's happy to be out here."

"No place she'd rather be," Brody said. "We've been doing a little work."

"It agrees with her." Val straightened, determined to ignore her sudden, inexplicable case of self-consciousness. Now that she wasn't looking at Honcho, she got a good look at Brody and just enjoyed the view. Brody's sleeveless T-shirt and army green athletic shorts left a lot of lean, tanned muscles bare. Her dark hair riffled in the breeze, and her steady, intent gaze was just as sharp as Val remembered. A small, neat caduceus with wings adorned her right upper arm. "I can guarantee she's having more fun than me."

Brody laughed. Nice laugh, deep and full. Her gaze never quite lost the careful, appraising edge though. Val wondered if it ever did.

"I have to say," Val said lightly, "running out here has it all over Manhattan. Even at five, in the park, it's busy. Out here…"

Brody laughed. "Yeah. Out here, not so much." She paused, gave Val a long look. "Manhattan. So you were living there?"

"Until just this summer. I went to Cornell for vet school, set up with a classmate in Manhattan, and had a little practice down there."

"A *little* practice in Manhattan?"

Val laughed. "Seriously—and literally. You know, dogs, cats, birds, exotics."

"Horses and cows and pigs and goats?"

"Not so much," Val said, raising a shoulder.

"I have to say, I didn't picture you as a farm vet. Of course, I didn't really think of you as a vet at all."

"Oh?" Val said, suddenly feeling on familiar ground. "How did you think of me?"

Brody colored. "I guess I figured you'd end up a lawyer or doctor or something business-y."

Val laughed at Brody's blush. Brody was uncomfortable. She kind of liked it, since she wasn't uncomfortable any longer. "Business-y. Well, that's me, definitely. And as you can see, here I am, in the business of horses, cows, goats, sheep, and other not so exotic animals."

"Why is that, since I sense a little reluctance in your voice."

"Not really," Val said quickly. That searching gaze wasn't all for show. Brody was quick and saw things. Something to remember. "Oh, you're right, it's absolutely not what I planned, but now that I'm getting into the swing of things, I'm enjoying it a lot more than I ever imagined."

"Being back? Or the work?"

Val shook her head. "You know, I'm not really sure." Time to turn this conversation around. She gestured to the tattoo. "What about you? How did you end up a medic?"

"Army," Brody said briefly.

"Must be a change being back here."

Brody's face closed, and Val realized she'd gone someplace she shouldn't have. Why hadn't she remembered the way Brody had left? Idiot.

"Too soon to tell." Abruptly, Brody said, "Honcho, let's go. I've got to get to work."

"Right. Me too," Val said.

"I'm running late, so if you don't mind, I'll just take off," Brody said, already in motion.

"Of course." Val eased back into a jog as Brody and Honcho disappeared around a bend.

She didn't think she'd ever said as much to Brody Clark in her life. Brody had always been in the background, often with Flann and Harper and their friends, and it was easy to understand why she'd gone unnoticed. At seventeen, Val had been into the flashy girls, the ones who were a little wild, the troublemakers, the daring ones. Flann had fit the bill, although most of the time Flann was never more than friendly. Brody barely registered. Somewhere between then and now, her tastes had changed. Flash was fine for a night or two, and that usually sufficed. After a while, though, the quick flame lost its power to please. Brody wasn't flashy in the least, and the smolder in her eyes was all the more intriguing for it.

Chapter Eight

As soon as Brody climbed into the trailer, she unlocked the hatch to Honcho's run. Honcho nosed the doggie door, apparently decided she'd rather nap on the sofa bench instead of under a tree, and stretched out with a world-weary sigh. The look she gave Brody was only mildly reproachful.

"Yeah, yeah, I know, it's not as good as the woods, but it's better than a tent, right?"

Honcho's ears twitched and her dark, liquid gaze tracked Brody as she pulled off her running shoes and stripped out of her T-shirt and shorts.

"And it's not like you weren't used to sitting around for hours waiting for something to happen. I was there, remember? I know from boring. So you're just gonna have to make do for a while."

She'd managed to talk the manager of the mobile home park into letting her have a spot underneath one of the few trees in the ten-acre tract that had been divided into haphazard lots by single dusty lanes with names like Oak Lane and Walnut Ave., even though the only trees in sight were straggly pines and leggy saplings. A little additional monetary incentive got her permission to put up a dog run around the tree behind her trailer. Now Honcho could come and go, inside or out, during the day. So far, she preferred being outside, although she usually waited until Brody left the trailer to push out through the hatch and set up camp under the tree where she could watch the perimeter of her new base camp. No surprise. Brody shared the same preference. After years of living in the desert, where sitting outside in whatever pitiful shade she could find was better than being inside a sweltering tent or mobile military shelter, she didn't like being inside either. She needed to find another place to live, though, one with real space for Honcho to run where she'd be safe.

Honcho was smart, but people…not so much. Brody didn't want her dog roaming where someone with a gun could decide the big, black four-legged beast was a coyote or a wolf. First, though, before settling on living arrangements, she'd have to decide if she was even staying. She'd give it a month or so.

And if she didn't hustle, she'd be late for her first shift. She hadn't counted on stopping to talk to Val.

The compact shower in the trailer wasn't bad, but the instant hot took a while to get going and she didn't have all that much time. The water was cold when she stepped under it. By the time she got back to the trailer, the morning temperature skirted close to eighty, so she didn't mind anyhow. She lathered fast and rinsed faster, the habit a result of years of having little time and less privacy.

As she pulled on her uniform pants and shirt and sat to lace her boots, she thought back to the conversation with Val. She could see her in Manhattan, in some glitzy office with plush chairs and coffee machines and designer water and minifridges, along with complimentary fruit and healthy snacks. Smiling to herself at the memory of chicken poop on Val's chin, she conjured the image of Val with straw in her hair and dirt on her knees after tending to some farm animal in a drafty barn. The picture made Val more real, more like the approachable woman Brody'd talked to that morning and less like the one she remembered. Hell, she could almost believe Val had been more than just casually friendly. Like, interested. A little.

Brody snorted. Not even back a week and she was courting impossible scenarios again. Val had been sociable—true. Making more out of it than that would get her nothing but sleepless nights and fruitless daydreams—and she'd already done that. Besides, she got the impression, although Val tried to hide it, that this turn in the road hadn't been in Val's plans, and she might not be staying here long either. What was it they said, you can't go home again? That sure felt true.

"See what happens when you start thinking about something other than the missions?" she said to Honcho. "You get your head turned around."

She scrubbed a hand through Honcho's ruff, grabbed her keys and wallet, and jogged out to the truck. Honcho raced outside and took up her position in the trees. As Brody backed out, she leaned out the window and called, "I'll be back in twelve hours."

When she pulled the truck into the same parking lot she'd sat in the day before, Jane was just getting off her motorcycle. Brody jumped out to join her. "Hey, all ready?"

Jane's smiled blazed. "I'm ready for anything that gets me into that helicopter."

"You lie awake all night thinking about it?"

"Could be." Jane's grin faded. "You know, it kinda sucks that the thing that really gets us going means something bad has happened to someone else."

"Bad things will still happen to people, whether we're doing this job or not," Brody said, "and if they're going to happen, they should have the best people on their side, right?"

Jane sighed. "I know. But you know," she said quietly, "sometimes I'm really glad I'm the one flying and not the one in the back."

Brody bumped her shoulder. "You know what? Me too."

The ER at a little before seven a.m. was probably as quiet as it would be all day. The night shift was getting ready to hand over care of the patients still awaiting results of tests or consults to the incoming staff. New patients would start trickling in soon, the ones who'd been feeling off for a day or more and finally decided they'd waited long enough. Then, as people drove to work or tackled the endless challenges of farming, accidents would happen and the traumas would arrive. By midday, the board would be filled with everything from common ailments and minor injuries to multiple traumas.

Right now, the board behind the central station was less than a quarter full with names, room numbers, and the names of doctors and PAs responsible for those patients. The board was no longer a whiteboard with hand-scrawled information but a big LED monitor that made the place look like a train station. It was a way station, of sorts, the point through which patients were shuttled into the hospital, back to their homes, or referred to other caregivers in the medical system. In a lot of ways, this was the beating heart of the hospital, although the surgeons would probably argue that point.

Brody sighed. And there to start her day off right was the surgeon she least wanted to see. Flann sat behind the counter in scrubs, leaning back in a swivel chair, talking to a young African American guy in scrubs.

"Morning," Jane said as they drew abreast.

Flann glanced over, then fixed on Brody. The smile that had started to form disappeared. "Morning."

"Coffee anywhere around here?" Jane asked.

"Around the corner on your left. Break room."

"Thanks."

"You had to do that," Brody said quietly as they rounded the corner.

"Hey, always best to get the first word in."

"Right." Brody shook her head. Flann had at least been civil, but seeing her in the flesh after all this time and being at the hard end of her anger left an ache in her midsection.

The break room was decent sized, with three round tables in the center, a sofa against one wall, a long counter with a refrigerator at one end and a sink next to that, the inevitable coffee machine with a jumble of coffee cups nearby, and the ubiquitous television tuned to some morning news show.

Jane opened the backpack she'd been carrying, pulled out a coffee cup with a big *J* on the side, and stuck it under the coffee machine. She put in a pod from the box next to the machine and programmed it.

"New cup?" Brody opted for one of the Styrofoam disposable cups in a stack nearby.

"Yeah—new place, new good luck cup. You really ought to bring your own cup," Jane said. "Tastes better that way."

"Yeah, but then you have to wash it."

"Think of the landfill."

"You're right, you're right," Brody said. "I'll bring a cup tomorrow."

"You don't have to." Jane reached into her knapsack again and pulled out a second cup, this one with a *B* on the side. "Here. I knew you'd forget."

Smiling, Brody put the Styrofoam cup back and took the one Jane offered. "Thanks."

"Yeah, yeah," Jane said.

"That's a great idea," a woman said from behind them. "The

initials. Someone's always stealing my cup, and of course, they never wash it after they get done using it."

Brody turned and, for a second, thought the woman was Val. In a millisecond more, she realized her mistake. The resemblance was there, but this woman was younger, and her features were softer. They didn't hold the elegant edge of Val's high cheekbones and angled jaw. Her eyes weren't quite the deep brown of Val's but close, and she was a little bit shorter. Attractive, but not breathtaking.

Jane, of course, got there ahead of her with an outstretched hand. "Hi, I'm Jane Montgomery."

"Courtney Valentine. Court."

"Brody Clark," Brody said, shaking her hand as well. She knew her now. Courtney was a couple years younger than her and had been a few years behind her in school. Not surprisingly, Courtney didn't recognize her.

"Hey, are you related to the vet?" Jane asked conversationally.

"Unfortunately, yes." Courtney's expression cooled. "You two are with Air Star, right?"

"Yes," Brody said, happy for anything to fill the awkward silence. She didn't know much about the Valentines, although she knew Courtney and Val hadn't been friendly. Something about a rift between their fathers. All she'd ever heard were the kind of things kids talked about when they didn't really know what was going on.

"I'm an ER resident, first year." Courtney's gaze slid over Brody and fixed on Jane. "I'm hoping I get to ride along with you sometime."

You and everyone else. Brody didn't comment. The who and when would be up to Matt. She didn't have a problem with residents, medics, and PAs flying along. She liked to teach. Courtney being Val's cousin was just a weird coincidence.

Courtney's beeper went off and she grimaced. "Okay, I'm up. Well, see you around."

She hurried away and Jane chuckled. "Guess she doesn't like Val. I thought they might be sisters."

Brody shook her head. "Cousins."

"What's it about, you know?" She took Brody's mug, slid it onto the coffee machine, and programmed in another cup.

"Nope."

"Is there a moratorium on talking about past history?"

"No, not a problem at all. Just nothing to say." Brody grabbed her coffee and tossed in a packet of fake creamer. "Let's get our preflight check squared away."

"Right," Jane said softly. "Let's do that."

❖

As soon as she'd finished her preflight check of the various instruments, med packs, and drug compartments in the EC145, Brody stretched out on the bunk in the call room they'd been assigned. She'd downloaded a couple of novels on her e-reader but first she wanted to scan the equipment manual. She needed to be prepared in the unlikely event of some mechanical or navigational failure in flight. After a quick look, she decided nothing differed too much from what she had been used to in the older helicopter she'd flown in with Air Star, which had felt luxurious compared to the Black Hawk. As she reviewed the systems in the new bird, she imagined a patient, and how she would move from one spot to the other in the cargo space, performing the orderly procession of treatment steps that were as natural to her now as breathing.

Jane came into the on-call room and dropped her backpack onto the narrow desk across from the bunk beds. "I knew you'd take the bottom bunk."

"You should've been here earlier. What have you been up to?"

"I've been getting acquainted with the staff. The place is pretty busy for this early in the day."

"That's a good sign. You want the ER to be busy to feed the hospital."

"True." Jane straddled the chair, folded her arms over the top and, resting her chin on her hands, studied Brody intently.

"What?" Brody asked after a few minutes.

"Just wondering if you're hiding out in here or if you're really, you know, *studying* that manual. Like, really, Brody?"

"I'm really studying the manual."

"Yeah, I figured. What about the hiding out part?"

Sighing, Brody closed the manual and put it on the floor next to her bunk. "I'm not hiding out. Exactly."

"How about un-exactly, then?"

"I just didn't feel like running into Flann again. Or…anyone else."

"Most of the staff is new, right, since you were here?"

"The ER staff, yeah. That's a new development. But the attending physicians come down here all the time to do consults—some of them I know."

"Did you used to hang out here a lot, when you lived with the Rivers family?"

Brody lifted a shoulder. She hadn't bothered to sit up and stared at the underside of the bunk above her. The mattress looked new and fresh. Everything in this brand-spanking-new ER looked that way. "Not a lot—the summer between my junior and senior year I volunteered. Flann and Harper did too. You know, pushing stretchers, running labs back and forth, getting lunch for people."

"Did you want to be a doctor like them?"

"No," Brody said pensively. "I'm not sure why, except maybe because they did, I didn't. Because look at me." She glanced over at Jane and grinned. "As soon as I got to the recruiting office, I knew what I was going to say. Maybe I just wanted to make it on my own."

"Is that why you left? To prove yourself? I can see how that might—"

Brody sat up. "No. That wasn't it."

"They don't know why, do they?"

"No, they don't."

"Jeez, Brody."

"Can we drop it?"

"Sure," Jane said with unusual gentleness. None of the gibe and poke that was so normal for her. "So I passed Matt on my way down here—he's going to start assigning ER staff as the second in-flight medics once we give the go-ahead on the bird and Devi signs off."

"Yeah, I figured we'd have fly-alongs soon. At least we've got—" The beeper clipped to Brody's pants went off. She glanced at Jane. "We're on."

"Yep." Jane jumped up and keyed her radio. "Ten-four, base. On our way."

Brody kicked into her boots, Jane had the door open by the time she reached it, and they sprinted down the hall to the elevator. She glanced at Jane. "Stairs?"

Jane grinned. "Yeah, let's do it."

On the way, Brody radioed Matt in operations for the info she'd need to prepare in flight for whatever was coming. "What have we got?"

"Scene call. Details coming in."

"Roger."

Their calls were either scene calls—traumas or accidents—or interhospital transfers. She always preferred the scene calls. She was winded when she reached the top of the fourth level a couple of steps ahead of Jane, but not too bad. She let Jane overtake her and get to the helicopter first. Jane would've already done a walk-around that morning, but she'd still need to do a preflight check. Brody climbed aboard and started her own check, happy now that she'd spent a little extra time with the manual. Everything seemed familiar.

Devi, wearing the blue Air Star shirt and pants and somehow managing to make the outfit look stylish, ran across the rooftop to the helipad and hopped in beside her. "Hi. I was with Matt."

"Here." Brody handed her a headset and put on her own. She plugged in her radio and signaled Matt's channel. "Mobile air one to base, over. Requesting coordinates and patient status."

"Mobile base to mobile air one," Matt responded. "Multivehicle crash, multiple victims, thirty miles northwest on Co-road 72. Crossroads Lee's Corner. First responders on scene. Prolonged extrication anticipated. Requesting air evac. No further victim info."

Jane settled into the pilot's seat. An area map came onscreen in the center of her instrument panel. "Mobile air one to base, requesting authorization for takeoff."

"Mobile air one," Matt said, "you are cleared for liftoff. IC on site, countrywide channel alpha-three."

"Ten-four, base." Jane's voice came through the intercom. "Prepare for takeoff."

The helicopter lifted up, smooth and fast, and banked northwest. Brody settled back and closed her eyes, the background chatter on the countrywide channel a familiar backdrop to the pulse of the rotor.

Twelve minutes later, Jane radioed ground command. "Mobile air one to ground command, requesting LZ, over."

"Mobile air one, this is ground command. Your LZ is just south of the intersection, west side Co-road 72."

"Ten-four, mobile air one, one minute out." Jane switched to Brody's channel. "That's a cornfield."

"Yep." Brody took in the rapidly enlarging view as the helicopter approached. Half a dozen highway patrol cruisers with light bars flashing blocked off the two-lane, blacktopped road in both directions. Emergency medical vehicles and three fire trucks crowded around the accident site. A pickup truck lay on its side in the gully beside the road on the east and firefighters hosed it down with foam. She could just make out the undercarriage and wheels of some kind of passenger vehicle in a ravine on the opposite side of the road. First responders in bright yellow-and-black-striped turnout coats swarmed around the shoulder above it. A big field of recently cut corn stretched from the far side of the ravine toward a series of tree-covered hills to the west. Their LZ.

She keyed her microphone to Jane's channel. "How close can you get to that overturned vehicle? That's gotta be our scene."

"A hundred yards."

"Fifty would be better."

Jane chuckled. "Always up for a challenge." She managed forty, the skids crushing six-inch cornstalks protruding from the ground as she set down.

Brody turned to Devi. "Can you slide the backboard out to me?"

"I'll come with you. That's a long run."

"Sure," Brody said after a moment's hesitation. She grabbed her trauma bag, slung her jump bag over one shoulder, and jumped out. Devi eased out the backboard and Brody hoisted one end. With Devi on the other, they sprinted toward the action.

"Stay back from the scene, okay?" Brody yelled over the noise of radios blaring, engines revving, and people shouting.

"No problem," Devi called.

A middle-aged guy with FIRE in big yellow letters on the back of his turnout jacket motioned to her as she assessed the overturned passenger van lying on its roof in a long, steep rocky ravine. None of the windows were visible, the roof crushed down nearly to the doorframes. A white shrouded form rested on the shoulder twenty-five feet down the highway.

"Ira Pratt, Incident Commander," he said, holding out his hand. "Driver of the pickup has nonthreatening blunt trauma. He's en route by ground already." As she returned the handshake, he tipped his chin toward the body. "One unrestrained passenger. The remaining male occupant is down there, wedged in the front passenger compartment. Extrication is tricky."

"Is he alert?"

"In and out. We can't see much. He said he can't feel his legs."

Brody grimaced.

"Yeah. We didn't think forty-five minutes via ground transport was advisable, and"—he grinned and glanced back toward the helicopter—"since you will be a little faster, seemed like a good idea."

"Can I get down there to see what I'm dealing with?"

"Go ahead. Our guys will give you whatever help you need."

The footing was treacherous, and Brody took advantage of the safety lines the first responders had strung to stabilize the vehicle, going hand over hand down the slope. The closer she got, the more obvious the precarious position of the vehicle became.

"Brody Clark, air mobile," she said to the firefighter directing the action.

"Billy Wiley." His jacket indicated he was an EMT.

"Patient status?" Brody asked.

"Fortysomething male, previously complaining of loss of sensation in his lower legs. Facial lacerations, unknown amount of blood loss. He's not responding to questions now."

"Do you have a collar on him yet?"

Brushing at the sweat running in grimy rivulets down his face, the young guy shook his head. "He's on the down side of the vehicle, and we just now got it stabilized. We're about ready to cut our way in."

"Can I get in there?"

"Vehicle's stable now, but I can't guarantee it will stay that way when we start extricating." He pointed to the loose rock and sand decline. "This place is like a waterslide without the water."

"I'd like to get a collar on him and an IV started before you start to pull him out. He's likely to get hypotensive as soon as we move him," Brody said. "Just give me a heads-up before you cut."

A muscle jumped in the firefighter's jaw but he nodded briskly. "Put on a safety harness and let us tie you off in case that starts to go."

"Roger that."

Brody strapped in, clipped on, and eased through the shattered driver's side window until she was kneeling on the angled center console. She had to bend double to avoid the crumpled undercarriage that now served as the roof. “Smells like a fuel breach in here,” she called over her shoulder.

“We’re foaming,” someone yelled back.

The patient lay with his legs folded in the wheel well, his back angled against the door. His eyes were closed and blood ran from multiple facial lacerations, soaking the front of his white dress shirt.

“Hey, can you hear me?” she called as she opened her pack and extracted IV tubing, saline, and a cervical collar. “I’m a paramedic. We’re going to get you out of here.”

He made no response as she carefully eased the cervical collar around his neck and secured it. She’d just gotten the IV in when Billy shouted in the window, “Get ready. We’re going to cut.”

Brody braced her legs against the edge of the seat, held the IV in with one hand, and gripped the patient’s shirt with the other to hold him still. The screech of tearing metal assaulted her ears, and the vehicle lurched, sliding a few feet farther onto its side. When the vehicle settled, she tore off a strip of tape to secure the IV. She barely noticed the sharp pain in the right side of her forehead until a drop of blood dripped onto her hand.

CHAPTER NINE

Val slowed as she rounded the corner and pulled up behind several cars already stopped. Light bars from a half-dozen cruisers, fire trucks, and emergency medical vehicles created a blinking red barricade across the center of the road.

"Damn it." She was already running ten minutes late, and now she was definitely going to be late for morning hours. If she turned around and backtracked to the nearest crossroad, she'd have to cut halfway across the county to get to the satellite office. There just weren't that many roads out here to begin with, and she was driving thirty minutes to the Hoosick office as it was. When Joe had asked her to come back and take over the bulk of the practice, she'd pictured herself in the Saratoga office, a fairly genteel practice in a bright, clean, air-conditioned clinic with nothing in the way of emergencies. She hadn't imagined he would still have a rural component to the practice, and definitely not one that had actually expanded since she'd been gone. Apparently as other vets in the area had stopped doing farm calls, Joe had stepped in to provide service. And look at her now. Rapidly becoming the most sought-after farm vet in three counties, staying up nights brushing up on state milk regulations, vaccination schedules for cows, prohibited drugs and nutritional additives in organic feed, and the most humane way to neuter goats.

She was not only sleepy, she was already behind in her day. After five minutes, she turned off the engine and got out of the car to see what was going on. Several of the drivers in front of her had already done the same and stood in a clump by the side of the road.

"Hey," Val said as she walked up, recognizing Mark Rappaport, one of the dairy farmers whose herd she cared for. "What's it look like?"

Mark frowned and shook his head. "Can't tell for sure. Something bad."

Val's stomach tightened as she got a better look beyond the clutch of vehicles, her worries about being late disappearing as she realized she was looking at a serious car accident and not a downed tree or a load of hay scattered across the road. Someone, probably several someones, she knew or at least knew of could be involved. No one around here was a stranger, at least on the surface. What lay beneath the surface was a different matter. "You know who?"

Mark shook his head, his hands in the back pockets of his khaki work pants. "Can't tell."

"How long have you been here?"

"About twenty minutes, maybe twenty-five. The fire truck and a bunch of the Staties passed me on their way here. I think if I'd been just a few minutes sooner, I might've seen the crash." He shook his head. "Really glad I didn't."

"Hey!" A teenager in cutoffs, a tank top, and sandals pointed excitedly, holding her cell phone in her other hand aimed at the accident site. "Something's happening down there. I think they're getting somebody out."

Val stepped a little closer to the shoulder of the road.

"Watch your footing," Mark said, coming to stand beside her.

A storm gully ran beside the narrow gravel shoulder and the ground dropped off sharply. Any vehicle veering off the blacktop would likely end up in the ditch. That must have been what happened to the overturned vehicle up ahead. Only a portion of the undercarriage and wheels were visible, and Val's skin prickled imagining what might have happened to the occupants.

"That's pretty bad, all right," she murmured.

"Haven't seen that before," Mark said, pointing into the nearby cornfield.

A helicopter with a big Air Star logo on the body sat in the middle of the cornfield with its bay doors open.

"That didn't take them long." Val thought she recognized Jane by the build of the person standing next to it. Brody must be somewhere around, and she scanned the clumps of first responders trying to pick her out. EMTs mingled with fire rescue, and she couldn't see Brody in the mix of responders climbing around the crumpled van. Her throat tightened at the sight of it. Could anyone have survived that?

"Look," the teen announced to no one in particular. "They got somebody!"

From where she was standing, Val could just make out the victim being secured to a backboard and slowly, painstakingly removed from the twisted wreckage. She shaded her eyes as another figure emerged from the car. The shock of midnight hair and lithe, agile body in the blue uniform clambering over the demolished van was clearly Brody.

Val narrowed her gaze, her pulse jumping in her throat. Even from here, she could make out the white gauze on Brody's forehead. As Brody grabbed the end of the stretcher and maneuvered it up the ravine toward the field, an expanding dark circle of red formed in the center of the bandage. Definitely a bandage, and she was definitely bleeding. Her breath caught. *She's hurt.*

"I think she's all right," Mark said. "She's moving okay."

Val flushed. She must have spoken out loud. "Of course, you're right."

And he was. Brody and the other paramedics hurried with the stretcher across the field toward the waiting helicopter. Another woman broke away from the crowd of onlookers and hastened along beside them. She said something to Brody, and Brody shook her head.

"She's fine," Val repeated. Still, she waited with the others and watched Brody load the victim into the helicopter and climb in, waiting for the second woman before closing the doors. She watched while the rotors spun, then the helicopter lifted off and, within seconds, disappeared in the direction of the Rivers.

She had absolutely no reason to be upset, none at all. Brody was obviously fine. The victim was headed for the best possible care. The only thing the least bit worrisome was her own inexplicable reaction.

"That was something, huh," Mark said as they walked back to their vehicles.

"It certainly was," Val said, still unable to shake the image of Brody climbing out of the smashed vehicle, and at a loss to understand her own lingering unease.

❖

"You're gonna have to get that taken care of," Jane said as she set the helicopter down on the helipad.

"Need to get this guy squared away first," Brody said.

The trauma team, several of them pushing a gurney, surged through the double doors on the far side of the rooftop and hurried toward the helicopter.

"Looks like they're about to take him off your hands," Jane said.

"I'll ride down with them," Brody said. "I need to fill in whoever's in charge."

"Then," Jane said, methodically shutting down the helicopter as she spoke, "you're getting it looked at, or I'm going to leave a boot print on your backside."

"Yeah, yeah," Brody said. "I'm fine."

"And I'll tell Matt to ground you."

"Come on!"

"You have a stick-um on your forehead, and you're bleeding."

"Hey…I had to put that on without looking. Give me a break." Brody's head hurt like a son of a gun, and her collar was soaked with blood, but facial lacerations always bled a lot. She really was fine. Her patient was stable but just barely, and she wanted to see him squared away. Jane, though, was relentless once she set a course. "Okay, soon as I can."

Devi'd been listening to the exchange with a grin while watching the trauma team approach and slid open the bay doors once they were clear to approach. Glenn and Courtney peered in.

"What have you got," Glenn said, catching the end of the stretcher as Brody and Devi angled it toward the door.

Brody jumped down. "MVA, multiple trauma, crush injury to the left lower extremity, closed head injury, loss of consciousness, possible cervical and/or thoracic spine injury."

"Vitals?" Courtney asked as they secured the patient still on the backboard to the gurney.

"BP running in the eighties, tachycardic to one thirty after two liters of saline. Pulse ox ninety-six on forty percent O2."

"All right, let's go," Glenn said, as they all grabbed on to the side rail of the gurney and began pushing it back toward the elevators. "Court, alert CT we're going to need head, spine, chest, and abdomen as soon as we're stabilized."

"On it." Courtney texted one-handed, and Mari, the PA, directed the gurney into the waiting elevator.

Brody piled onto the elevator with them, needing to ride things out. Once she was sure the patient was stable, and she'd done everything that should have been done in transport, she'd restock the helicopter in preparation for the next call, and then she'd get a look at the damn cut on her forehead.

"What happened to you?" Glenn said, indicating Brody's forehead with a tilt of her chin.

"Must've banged it when they were chopping," Brody said. "Nothing serious."

"You look like you've been hit with a machete," Glenn said.

Brody winced. "That bad, huh?"

"Impressive. You're going to need a new shirt."

"And stitches," Courtney said. "Anything bleeding that much is going to be deep." She grinned. "I'm good with stitches."

Brody laughed. She wasn't sure why Courtney had reminded her of Val. Some resemblance, sure, but Courtney was all casual cocky and Val…Val was elegant confidence. Untouchable, she ought to remember. Or she had been. "I'm sure Steri-Strips will do."

"I'm with Court," Glenn said. "That much blood? Stitches. Just suck it up."

Brody sighed. "Let's wait and see."

An ER resident met them in the hall, a mask hanging around his neck, an eager look on his face. "Trauma one."

They wheeled the patient into one of the two new, fully equipped trauma rooms where more staff awaited them. Within seconds the patient disappeared beneath the scrum and Brody was forced to the sidelines.

Abby Remy appeared beside her from the hall. "What's the status?"

Brody repeated the field report.

"How did it go out there?" Abby asked.

"No problem. The first responders made a good call for air transport. This guy needed immediate evac. I intubated him en route when his SATs started dropping."

"Good," Abby murmured, her gaze on the monitors tracking the patient's vital signs. "We're going to have to medically justify every callout as well as your treatment for the insurance reviews."

"For how long?" Brody knew some calls were more for convenience rather than necessity, but those were in the minority. She also understood the economics of sending out a helicopter. Insurance companies didn't want to foot the bill unless they had to.

"As long as they say," Abby muttered. "Glenn—how's it going?"

"His SATs are trailing down and his blood pressure's erratic."

"Let's move the portable machine in and get a chest X-ray to check the tube position," Abby said.

Brody looked around as a tech swung a portable X-ray arm out from the wall. "You have your own machine down here?"

Abby smiled. "State of the art."

"Nice."

When the X-ray was done, Glenn said, "We need to tap the belly before he goes to CT. His belly feels tense to me, and we don't want him crashing downstairs."

Abby nodded. "Courtney, why don't you set up for an abdominal paracentesis."

"Me?" Courtney said eagerly.

"Yes. Glenn will assist you."

"Yeah, sure," Courtney said, nearly breathless as she hurried to the equipment locker to pull out the appropriate equipment packs.

Abby leaned closer and said to Brody, "We should take a look at your head."

"There's no rush. I have to go restock the helicopter, just in case we get another call."

"Maybe you should take yourself off the call list today."

Brody frowned, and winced before she could stop herself. Moving her forehead was not such a great idea. Plus, arguing with the boss was not a good idea either, especially not on her first day. "It's nothing to put me out of commission, but I'll get it looked at."

Flann walked into the trauma area. "I heard you had a trauma. Something for me?"

"Maybe," Abby said. "We're tapping the belly right now."

"Want to do it open?"

"Courtney's doing a transabdominal tap right now. Let her finish that and if we're equivocal, I'll let you cut."

"Okay, your call."

"But," Abby said, "you can take a look at Brody's forehead since you're here."

"No," Brody said quickly. "Really, it's—"

Flann frowned at her. "Room three is open. Let's go."

"It's—"

"The sooner we go, the sooner we'll be done. Let's not waste any of our time."

"Right." Brody glanced once at the patient, then blew out a breath and followed Flann.

"Juan," Flann called to an ER nurse as she led the way down the hall, "can you set up a suture tray in room three for me. The usual."

"Sure thing, Doc," the ER nurse said. "Want a hand?"

"I can handle it, thanks." Flann pulled the curtain aside and waited wordlessly as Brody passed her and hopped up onto the stretcher. Flann washed her hands, pulled on gloves and, still without saying a word, removed the gauze from Brody's forehead.

Brody winced as the tape pulled at the wound, and she felt another warm trickle run down her temple. She didn't say anything either.

Flann gently blotted the stream. "What happened?"

"MVA. The van looked like the Hulk had crushed a Coke can. I must've hit my head on something inside the vehicle when fire rescue employed the can opener."

"You were inside?" Flann said evenly, tossing the gauze and gloves aside and donning fresh gloves. She picked up the local Juan had left for her on the instrument tray. "This will smart some."

Brody sucked in a breath. Damn, that stung. She talked just to keep her mind off the burning. "Yeah, the extrication was tough. The van was upside down in a gully out on 72. Right before that curve by the tractor place."

"We've seen a lot of accidents around that stretch." Flann regarded her evenly. "Your crash was out near there, wasn't it?"

Brody tensed. "A little closer to town."

Flann nodded. "So you were inside the vehicle with the victim."

"That's right."

"Risky."

Brody shrugged. "That's the job."

"Well," Flann said briskly, sliding the syringe into the sharps container, "you've got a six-centimeter laceration through the muscle at one end. Luckily, it's right in a skinfold, so you'll have a scar, but it won't be bad. You'll be able to impress the girls with it."

Brody laughed. "Probably help me out."

For a second, Brody thought Flann was going to say something else, joke with her a little bit, tease her about her lack of game, like she'd done when they'd been teenagers. Brody'd taken the ribbing back then. She hadn't been trying very hard, but Flann didn't need to know that. Or why.

But Flann turned her back, got her instruments set up, and said, "Lie back. This won't take long."

Brody knew what was coming. She'd had plenty of superficial wounds closed, most of them under a lot less comfortable conditions than this. Even when the Black Hawk teams weren't taking direct fire, running through a battlefield was fraught with danger and she'd incurred shrapnel wounds and burns on a regular basis.

When Flann was finished, she applied a transparent wound glue over the stitches.

"You know the drill," Flann said. "These can come out in five days."

"Right. Thanks."

Flann pulled off her gloves. "Next time, watch your head."

"I'll do that," Brody called as Flann walked out.

Brody sat up, sweat trickling down the center of her back. She hadn't been bothered by the injury, or the sutures, or Flann's cold regard. She should have been prepared for Flann or someone else to bring up the accident. After all, Flann had no reason to know she'd just spent a decade trying to forget it.

Chapter Ten

"Are you heading over to the fairgrounds?" Jane said at the end of shift.

They hadn't had another callout, and once Brody had restocked the helicopter, they'd spent the rest of the day talking to the ER staff who were interested in getting flight experience. Two residents, one of the nurses, and several of the PAs all wanted to rotate with them. Matt had put Brody in charge of drawing up a training syllabus. She'd decided the easiest way to do that was to create the same kind of program she'd gone through in the Army. When she'd told the hopefuls they were going to need to learn how helicopters operated as part of their training, they'd all been surprised but still just as eager to get going. Brody'd promised to get Abby's approval to set up a rotation schedule as soon as possible.

"What time are we supposed to meet the organizers?" Brody asked. "I'm going home to get Honcho first."

"About forty-five minutes. You think Honch will be okay in the new surroundings?"

"The crowds won't be bad tonight, so she'll have a chance to get used to it, and she needs exposure to more stimulation. Besides, she's getting bored, and pretty soon she'll be lazy and then she'll get fat."

Jane laughed. "I doubt it. Hasn't happened to you yet."

"Are you saying I'm bored and lazy?"

"I'm saying you could probably use a little more excitement in your life."

Brody rolled her eyes. "I'm doing fine."

"Aha. So you say." Jane cocked her head. "How's your head?"

"It's fine. It's nothing."

"I heard Flann Rivers sewed you up."

Brody tried to make light of it. She'd have to get used to everyone knowing her business too. "Nothing but the best for me."

"How was that?"

"Fine." Fine except for the casual mention of her past, which was going to come back to haunt her relentlessly as long as she was here. "I better get Honcho. See you at six thirty."

Jane looked like she wanted to say more but finally nodded and grabbed her gear bag. "I'll walk out with you. I hope the concessions are open. I'm starving."

"The fair doesn't officially open until nine tomorrow morning, but a few of the concessions ought to be open."

"Well, if not at least I won't get fat and lazy."

Brody opened the door to the truck and leaned on it as Jane pulled on her motorcycle helmet. "You can stop worrying, you know. I'm okay."

Jane laughed, but her eyes were serious as she regarded Brody. "Okay. I'll see you there."

When Brody pulled in next to the trailer, Honcho raced over to the side of her run and stared at the truck.

"Really want to get out of here, huh? Just give me five minutes." Brody hurriedly changed into jeans and a polo shirt with an Air Star logo over the left breast pocket. Honcho rode with her head out the window, and they made it to the fairgrounds early. When she pulled in to the gate and showed her the pass Matt had provided, the girl at the gate directed her to a staff lot adjacent to the grandstands. She bounced across the hayfield that now seconded as a parking area and turned to Honcho, who sat upright in the passenger seat with tense anticipation.

"So listen, this is like a big Army base. Lots of buildings, lots of smells, lots of people. Probably a lot of loud noises. You know what to expect. Just remember your training. You'll be cool."

Honcho's ears stood up straight and she lifted her snout, already searching the myriad new scents for the one that could spell death.

"Not here—not anymore," Brody murmured. "You'll figure it out one day. Come on."

Brody jumped out, came around, and clipped the short leash to Honcho's collar. She stood for a second regarding the fairgrounds.

Nothing had changed. The animal barns and commercial buildings were still in the same place with the same damn weathered signs denoting 4-H, Arts and Crafts, Schoolhouse, and a dozen other functions. Concession workers readied their fryers and grills and popcorn machines, and the scents mingled into the unmistakable miasma of fair food. Roustabouts scrambled over the rides, preparing them for the opening day, and the midway barkers unfolded their tents and readied their booths with hundreds of cheap prizes.

"Lucky us, Honch, all these people have to eat," Brody said as they crossed the field, the grass already rutted from the heavy machine traffic. "I smell hot dogs."

The grandstands, six sections long and two dozen tiers high, were empty but they'd be full tomorrow night, with fans cheering the tractor pulls and demolition derby and barrel racing. The county fair was one of the biggest events of the summer and everyone would be there, some probably every night. A twist of longing struck her unexpectedly, and she chased it away.

Memories could be deceptive, especially the good ones.

"Let's go find our command post, Honch."

She wended her way down the dusty paths marked with signposts proclaiming Chicken Roost Road, Hog Valley, and Goat Hollow. The Rivers hospital tent was exactly that, a canvas hospital tent with a large red cross stenciled on two sides, the front flaps turned back to reveal several chairs inside in the shade and a long table outside. Impossible to miss.

"Well, looks like we're free for a while," Brody murmured, surveying the deserted tent. There were supposed to be boxes of flyers and other information, but she didn't see any. Jane hadn't arrived yet either.

"Guess we're all early," Val said as she stepped out of a smaller tent directly across from the hospital tent.

Brody turned. "Hi, Val."

Val looked great in casual gray cotton pants, a short-sleeved floral patterned shirt, and sturdy but not too clunky sneakers. Her hair was loose and her oversized sunglasses looked hip as well as functional. As usual, Val managed to be stylish no matter the occasion. Brody wished she'd worn a better shirt and jeans that weren't five years old.

"Are you sightseeing or…"

"Oh no," Brody said. "I've been volunteered."

Val laughed. "Me too." She gestured over her shoulder. "I'm working with the local shelters to run adoptions. I'm on call for the farm association people for the duration, so I was going to be here most of the time anyhow. You?"

"In between shifts, I'm…uh…doing outreach."

Val grinned. "That sounds like something Presley or Abby organized."

"Yep. You know them?" As soon as she asked, Brody knew the question was dumb. Of course Val would know all the important people in the area. That was her crowd, after all.

"A little. I got to chat with them some at the weddings this summer."

"I guess we can't possibly run away, then," Brody said.

"Interesting thought," Val said slowly, color rising in her face. "I'm afraid not."

"Well, whoever I'm supposed to meet isn't here yet, and I'm ready for food." Brody hesitated, considering something she'd thought about hundreds of times and never had the guts to do. But she wasn't seventeen anymore. "How about you? Can I treat you to a hot dog?"

Brody braced for the rejection. A hot dog? Really? That was the best she could do?

"That sounds like the next best thing to running away," Val said.

Brody let out a breath, a lightness taking the place of the dark she'd anticipated. "Okay then."

"Okay then," Val said with a laugh, as if she was surprised herself. "Let me text the kids. They know what to do in case someone shows up while I'm gone."

"Right. Me too." She texted Jane. *Gone for a walk. Be back soon.*

Val walked over and knelt down by Honcho. "Hello again, gorgeous. How are you doing?"

"She hasn't learned that she doesn't always have to be on the lookout for danger yet," Brody said.

"I bet she knows she's safe with you." Val glanced up, her dark eyes shimmering with gold where the shafts of setting sunlight angled across her face.

Brody's breath caught in her chest. Maybe that showed. Val's smile softened and her whole expression tilted in a heartbeat from just plain beautiful to gut-churningly seductive.

"I hope so," Brody murmured.

Val rose. "So, are you feeding us?"

"Yes, right." Brody struggled to clear the fog from her brain as they rounded the grandstand and ambled toward the midway. "Seriously, though, you don't have to have a hot dog. I can offer cheesesteaks, chicken tenders, pizza, candy apples, and, of course, everyone's favorite, corn dogs."

Val laughed. "You left out the sausage and peppers, hamburgers, and ribbon fries."

"Of course. How could I possibly forget ribbon fries."

"I imagine it's not something you had much of a chance to get in the military."

"Honestly, the food wasn't bad, at least at the big bases. We weren't even eating MREs most of the time when we were deployed."

"How long were you over there?"

Brody shrugged. "Being a medic, we were pretty much always in demand. I did three tours altogether."

"You make it sound simple—I don't imagine it was." Val drew a breath. "I want to say I'm impressed, which I am, but I bet you don't see it that way."

"Thanks," Brody said, "and I guess you're right. I was just doing my job."

"And now you're here doing it." Val shook her head. "Does it ever strike you as just a little surreal?"

"Which part?" Brody said.

Val waved her hand. "This, being here. Who would have thought—not me, that's for sure. It looks just the same, doesn't it?"

"I was just thinking the same thing when I got here. If I don't think about it too hard, I feel like I've never left." Inwardly, Brody shuddered. That was exactly the problem. Part of her was still looking over her shoulder for the blow she knew was coming.

"I get that feeling too, sometimes," Val mused. "But I'm not at all the same person. At least, I hope I'm not."

Brody cocked her head. "How so?"

Val colored. "Oh, well, I think I was a bit of a jerk, probably."

"Hey," Brody said, "that's kind of the definition of a teenager, isn't it?"

Val met her gaze. "Nice of you to say that."

"I didn't know you then, but you seem to have turned out respectably enough."

"I hope so." Val rolled her eyes.

"So," Brody swept an arm to take in the midway, "have you decided on the first evil of the week? Remember now, you've got six days to indulge."

Val groaned. "Oh my God. This is going to kill me. Between fair food and the kids wanting to eat every two hours, I'll just have to give up any idea of eating healthy."

"Come on, it's not all that bad. Look"—Brody pointed—"I think the gyro place is open. What do you say? Or are you vegetarian?"

"No, I have no particular exclusions. I just *try* not to eat ice cream at every meal."

Brody grinned. "I don't know, that sounds like it might take a lot of willpower."

"You have no idea. You should try working with two teenagers three days a week."

"If it was those two, I don't think I'd mind."

"You're right about that," Val said. "It's fun. I like teaching, and they're both incredibly smart and motivated."

"I remember Margie was well on her way to being another Rivers star."

"She must've been pretty small when you—" Val swallowed her sentence. "Sorry."

"For what?"

"I feel like I'm prying."

"There's no use pretending we don't have a past, right?"

Val sighed. "Well, that's certainly true. Although there are parts of mine I wish I could forget."

"Me too," Brody murmured.

"So shall we? Forget it, for now?"

As if she could. But hell, for a night? Especially for a night like this, that was more a dream than reality anyhow? Brody nodded briskly. "I think that's an excellent idea." She held out her hand, and Val looked at her curiously. "Hi, I'm Brody Clark. I'm new in town."

Val's eyes brightened, and she grasped Brody's hand. "Brody, I'm Val. You know what, I'm pretty new here too. First time at the fair?"

"It is. You want to explore? Maybe get something to eat?"

Val's fingers squeezed hers for a moment, warm and strong and inviting. "I'd love to."

❖

Brody walked up to the food truck window, one of the half dozen open in the long line of vendors flanking the center aisle of the midway. The guy inside was smiling, but with the temperatures predicted to be in the eighties every day, she suspected that wouldn't last long.

"What will it be?" he said.

"Ribbon fries with…" She glanced at Val. "Sour cream and bacon?"

"Oh, absolutely," Val said. "While you're getting that, how about I get us some lemonade."

"Perfect," Brody said.

"Meet you at the picnic tables by the bandstand?"

"Good enough." Brody watched Val walk away, not quite believing she was about to have dinner at the fair with Val. She'd probably stood in this exact same spot a few dozen times in her life. Every single time when everyone else was pairing off, even when they pretended to be in groups, she'd wanted to be the one buying Val an ice cream or a hot dog or, hell, anything. And now she was. She shook her head. If this was a dream, she was damn well going to enjoy it. After all, how many times in her life were dreams going to come true?

"That'll be eight bucks," the guy behind the window said.

She handed him a ten. "Keep it, and good luck this week."

"You enjoy now," he said.

"I will," Brody said under her breath. She carried the paper plate piled six inches high with swirls of deep-fried ribbon potatoes doused in sour cream and honest-to-God bacon bits toward the picnic area in front of the bandstand. She wasn't going to think about why Val had accepted her invitation. Probably because she'd wanted to get something to eat. That answer was exactly what she needed to keep her feet on the ground and her head out of the clouds. All the same, she scanned the smattering of locals running concession stands, farmers getting their stock into the show barns, and fair organizers directing exhibitors to the appropriate buildings with a surge of anticipation unlike anything she could remember.

She found Val at a table in front of the empty bandstand. This time tomorrow, artists from all along the East Coast would be performing country-western music, pop songs, Elvis impersonations, and dance numbers to full tables. Right now, only a few tables were occupied.

"Oh my God," Val said with a note of reverence when Brody sat down across from her. "That looks awesome. Oh, here." She slid a gigantic plastic cup with a green flexy straw over to Brody. "I took a chance and told them not to add any extra sugar to yours. Because we're being all healthy and all."

Brody laughed. "That's great, thanks." She passed Val some napkins and they attacked the huge plate of fries from opposite sides. They were as good as she remembered, and the company made them even better.

"It's nice, isn't it," Val said between bites, "being here when it's not really open. I've never done that before. Have you?"

"Nope. I pretty much never missed a night, or most afternoons for that matter, but only during regular hours. And then, you know, when you're a kid it's different. You don't see things the same."

"Sometimes not at all," Val said quietly.

Brody looked up. Val was studying her, almost as if she was searching for something. Brody ducked her head. Whatever was there, she wasn't sure she wanted Val to see.

"You think we should see if whoever we're meeting is waiting?" Brody's attempt to cover up her discomfort was lame, but Val let it go.

"Margie and Blake can talk to the shelter people. They know what we need to do to get set up. How about you?"

"Jane will call me if she needs me."

"So we can play hooky a while longer," Val said.

Brody grinned. "I guess we can."

"Did you ever do that, at school?"

"Now and then, not much after I moved in with the Riverses, though. Ida would've...Well, she wouldn't have thought too highly of that."

Val laughed. "From what I know of Ida Rivers, that would be putting it mildly. So how is it, being back there?"

"Sorry?"

"I was just wondering how it felt being back, you know, with everyone grown up and only Margie at home now."

"I'm not staying there," Brody said quietly.

Val paused, blinked once, and shook her head. "Boy, I really do have a knack for putting my foot in things with you."

"Not at all. It's a logical assumption, I guess. But it would be awkward."

"So where are you staying?"

"At the trailer park on twenty-two."

"You're staying at the trailer park, in a trailer." Val laughed. "Why? No apartments around?"

"I couldn't find one to take Honcho. And hey, we like the trailer." Brody grinned and dropped one hand on Honcho's back. "I brought it all the way from Ohio."

"You're full of surprises."

"How about you, staying at home?"

Val broke off a section of ribbon, managed to get it into her mouth without getting a drop of sour cream on her, and shook her head. "No. I love my mother, but we can't be in the same house for more than a few hours without disagreeing on just about everything. I learned a long time ago overnight was the max when I was visiting, and even that was pushing it."

"Your dad," Brody said slowly, "is he…"

"Yeah, heart attack, when I was in college."

"I'm sorry."

"Me too. Like I said, I love my mother, but my father always seemed to be the one who got me…Well, mostly." Val broke off another section with just a bit of bacon and looked at Honcho. "Can she…?"

"Sure. So why did you come back?" Brody asked as Honcho carefully accepted the offering.

"Joe Finnici—he had a double hip replacement, got a postop infection, and has been really slow to rehab. He needed help or he'd lose the practice. Plus, all the cows around here really needed me."

Brody laughed. "I believe it. Lucky cows."

Val tilted her head, smiled softly. "You think?"

"Absolutely," Brody said, totally serious.

The silence drew out, and Val finally made a show of picking apart another ribbon of potato. "Well, I know what you're doing here. I saw you in action this morning."

"What do you mean?"

"I got caught up at the accident site on my way into work this morning. That was you, wasn't it, getting that guy—I guess it was a guy—out of the car?"

"Yeah."

"I didn't realize flight medics did ground work too."

"We'll pretty much get involved with anything necessary to get the patient into the helicopter and back to the hospital. Field evaluation and treatment, extrication, you name it, especially if the other first responders are handling multiple victims or a fire, or like today, a vehicle that needs to be opened up."

"You were inside while they were working on it, weren't you?"

"For a bit, yeah."

"Is that where you got the laceration?" Val asked.

For a second Brody wasn't sure what she was talking about. She brushed the stiff glue over the suture. "Oh, that, yeah, bumped my head."

"Looks like it was a pretty good bump."

"Looks worse than it is."

"You do know you're getting a black eye."

Brody winced. "I was afraid that was going to happen. So it looks doubly worse than it is."

"Uh-huh. Well, I'm glad it wasn't worse. It looked scary out there for a little bit."

Not sure what to make of the slow, soft thrum in Val's voice—or afraid she was making too much of it—Brody said, "You must get quite a few bumps and bruises in your line of work too."

"Bumps and bruises, true," Val said. "But I'm usually not in serious danger."

"Me neither, not anymore."

"You're quite the hero, aren't you, Brody Clark," Val said softly.

"Not in the least."

Val just smiled.

Brody's phone beeped. "That's Jane. I'll have to get back."

"Me too. I enjoyed dinner. Thanks." Val stood, brushed crumbs off her lap, and waited until Brody came around the end of the table with Honcho.

"It wasn't much of a dinner," Brody said.

"It was great. I haven't had such a good time in quite a while." Val leaned close and kissed Brody's cheek, the barest whisper of warmth against her skin. "Next time, let's go for the corn dogs."

CHAPTER ELEVEN

Hey," Jane called as Val and Brody approached the Rivers tent. "Tell me you brought me a hot dog."

Val glanced at Brody. "Uh-oh."

Brody grinned a little sheepishly. "Uh-oh is right. I guess I should have been paying more attention. I sort of lost track of…things."

Brody sounded slightly stunned. Maybe she wasn't talking about Jane's missed dinner order at all. Maybe she was talking about Val's out of left field kiss.

Val was feeling a bit stunned herself. She'd just kissed Brody Clark, a woman she hadn't seen in more than a decade and who she'd barely known even then. While it wasn't exactly a kiss-kiss, it was more a thank-you-for-an-unexpectedly-nice-time kiss, it still counted as a kiss if lips touched a body part. Which hers had done. Totally spontaneously, and she wasn't really the spontaneous type. Especially when it came to kissing.

She'd kissed women she didn't know all that well before. She'd actually kissed a lot of women, not all of whom she even wanted to know better, when she was a lot younger and hopefully a lot dumber. She hadn't exactly been the school slut, but she'd gotten started going farther a lot earlier than a lot of her friends. First with boys, until she'd realized she preferred the girls, and then there'd been plenty of girls who'd been willing to experiment at least. Looking back, which she didn't spend a lot of time doing, she couldn't remember what had driven her wild behavior, if she'd ever really known. She only remembered being angry. Angry at her father at first, for ruining her entire high school experience, and probably her whole life. That's how ending up in high school in cow country had felt to her then. Of course, she'd been thirteen at the time and maybe should've rethought it before she reached her twenties, but hadn't.

Maybe the anger came from something that swirled around in her family like an undercurrent, always there, rolling in when least expected and pulling her under. Her father's festering rage was fueled by the rift with his brother, and part of her mother's from the social pressures of so public a blot on the family. Val couldn't help but wonder if her youthful ire hadn't just been inherited.

She knew exactly when the mantle of self-destructive unrest had lifted, and the abrupt turn her life had taken as a result. She'd been almost eighteen, just out of high school and looking forward to a summer of partying and Flann Rivers finally working her way through every available girl in the class and noticing what she'd been missing. Namely Val. She'd been furious when her father'd announced he'd set her up with an internship for the summer that would look good when she got ready to apply to law school. She initially refused—spending the summer working for a vet, he had to be kidding—but then he'd said no internship, no money. He'd meant it, and she'd trudged off to Joe's animal clinic with an attitude. And that first night, everything changed. They'd had an emergency call, a calving gone wrong, and she'd gotten stuck going along with Joe to the farm. The low moans of the distressed cow, the heat and acrid scent of the barn, the blood and the mucus and the never-ending swirls of dust coating her skin and hair—all of it disappeared when Joe delivered the calf, a weak, gangly, snot-covered miracle who staggered about for a few minutes until gently nudged into place beneath his mother's udder. Val's wonder, the first unadulterated happy moment she'd ever experienced, transformed into pure joy, and for the first time in her life, her spirit soared.

She waited three years to tell her father his tuition money wasn't going toward a law degree, and by then it was too late. She'd won her freedom and her future. She'd needed a while longer to shed her habit of casual hookups and superficial relationships, but she'd eventually grown more cautious about getting involved. She wasn't interested in drama, and when she decided to kiss a woman, or more than kiss, she made certain she'd accounted for any potential fallout first.

Thus the non-kiss kiss that came out of nowhere was totally out of character. She was more bemused than worried—after all, it *was* only a little thing. But how odd that Brody had subverted her careful approach to women without her having the slightest warning. That was something to consider. Sometime other than when Brody's friend Jane was studying them both with narrowed eyes.

"Hi, Val," Jane said.

"Hi, Jane."

"You both look guilty," Jane said.

Brody flinched. Val nearly laughed. Were they back in high school again for real?

"There was food involved, wasn't there," Jane said accusingly. "Food that you did not share with your friend and coworker."

"Sorry," Brody said hastily. "Why don't you grab something to eat now. I'll be here if the…" She looked flummoxed. "Whoever we're meeting comes by. Who are we meeting?"

Jane snorted. "The unit commander of the local fire rescue crew to set up a rotation with us to cover…" She waved a hand at the tent. "This. And the grounds people want to meet with us. I didn't get the story behind that—maybe you can call Matt for a sit rep."

"I will. Go eat," Brody said. "Honcho and I have this."

"Bye, Jane," Val called as Jane ambled off. She had no doubt Jane would be probing Brody for details of their impromptu walkabout later. She wondered what Brody would say, if she'd mention the kiss. Not that she'd mind, but maybe Brody wasn't the kiss-and-tell type. Especially when it was a not-kiss kiss. Just a little thank-you, like a handshake. Although usually, her fingers didn't tingle the way her lips did now after just brushing against a woman's skin. As tanned as Brody was from years in the desert and working outside, her skin was unlined and surprisingly soft. The softness of her skin made a striking contrast to the hardness of her body. Just looking at her it was obvious she was fit, but from the few times Val's fingers had strayed to Brody's arm as they'd talked or when their bodies had brushed together when walking, she'd sensed just how strong Brody was. She'd have to be, to lift injured troops off a battlefield, wouldn't she? Val'd gotten a lot of information from that causal dinner and the even more casual not-kiss. Intriguing information she'd think about later. A lot later.

Time to at least pretend she wasn't thinking about another not-kiss. The kids were waiting, slouched in chairs behind the table, scanning their phones and chatting.

"I guess I better go talk to the kids and try to get organized."

"Right," Brody said. "Me too."

"Well, thanks again." That sounded lame even to her, but she'd already tossed out a card, right? Next move was Brody's.

"So," Brody said, "I guess we'll be neighbors for a while."

Val smiled. "I guess we will."

"We should definitely try for the corn dogs."

Val's middle skittered just a little but she didn't let the ripple of excitement show. There it was—the next move. "We absolutely should."

With that, she turned to Margie and Blake. She sensed Brody still watching her, and the pleasure swirling inside ratcheted up a notch. She hadn't been really watched by a woman in a very long time. "Hey, you two—what did I miss?"

Blake straightened. Margie seemed content to let him take the lead where the animals were concerned, not that she ever took a back seat. That just wasn't in her DNA.

"One of the shelter people stopped by. They're bringing the crates and food and stuff around tonight so we can get everything all set up."

"The animal vans will be here at eight tomorrow," Margie added. "We're expecting fifteen dogs and twelve cats."

Val blinked. "Twenty-seven. Well, that's going to be a lot of feeding, cleaning, and walking for you guys for the next week or so."

Blake shrugged. "No problem. We've got it covered."

"Yeah," Margie said, "we offered week passes to some of our friends for walking duties."

"You did, huh." Val smiled. "And who's paying for that exactly?"

Margie glanced at Blake.

He took over the explanation. "Well, we kind of got the fairground people to donate the passes, and the shelter people will give them a letter that it's a donation."

Val couldn't see anything dicey about that—in fact it was damn clever of them. "Good thinking."

Their grins were electric. Not for the first time and probably not for the last, she envied them. "Did you two eat?"

"No, we didn't want to leave here in case somebody else came by to talk to us."

"There's food in the midway. Why don't you take off."

"Great," Blake said jumping up. "I want to check out the 4-H building anyhow. I need to know when to bring Rooster around."

"You still think he can take the crowing contest?"

"Absolutely. What he's missing in the mobility department, he makes up for with sound."

Val laughed. "All right, go on."

"We'll be back in time to help unload the van. Steve and Sarah are meeting us here too."

"I'll keep an eye out for them." Left with nothing to do, Val wandered back over to the hospital tent and waited while Brody finished talking to someone on her cell. "I'm all squared away temporarily. What about you?"

Brody slid the phone into her pocket. She hadn't expected to have another chance to talk to Val alone until she didn't know when. Now it was just the two of them again. She'd never been lucky in her life, but that seemed to have changed. Hopefully her luck would hold. She liked being around Val even more than she'd imagined she might when the idea was just wishful thinking. "In a holding pattern waiting for the grounds people to come by. That was my boss I was just talking to—apparently the plan is for Jane to bring the helicopter in here for some show-and-tell."

"Wow. That's kind of amazing."

Brody shook her head. "A big headache is what it is."

"Why?"

"Logistics, mostly. We need an LZ and someone who knows what they're doing so we don't end up landing on a bunch of livestock. Or worse, people."

"I never thought about that. Still, it's a great idea."

Brody laughed. "Why exactly?"

"Everyone will want to see the helicopter, so you'll meet the whole community. The sooner you're seen as part of the community, the easier the extra costs will go over." Brody's face took on that shadowed look that signaled they'd strayed into unwelcome territory, but Val was at a loss to know what she'd said to trigger it. "What?"

"Nothing." Brody gave a start. She didn't see any point in explaining she didn't want to interact with everyone in the community. She'd already done that once and it had almost gotten her killed. "I didn't think about what all this must be costing the locals. I figured since the hospital system was private and the emergency room was independent, that pretty much covered it."

Val's look said she wasn't totally buying it, but she didn't press. So far she hadn't, and that made it a lot easier to talk to her. And to forget herself and say more than she intended.

"You're right," Val said, "but the town infrastructure needs to accommodate all the increased traffic—road maintenance, local law enforcement coverage, even food and lodging. Some of that requires increased revenues, which means more taxes."

"I can see why the hospital management wants to parade us around, I guess," Brody said.

"Oh yes." Val laughed. "Presley won't pass up an opportunity to remind everyone the Rivers is going to save this area."

"Is she right?" Brody asked.

"I think so." Val gestured to the shelter tent. "You'll help *us* out right away. The showier you get, the better for us. More traffic coming by our tent means we'll be able to attract more potential adopters. We're going to have a boatload of animals that need homes."

Brody automatically scratched behind Honcho's ears. Honcho continued to scan up and down the dirt track but teased her muzzle into Brody's hand for a second. "Hear that, Honcho? You're going to be a star pretty quick."

"Will she handle the attention okay?" Val asked.

"Oh yeah. The crowds won't bother her, but with all the activity, she'll think she has to work all the time. When she's so focused like that, she forgets to eat and doesn't sleep very well. And she just doesn't need to work that hard anymore."

"I know you don't want to use medication and that's fine. How about this—will she wear a lightweight vest?"

Brody laughed. "Are you kidding me? When we were in the field, she wore a Kevlar vest and a pack with her gear, just like the rest of us. She won't even notice one. Why?"

"Let's put a twenty-four-hour heart monitor on her. Then we'll know how anxious she really gets. I'm not saying it's you, but maybe…"

"Are you trying to tell me I'm an anxious parent?"

"I doubt with your experience much of anything makes you anxious."

Brody touched her cheek were Val had kissed her. Her nerves still jangled from the adrenaline rush. "You might be surprised."

Val pursed her lips, gazing at Brody from beneath half-lowered lids. "Is that right? Were you?"

Her tone was low and teasing and Brody couldn't miss the glint in her eyes. "Yeah."

"In a good or bad way?"

Brody ignored the sirens blaring in her head, warning her to be cautious. What did she have to lose, after all? Val might be flirting with her, but that's what Val did. She didn't mean anything by it. "Definitely good."

"Good," Val said. "I try to make it a habit of only surprising women in a good way."

"Mission accomplished."

Val looked like she was going to say more, but Jane appeared around the corner with two hot dogs balanced in her hand. A big panel van with pictures of dogs and cats on the side trundled across the field toward them from the opposite direction.

Brody reluctantly said, "I'll let you get to work."

"I'll see you later?" Val made it sound like a question as she waved the truck down.

"Sure." Brody crossed back to her side of the lane and sank into the chair opposite Jane. Val was just being neighborly. She knew that, as long as she didn't think too hard on the kiss. She didn't quite know what to make of that. Best to just chalk it up to being friendly. Yep, friendly and neighborly. Nothing more.

❖

"Looks like Honch is going to have some company." Jane lounged with her jeans-clad legs crossed at the ankle, her motorcycle boots dusty from the ride over and tromping through the fairgrounds.

"Uh-huh." Brody had been watching Val, Blake, Margie, and two middle-aged volunteers from the local animal shelter unload crates, water bottles, bags of food, tarps, and other paraphernalia for the last twenty minutes.

"The vet's going to be busy too," Jane added.

"Uh-huh." Val laughed at something one of the kids said, her voice for some reason rising above all the others, striking Brody like a clear bell ringing on a still spring morning.

"She's probably going to need a lot of help, taking care of all the animals."

"Yep." Brody slid her hands into her pockets, trying to relax, as Val pointed to the open space beside the tent and Margie and Blake started dragging around crates and stacking them.

"You should probably go over there and lend them a hand," Jane said. "Instead of drooling over the vet."

"Uh-huh." Brody touched the spot on her cheek, wondering if there was a mark. Maybe a lipstick smear. She smiled to herself. Lipstick on her collar. Well, not exactly. She was pretty sure whatever shimmered on Val's lips when the light was just right wasn't actually lipstick. Lip gloss or something. Nice. Would probably taste nice too. Jane's comment finally registered. She glared. "I'm not drooling."

Jane pointed a finger. "Yes, you are. I can see it on your chin." Reflexively, Brody wiped her face and Jane laughed. "Wow. She must have some mojo. You look poleaxed."

"Will you cut it out—she might hear you."

"The *she* in question is busy working over there. Go ahead and help. You know you want to, and we're not doing anything."

"I already deserted you once," Brody protested weakly.

"And for that you will not soon be forgiven, considering that you were eating and I was not."

"I'm sorry about that. I should've—"

"I'm kidding, Brody. I wasn't even here yet. Will you relax."

"I'm relaxed, I'm relaxed."

"You really look a bit…smitten. Something happen?"

"No," Brody said more forcefully. She was not smitten, or anything else. Not again.

"Okay, if you say so." Jane smirked. "Look, I'm stuck here waiting for the grounds manager, but you might as well do something useful. Really, they could use another hand."

Brody happily jumped on a change in topic, anything to keep the focus off Val and her. About which there was nothing to say. "You really think it's a good idea to bring the helicopter in here?"

"Technically, there's no problem. No electrical wires, plenty of space to land if they cordon off an LZ, but I'm worried about not having a ground crew. It's one thing to bring it down on the helipad on top of the hospital that's been cleared for us, but down here?" Jane shook her head.

"Maybe you should talk to Matt about that."

"He and the CEO hatched this plan together and he thinks it's a great idea. Especially since somehow, God knows how, the fairgrounds have agreed to assume liability should anything happen."

"Right. Which means we have to be sure nothing does."

"Yeah." Jane pointed to Val. "You're trying to change the subject."

"I'll be right over there," Brody said.

"I can see that." Jane made a shooing motion. "Go, go. I'll keep an eye on Honcho."

"Thanks." Brody hurried over to Val. "Can I offer a little muscle?"

Val smiled. "Most definitely. If you're sure?"

"Totally. Just tell me what you need."

Val's smile deepened and Brody's pulse zigged a little. "We've got some aluminum trash cans in the back of the van to use for the animal food. No point inviting critters for dinner. If you could set them up out behind the tent and empty a couple of the bags of cat and dog food into them, that would be great."

"No problem," Brody said. "Do you have a marker or something I can write with on the cans so you'll know which one is which?"

"Somewhere around here," Val said. "Wait a minute."

She pulled a voluminous leather bag up onto the table and rummaged through it, emerging a second later with a black marker in her hand. "Here you go."

"Thanks." Brody held out her hand and Val placed the marker across her palm. Now her hand tingled, a little bit like her cheek. That shouldn't be possible. Had to be the August heat. Or something. She closed her fingers around the marker, and Val's hand brushed across her knuckles. The tingling spread.

"You're welcome," Val said softly.

Brody hurried to the van. Blake jumped down with a forty-pound sack of dog chow on his shoulder.

"Hey, Blake," Brody said. "I'll give you a hand. Val wants the food around back in the cans."

"Great. You got the cans?"

"On it," Brody said.

An hour later, Val handed her a water bottle. "Here. Drink." She tossed one to Blake. "You too."

Brody wiped sweat from her forehead on her sleeve. "Thanks."

"The last thing we need to do tonight," Val said as Margie emerged from inside the tent, "is string a tarp over the animal crates to keep the sun off them and hopefully keep them dry if it rains. Are you game for that?"

"Stringing tarp is something I'm really good at," Brody said.

"I guess you probably are." Val pointed to a pile of canvas, ropes, and other equipment. "The fair people left us this stuff. I don't pretend to know a thing about pitching tents or tarps, but I'm a good assistant."

Brody surveyed the assortment of tent poles, ropes, tie-downs, and stakes. "I ought to be able to find something to work with here." She grabbed a stake and said, "You hold, I'll pound stakes."

"Perfect."

Brody dug a rubber mallet out of the pile and knelt down to pound in the first stake. Once she had everything positioned, she motioned to Margie. "Want to grab one end of the tarp and we'll hoist it up on the poles. Blake—you'll handle the tie-downs."

Brody leaned over to shake out the tarp. A gust of wind blew grit in her face and she hastily wiped her face on her sleeve again.

"Be careful with your stitches," Val murmured.

"Forgot about them." Brody grinned. "It's not bad, really."

"So you said." Val's mouth tilted into a soft smile and the appraising look in her eyes was a punch to the gut.

Brody swallowed. "Right. So I should get this tarp up."

"You know, after all this hard work, you deserve a reward," Val said slowly.

Brody stopped in her tracks.

"How about a drink. You and Jane, my treat."

Brody's breath whooshed out. Just being friendly. "Sounds great."

"Good." Val grabbed another corner of the tarp. "Then let's get this done."

Chapter Twelve

You coming with us, Jane?" Val said as the shelter van pulled away and Margie and Blake took off like rockets with their friends. The evening had pretty much gotten away from her, and it was closing in on night. She was tired from lifting crates and stacking supplies, and had a busy early morning the next day with more of the same, but she had nothing to go home to except a half-read book and a glass of wine. Usually she didn't hunger for company in the evenings. She spent most days talking to animal owners or otherwise surrounded by people asking questions, needing reassurance, or just wanting to pass the time of day. Half the week she had Margie and Blake, and as much as she enjoyed their company, she wanted them to get something out of the experience. She didn't need to teach either one of them about respecting and caring for animals, but she hoped to instill an appreciation for the science behind the medicine. Both of them were avid students, which made the job easy. All the same, she was totally talked out by seven o'clock at night. Tonight, though, her usual routine held no interest.

"Absolutely," Jane said. "This place, does it have food?"

Val laughed. "What, the two hot dogs didn't do the trick?"

Jane grinned, a mischievous know-it-all kind of grin, and a wave of confidence and innate flirtatiousness rolled Val's way. Jane wasn't flirting with her, at least she didn't think so. Jane just had a megadose of natural charm that made everyone feel just a little bit special when she turned her attention their way. Val wasn't particularly susceptible to that kind of attraction, and with Brody standing a few feet away, hands in her back pockets, her dark intense gaze fixed on Val, she was even more immune.

"Oh," Jane said, "the hot dogs were excellent, and I plan to repeat the meal, but that was…" She looked at her phone. "Almost three hours ago. Time for more fuel."

Val glanced at Brody. "Is she serious?"

Brody nodded, amusement lightening her features for an instant, making her look carefree and surprisingly vulnerable. "Jane has an off-the-charts metabolism that needs frequent feeding or she gets extremely cranky."

"Hey," Jane said, sounding offended. "You're exaggerating."

"Nope. Trust me, you do."

"Then you don't have to worry," Val said, thinking the two of them were like siblings. Or lovers. She'd wondered about that earlier and considered it again now, a spark of annoyance flaring as she did. She could see them together, Jane's fire and Brody's ice. There'd be heat on both sides of that. Jane's brows rose, and Val quickly averted her gaze. She must have been staring. Hopefully not sending daggers. Really, not her place. "The menu is pretty standard—burgers, fries, chicken tenders, the usual. But decent quality."

"Let's go, then," Jane said. "Val, you want to ride over on my bike?"

"Ah, I can't, but thanks. I've got my car here."

"Some other time, then," Jane said. "You can show me around all the best back roads."

Brody's brows lowered, and she shot Jane a half-annoyed look. Val quite enjoyed that, but she might be reading Brody's little bit of surprise—or annoyance—all wrong. Maybe Jane's flirting bothered Brody because Jane was Brody's girlfriend. Val sighed. That would well and truly be a shame.

She shook off the thought. Really, all she could do was wait to find out. But Brody would've said something earlier, wouldn't she? They'd had an almost date. And a kiss. Even though the little kiss was very little, it was still a kiss. She probably should've just asked first if Brody was attached—she would have with anyone else she was interested in. But if she'd known she was going to do it, she wouldn't have done it at all. She wasn't in the market for anyone of interest. She'd just arrived back in town in a new job, and her plate was full to overflowing. And Brody didn't seem to be the sort of woman to trifle with—which was the only kind Val had time for right now.

"Okay then," Val said, giving up her constant questioning for lack of answers. "Brody, do you remember Bottoms Up?"

"Still the same place?" Brody asked.

"Same place, same owners, probably the same crowd."

Val laughed. Brody didn't. Something there. Every time anything related to the past came up, Brody went cold and dark. Val wanted to know why. Not out of curiosity—well, not entirely. Sure, she was curious to know what Brody was thinking behind her hooded gaze, what interested her, what she wanted. All natural reactions to finding someone attractive. And that was just natural too—biology, after all—and nothing to require explanation. But beyond that, she was bothered by knowing something still wore at Brody, still troubled her. She'd never particularly wanted to know anyone's secrets before, but she wanted to know hers. She had a feeling when Brody shared her secrets, it was only with the very few. She wanted to be one of those few. She hadn't the slightest idea why.

"I have to swing by the trailer and leave Honcho," Brody said as they all walked to the parking area.

"Jane, you can follow me over, then," Val said.

"Roger that," Jane said.

Brody broke off to go to her truck. "I'll meet you there."

The half-mile drive took all of five minutes. Val pulled into the parking lot beside a low-slung building that might have been a garage in an earlier life. The painted white concrete walls were interrupted by windows displaying neon beer signs now. The front door stood ajar and a wash of noise tumbled out. Jane backed her motorcycle in beneath a stand of pines and climbed off.

"Nice bike," Val said.

"Thanks. You ride?"

"Only on the back, and not for a long time." Val smiled, thinking of the few times she'd managed to get Flann to take her somewhere on her motorcycle. She wondered if Flann even had that old Harley any longer.

"Offer stands," Jane said.

"I'll remember."

Brody turned in and Val and Jane waited while she parked. The large room with a bar running along one side and mismatched tables in the middle was mostly full, being one of the few places still open at that time of night serving alcohol and food. Val spotted an open table, and they dragged three chairs over to it.

"I'll get the drinks," Brody said. "Val? What are you having?"

"Usually I have wine this time of night, but I've had the wine here. So, no." As Jane laughed, Val went on, "I'll have a vodka tonic with lime."

"Got it. Jane—beer?"

"Yep. Whatever pale ale they've got on tap. And can you get me a burger and fries?"

"Sure. Be back in a minute."

"So you and Brody go way back," Jane said as Brody threaded her way through the tables and edged between a couple of guys standing at the bar.

"I guess you could say that." Val picked her answers carefully. Jane wasn't being very circumspect about fishing for information, and she didn't have anything to hide, but talking about Brody seemed a little bit like walking through a minefield. Brody's story was hers to tell and Val didn't even know what it was. What she *did* know probably wasn't all that accurate, and she didn't want to inadvertently violate Brody's privacy. Best to stay safe and stick to the basics. "We went to school here, same class. I didn't live in town, though, and I didn't know her all that well."

"Gee, I'd think in a place this size everybody would know everybody else."

"You'd think so, wouldn't you? But you know, just like everywhere else, people form their little groups."

Jane leaned back in her chair and scanned the room. "I know what you mean. I went to a big city school and didn't know most of the kids in my classes, but it wouldn't have mattered anyway. I only hung out with a couple of people. It's funny, you'd think things would be so different between a place like there and here, but not so much."

"Only on the surface, maybe." Val figured she might as well get a little information herself. "Did you know Brody in the service?"

"No, big country over there, different branches of the service. I was Navy, Brody's Army. But we both started at Air Star about the same time. I was maybe four months ahead of her." She smiled as she watched Brody head back with three drinks expertly balanced between her hands. "So we've been crewing together three years now. Sometimes it feels like forever."

"I guess when things really work, that happens."

Jane met Val's eyes across the table. "Well, she's pretty special."

Val smiled. "No argument there."

"Here you go," Brody said as she slid the drinks onto the table. "About fifteen minutes for the burger, Jane."

"Thanks."

Val sipped at the vodka tonic. Not her usual drink, and she was driving. She'd suggested the drinks more to continue the evening than for any other reason. She was glad she had. Jane was interesting and funny and insightful, and someone she'd enjoy getting to know. She hadn't reconnected with any of her old friends from high school since she'd been back, and none had reached out to her. Looking back, she recognized they hadn't been friends as much as co-conspirators. All of them participating in an unspoken competition for the attention of boys or girls, and all the other nameless and ultimately forgettable glories of high school. Bitter much? She smiled to herself. Not nearly as much now as then. "I don't know about you two, but I for one feel like I'm getting old. It's ten at night, and I'm tired and have a distressing tendency to reflect on my lost glory days."

Jane snorted. "Age is just a state of mind." She stretched her arms behind her head and managed to look cocky and self-amused at the same time. "Who needs sleep? You can sleep when you're dead."

"Farmers get up at three a.m." Val sighed. "And so do their vets. Or at least, they expect me to."

"You know what it is," Brody said quietly, drinking her beer at a pretty sedate pace also. "It's being back and running smack-dab into your old self."

"You think if you'd never left, you'd feel the same?" Jane asked. "Because everyone grows up. Maybe you'd still look around and see the ghosts."

Val caught the echo of some hidden pain in Jane's voice. She was right. Everyone had their pasts. "I'm kind of embarrassed to say I don't really know if I should recognize most of these people or not."

Brody sipped her beer, watching Val. "I guess your group stayed pretty tight."

"Nice way of putting it."

"Pretty normal, really." Brody smiled.

Val appreciated the unspoken peace offering. Maybe Brody's memory of her wasn't as critical as her own. Or maybe Brody never thought of her in any way at all. "I've been back a little longer than you, and as much as I sometimes get these strange feelings of déjà vu I'd rather not have, I'm enjoying it a lot more than I thought I would."

"Jury's still out," Brody murmured.

"Beer's pretty good," Jane observed as she took a bite of her burger a guy from the kitchen had delivered. "And the burgers are excellent. That speaks well for this place."

Val sensed someone stop by her side and looked up.

"Slumming, *Sin*?" Courtney said.

"Hi, Court," Val said evenly. She hadn't seen Courtney before now, so she must've just come in. And couldn't wait to continue her verbal barrage. Wonderful.

"Courtney," Jane said brightly. "You here by yourself? Want to sit down?"

Courtney shook her head. If her eyes had been laser sights, they would've painted a red spot in the center of Val's forehead. "No thanks. The company's not to my taste." She glanced at Brody. "Will you have the flight schedule soon?"

"As soon as Matt and Dr. Remy give the go-ahead."

"Good. I'm looking forward to it." Pointedly ignoring Val, she said, "See you tomorrow."

Jane let out a breath. "Boy, she isn't too subtle."

"You mean about the fact that she can't stand me?" Val said quietly.

"Yeah, that. What's the deal?"

"Jane," Brody said quietly.

"Hey, no problem," Val said. "It's ancient history, really. She doesn't even know me, and to tell you the truth, I don't know her either. We haven't seen each other in years. I don't think the opinions of a fifteen-year-old really have much validity now."

"She seems to think so," Jane said, dipping a fry in her ketchup. "Sorry if I was being nosy. Well, I *was* being nosy."

"The short story is our fathers are brothers. Actually, half brothers. My dad is the younger brother from the second marriage, and I guess Courtney's dad felt that he got pushed aside when his father remarried.

Something about him needing to sacrifice what he wanted to do so my dad could go to college." Val grimaced. "Honestly, I have no idea if any of it is true after all this time."

"Wow," Jane said, pushing aside her plates. "It's a variation on the second son thing, right, only in this case the second son was the golden boy?"

"I gather Courtney's dad thought so. Whatever the breach, it was passed down, at least on Courtney's side of things. My dad never really talked about it."

"Families." Jane shook her head. "Funny how no matter where we go, they're always part of what we do."

"Seems that way." Val glanced at Brody, whose gaze had gone distant. Was she thinking about her family or the time she'd spent living with the Rivers family? As hard as she tried, Val still couldn't come up with why Brody had ended up with the Riverses. She'd never been all that interested at the time, and now the missing pieces of Brody's past kept niggling at the edges of her consciousness. She couldn't ask, even though Brody might answer. She'd wait until Brody was ready to tell her.

Brody cleared her throat. "Val is going to hook up a vest for Honcho so we can monitor her reactions at the fair. Heart rate, breathing, that kind of thing."

Jane's brows rose, but she didn't comment on the change in topic. "No kidding. That's an awesome idea. She seemed fine tonight, didn't you think?"

"She did great."

Val relaxed as the tension of Courtney's impromptu visit faded. "If we get a break at the fair tomorrow, we can run over to the clinic and try one out on her."

"Sounds like a good—"

"Brody Clark," a man said as he stepped up to the table. "Never thought I'd see you back here again."

Brody stiffened as Val and Jane both stared. He was big, six five, broad shoulders, already showing signs of a beer gut beneath the T-shirt emblazoned with the logo for a roofing company. Val couldn't place him, but he looked familiar. How was it she was surrounded by the strangers she'd grown up with everywhere she turned?

"Lloyd," Brody said quietly.

"Hey." Lloyd dropped a heavy hand onto Brody's shoulder. His fingers closed. His grip had to verge on painful. "Nice of you to bring your friends along."

Brody said nothing.

He grinned and gave Jane a long look, then his gaze slid, like cold, damp fingers trailing over the back of her neck, to Val. "Dr. Valentine. I heard you were back too. A pleasure to see you visiting the old stomping grounds."

Before Val could reply, he slapped Brody on the back. "Well, I'll be seeing you around."

He disappeared as quickly as he'd come, leaving a cloud of violence hanging in the air around them. Brody shivered as if shaking off something unpleasant that clung to her skin.

"Am I right in thinking that guy's an asshole?" Jane glanced at Brody. "Who is he?"

"My cousin," Brody said quietly.

"I guess it's a night for crappy family reunions," Jane said.

"You two ready to leave?" Val rose and laid a twenty on the table. "I've got an early morning."

Brody hurriedly stood. "Me too."

"Sure," Jane said. "I'll get us next time." She waved across to the bar to where Courtney stared in their direction. "Can't let the wildlife scare us away."

Val followed Brody out and nearly walked into her when Brody jerked to a halt.

"Son of a bitch," Brody muttered.

"What?" Val edged around her and squinted into the dim lot. "Oh, hell."

Brody's truck sat on four flat tires.

Chapter Thirteen

Flann gripped Abby's shoulders with what little bit of strength she had left and buried her face in the curve of Abby's neck. Abby stroked her back, her fingertips dancing along the ridges of her spine and shoulder blades, finally coming to rest in the hollow above her ass.

"Welcome home," Abby murmured in her ear.

Flann chuckled. "It certainly was. Did I do anything special to deserve that? Because I want to be sure to do it again soon."

"If I tell you, you'll only get a big head."

"Bigger, you mean?" Flann kissed Abby's jaw. "I love you."

"Mm. Really, I just don't want to waste an opportunity, especially when we have the place to ourselves." Abby inched her thigh between Flann's. "I was afraid you were going to end up in the OR all night when that girl with belly pain came in."

"Even if I'd had to take out her appendix, I still would've gotten home before the kid if I'd known you were here waiting."

"You might be fast, baby," Abby patted her butt, "but that doesn't mean the OR would have been."

Flann eased her weight onto one arm and rested her head on her bent elbow. "Yeah, funny how that works." She kissed Abby. "How did things go with the new crew today?"

"Better than I expected. Matt and his people know what they're doing. This isn't their first assignment and they settled in right away."

"I checked on the guy they transported from the car accident right before I left," Flann said. "His belly still looked pretty quiet. He's got neurological loss from T-12, though."

Abby sighed. "I know, I talked to the neurosurgeons too. Wait and watch, I guess."

"So far. It made a difference, him getting here by air mobile. Every minute counts with that kind of injury." Flann idly twirled a lock of Abby's hair around her fingertip. She wasn't happy to have Brody back out of the blue, and right in the heart of her universe at that, but she couldn't argue with having an air mobile unit on-site. Their trauma and ER census would skyrocket, and with residents and PAs to train and a bottom line to shore up, they needed the patients.

"I agree," Abby said, "and I called the fire rescue incident commander to let him know his team made the right call handing off to air mobile, *and* they'd made a difference in that man's outcome."

"How'd he take it?"

Abby laughed. "You know there's going to be a bit of a turf scuffle. But these guys have seen plenty out there, and they know what the red zones are in time to definitive care. I trust them to make the right calls, even when there's a little growling going on between the big dogs."

"Matt strikes me as being a pretty good politician. He seems to have gotten everything he wanted here so far—a slick new helicopter, his own crew, and operational control."

"You mean he got everything Presley wanted him to get."

"That might be a better way of putting it." Flann laughed and stroked the curve of Abby's breast. She was getting a second wind.

"I take it there was nothing too serious with Brody Clark's injury."

Flann tried not to stiffen up but she couldn't help it. Knee-jerk reaction to anything having to do with Brody. "She had a pretty good laceration, but nothing serious. She's got a hard head, and I imagine she had worse bruises in Afghanistan."

"That bothers you, doesn't it? The danger she was in over there."

"Hey, her choice. But I wouldn't have wanted her to get hurt." Flann knew every time Brody sent a letter home, and every time her mother mentioned it, she'd gotten pissed all over again. Brody could have gotten killed over there, and none of them would have known for months.

Abby slid her fingers into Flann's hair and massaged the back of her neck. "Are you ever going to tell me the rest of the story?"

"There isn't anything to tell. She left. Forgot about us."

"How do you know that?"

Flann sat up, wrapped her arms around her knees. She wasn't going to contaminate what they'd just shared with her anger and tried to let it bleed off into the dark. "If she hadn't forgotten, then we would've heard from her, seen her, known what the hell she was doing before now."

"She reached out to your mother, though, right?"

"Oh yeah, once a year. Big deal. People you barely know send you a Christmas card."

Abby stroked Flann's back again, and her touch was as soothing as always. Flann loved Abby for more reasons than she could count, but she adored her for never trying to talk her out of her anger. Sometimes, being allowed to rage was the fastest way to get rid of it. She flopped back onto the bed and pulled Abby against her side. Abby curled into her the way she always did, her head on Flann's shoulder, her arm wrapped around her middle. Flann rested her cheek against Abby's head and closed her eyes. "I don't know what's going on. I don't want to be glad to see her, but I am. Glad to know she's still walking around, that she's healthy, and look at her. She's a freaking hero."

"Maybe you should try telling her that."

Flann snorted. "No way."

Abby kissed her jaw. "Well, just think about it a little bit."

"You mind if I think about something else right now?"

Abby pulled Flann on top of her, wrapped her legs around Flann's. "I very much do not mind. In fact, I—" She groaned at the thud of the front door banging open and shut. "Damn, damn, damn."

Flann rested her forehead against Abby's. "Do you suppose if we're really, really quiet—"

"I don't like to be quiet." Abby kissed Flann and gave her a little shove. "Besides, we ought to check in."

"You're right." Trying to ignore the pressure in her groin, Flann rolled out of bed, found her jeans, and pulled them on along with a T-shirt. Abby followed close behind as Flann walked barefoot from their bedroom into the large common room that had once been the main part of the schoolhouse they now inhabited.

Blake already had his head in the refrigerator and looked over his shoulder when he heard them coming. "Hey. Did I wake you guys up?"

"No, we were…" Flann glanced at Abby. "Reading."

Blake smirked. "Yeah, I bet."

Abby smacked him lightly on the shoulder. "Don't be a wise guy."

Blake came out with a quart of milk in a glass bottle. Never having had milk in a bottle in the city, he was convinced this milk was better and wouldn't drink anything else. He took off the cap and Abby pointed a finger.

"Do not drink that out of the bottle."

"Hey." He held it up and shook it. "There's only like a quarter of it left. I was going to drink it all."

"Not out of the bottle. You're turning into a heathen."

Flann laughed. "Why dirty a glass?"

Abby shot her a look. "Really? Is that helping?"

Flann pulled out a pizza box and fished out a piece of cold pepperoni pizza. She leaned against the counter and took a bite. "Can't see that it really hurts anything."

Blake took a swig and Abby rolled her eyes. "Fine. Give me a slice of that."

Flann handed her and Blake each a piece, and they all stood around eating.

"So?" Flann said. "Let's hear it."

"What?" Blake said.

"What did you do with your day?"

Blake instantly launched into a rhapsodic recounting of farm call with Sydney Valentine.

"Wow," Abby said, "she let you do the venous puncture, huh?"

"Well, she helped," Blake said. "It was amazing. Like, you can't really feel the veins or anything, but if you find the pulse in the neck, the vein's going to be right near there and you take this eight gauge needle and it's five inches long, and you go right next to where you feel the pulse."

"So what was the deal?" Flann said.

"Oh, the cow had just calved, and they get this thing called milk letdown, where so much calcium goes into the milk, they get really weak. So you have to give them an infusion."

"Okay," Flann said. "That's pretty impressive."

Blake narrowed his eyes. "You knew about that, right?"

Flann grinned. "Well, I've known a few farmers in my life."

"The rest of the day we had clinic and then had to get ready for the adoption booth."

"How are things over at the fairgrounds?" Abby asked.

"Good. We're right across from Brody and the hospital tent," Blake said. "She helped us set up."

Flann stopped chewing. Was she going to run into Brody every single time she turned around? First her wife was going to be working with her every day, and now the kid?

Abby's hand landed on her forearm and squeezed gently. Flann let out a long breath. Okay, Blake wasn't part of whatever the hell had happened in the past. No reason to drag him into it. If he and Brody hung out a little, no harm. Maybe. Just something to keep an eye on.

"And Honcho was there," Blake went on. "That's her dog? She's a vet too, from when Brody was in Afghanistan."

"You know quite a lot about that already, don't you," Flann said carefully.

"Yeah, she was telling us about that earlier."

"Earlier," Flann said flatly.

"At the ice cream place." Blake dragged the last piece of pizza out of the box. "You guys want to split this?"

Abby laughed and shook her head.

Flann had already lost her appetite. "No, go ahead."

"Anyhow, I might be doing some dog duty for Brody, after the fair. You know, because Honcho's at the trailer park all day long. And I can stop by and walk her." Blake stopped, shrugged. "Maybe, Brody said."

"Brody is living at the trailer park?" Flann said.

"Yeah."

Flann snarled inwardly. Well, that was just perfect. Brody had come back, but she hadn't come home. Why was she surprised?

❖

Brody clenched her fists, a sense of violation rushing through her she hadn't experienced since she'd walked out to Route 40 and hitched a ride into the city to enlist. The close-on wave of helpless fury burned an acid trail down her spine. "Looks like I'm going to need a ride home."

Jane headed toward the truck. "That or a whole mess of work in the dark."

"Oh my God, Brody." Val grasped her arm, just as quickly removing it as if realizing what she had done. "Who would do this?"

"No idea," Brody said, the lie coming easily. Without proof, the truth was only empty words.

"Got all four of them," Jane called. "Punctures, not slashes. Possibly fixable." She got up from where she was kneeling by the front tire and strode toward Brody. As the light from the neon signs caught her face, her eyes glowed in the red shadows, hot and fierce. "You know what this is about?"

"Nope," Brody said.

Val said, "Could it be random? Just someone acting out?"

"Sure. Could be." Brody walked to the truck, checked that the doors were locked, and turned around. "I guess I'll be riding on the back seat tonight after all, Jane. I'll see about getting some spares out here in the morning."

"You have to call the police," Val said.

"For what?" Brody said. "There's no way to tell who did this."

"Maybe they have security cameras," Val said, spinning around to search the side of the building.

Brody chuckled. "We're not in New York City, Val. High-tech security isn't a big priority here. Maybe inside a convenience store, but outside a beer joint like this? No."

"She's right, Brode," Jane said, closing ranks with Val. "The police need a report, for insurance if nothing else."

"I'm not using my insurance for this," Brody said. "Probably time to get new tires anyhow."

Val took a slow breath. She didn't want to argue or press Brody, who had to be already stressed to the max, and she didn't want to look like she was ganging up on her, either, but this…this, whatever it was…went beyond simple vandalism, if there ever could be such a thing. This felt dangerous. "Brody, hold on a second. No matter what this was—random or something else—we can't just pretend it didn't happen."

Brody jammed her hands in her pockets. "There is no *we* here. I appreciate your concern—both of you—but this isn't something you want to get involved in."

Jane glanced at Val. "She isn't always an asshat, just when she gets her back up about something."

"All right, Brody," Val said reasonably. "I'll call, then."

"God damn it, Val," Brody said, heat in her voice. "You don't want to be mixed up in this."

Val gave her a long look. "I already am."

She thought she heard Jane laugh but kept her gaze on Brody. She hadn't intended to get involved, but she was. Somehow, she had been drawn to Brody since the first moment she'd seen her walk into the Riverses' kitchen. A stranger who'd touched a chord, a memory she hadn't even known she had. And Brody wasn't a stranger any longer. They had memories, not the same ones, but of the same things, the same people, the same place. They'd shared the same world during a critical part of their lives, but more important than that, they'd shared something in the present when old connections like random threads of a worn tapestry had rewoven while no one was looking. The weave was tighter now, their paths converging, the pattern stronger than before. "I can't pretend I didn't see this."

Brody let out a long sigh. She wasn't winning this argument. Jane and Val were like an immovable wall, both of them staring her down, wearing her down with their caring. And as much as she wanted to keep them both away from whatever was happening here, she only knew one way to do that, and she'd already tried that once. She'd run then. She wasn't ready to do that again.

"All right, I'll make the call."

It didn't take long for the cruiser to pull into the parking lot, lights flashing but, thankfully, no siren. The town officer who emerged was twenty-one if he was a day, but he joined them with a self-assured nod and an outstretched hand to Brody. "You the one that made the call?"

Brody shook his hand. "That's right, Brody Clark. That's my truck over there."

"Tom Kincaid." He put his hands on his hips and tilted his head, taking a long look. "Looks like somebody did a number on it."

"'Fraid so."

He turned on his Maglite, shined it on each tire in sequence as he walked around the truck. "No other damage that you saw?"

Brody shook her head. A small crowd gathered behind them, curious bar patrons stopping on their way to their cars to see what was going on. Great, an audience. Just what she wanted for something like this. By the morning, half the town would know what had happened. Correction, probably the whole town.

"Doors are still locked, body looks to be fine. Any idea who might have done this?"

"No," Brody said.

"Funny they'd pick out a vehicle in the middle of the lot, if it was just some random vandalism."

Brody held his gaze. "Guess I'm just unlucky."

"Okay." He nodded. "Probably nothing in the way of forensics here. Plus, we have to send that stuff out, and it's expensive."

"I didn't expect you to do anything like that," Brody said. "Anything you got off the truck would be inconclusive anyhow. Sitting out here in the parking lot, anyone could've touched it."

Kincaid rubbed the back of his neck. "My thinking too. I'll take some pictures, write up the report. What time did you get here?"

Brody filled him in on their arrival time.

He looked over her shoulder at the people gathered around. "Anybody see anything out here?"

A mumbled chorus of negatives ensued.

"I'll talk to the people inside," he said, "but…"

"I understand," Brody said. "I'd like to wait till the morning to see if I can get tires over here before I tow it."

"I'll talk to the bar owner," Kincaid said. "He's not going to make a fuss about you leaving it here all night. I'll let the other officers know to keep an eye on it."

"I appreciate that."

He studied her, impressively astute for someone she initially took as green and possibly not on her side. "Well, if you think of anything else, you let me know. Call me when you're coming over in the morning."

"Won't you be off duty by then?" she said.

He grinned and suddenly looked much younger again. "I live in town. Call me."

"Sure."

As he walked off toward the bar, Brody turned to Val and Jane. "Satisfied now?"

"Thanks," Val said. "I'd be happy to drive you home."

"I appreciate it," Brody said, "but Jane's going in the same direction, so—"

"Of course." Val hesitated. "You'll probably think this is really silly, but will you text me when you get home? Just so I know you're both okay?"

Brody swallowed. "Sure." She pulled out her phone and passed it to Val with a contact window open. "Want to put your number in?"

"Thanks." Val typed and handed the phone back. "Night."

Val hurried away and Brody watched her go.

"You know," Jane said, "I happen to know you hate riding back seat. If I didn't know better, I'd think you were avoiding being alone with her."

Might be true, but right now she had other reasons for wanting Val safely away. "Just making sure she doesn't get dragged into anything she's not prepared for."

Jane handed her an extra helmet she'd pulled from a pannier. "You think there's some trouble waiting back at the trailer park?"

"If I did, I wouldn't have hung around. No one knows where I'm staying, and Honcho can take care of herself. But I'll feel better once I'm sure."

Jane straddled the motorcycle, and Brody climbed on behind her. "Then you'd better hold on."

Brody snaked an arm around Jane's middle. "Always do."

Chapter Fourteen

Brody kept her head tucked close to Jane's, cutting down on the wind hitting her exposed neck and chest. Even on a summer night, the air bit through most everything except leathers, and she hadn't worn those in a lot of years. She wouldn't have ridden with anyone other than Jane, but Jane was her pilot, and she trusted her with her life every time they went up in a helicopter. Riding behind her now was no different. She joked with Jane about the bitch seat, but the real reason she objected to sitting back seat was the way her stomach squirmed and a sweat broke out between her shoulder blades. She could surrender control of the stick—or the grips, in this case—but she couldn't wipe out the flashes of memory of the last time she'd been on a motorcycle on these roads. She'd been closing in on eighteen, riding at dawn, and she'd only had a second to see the truck closing in behind her. She saw it, though, long enough to remember the faces. Time hadn't dulled the images of the silent laughter.

She'd told Jane she didn't expect a problem at the trailer, but the hard fist clamped down on her chest didn't ease until Jane turned into the lane that led to the Gulf Stream. The trees behind the trailer extended fingerlike branches over the metal rectangle, creating ominous shapes reminiscent of the skeletal remains of bombed-out vehicles abandoned in the desert. In the scant glow of the moonlight, Honcho's dark shadow flickered in and out of the patches of silver, sleek and agile, patrolling, watchful. Unharmed.

Jane stopped her bike and put a leg down on either side, twisting to look back at Brody as she stepped off. Brody yanked off the helmet and took a deep breath, relaxing a fraction as the knife edge of discomfort bled away.

"Thanks for the ride," Brody said.

Jane removed her helmet and tucked it under one arm. "You want me to walk around with you?"

Brody shook her head. Honcho sat just inside the fence now, her head cocked to one side, her eyes gleaming in sharp counterpoint to the dark body blending into the night.

"If there was anything going on here, Honcho would've already taken care of it. And she'd be letting me know about it."

"So," Jane said, making no move to head off to her temporary lodgings on the other side of the park. "You really don't know what that was all about?"

"Not for sure, no."

"But you have some idea?"

Brody shrugged. "Nothing I can swear to. Not even close."

"'Cause, you know," Jane said conversationally, "seemed like kind of a big coincidence after that dickwad gave you a hard time in the bar."

"Like I said, no way to know." Brody wasn't going to insult Jane by arguing when she had the same suspicion. She hadn't seen Lloyd the morning she'd crashed her bike, not for sure, but she couldn't shake the feeling he'd been there. Like tonight.

"Is there more of this crap headed our way?"

"Hope not."

"Well, let's just make sure we've got our heads on the swivel."

No way was Brody going to be able to convince Jane to stay out of whatever might come. Jane would have her six just like she'd have Jane's, and as Jane suggested, she'd be looking out for trouble. "Roger that."

Jane jammed her helmet on and kicked her bike's engine over. "See you in the morning."

Brody watched her ride out of sight before going inside to check out the trailer. She moved through quickly, examining windows, the bedroom, the two closets. Nothing had been touched.

As Honcho appeared through the hatch, Brody asked, "Everything quiet out there?"

Honcho brushed against Brody's thigh, and she buried her fingers in the ruff around the dog's neck. Honcho's strong shoulders and calm, steady presence dispelled the rest of Brody's lingering unease. She didn't for a second think the attack on her vehicle was random. Someone had sent a welcome home message, and a not too subtle suggestion that she might not want to stay.

She dropped onto the narrow red and green sofa bench on the wall opposite her screen door and stared out into the night. She was too far from the road to hear any traffic, and the closest trailers were all dark and quiet. Fireflies flickered around the small light over her door, and somewhere close by coyotes howled. She wasn't much for trying to figure out what the future might or might not hold. War would do that to you. Worrying about what hadn't happened was just a waste of energy. So was the anger that swirled in her chest. Embracing powerlessness only clouded your judgment and slowed your reflexes. She'd had plenty of practice dealing with real enemies, and she'd wait until she had one to focus on before wearing herself out planning for something that might never come. Besides, she had a lot more important things to think about.

Her phone sat in front of her on the little dining table that took up most of the middle of the living area.

Val had asked her to text an all clear. Strange, someone other than Jane wanting to be sure she was squared away. Even stranger that it was Val. Thinking about Val's reason for making the request was asking for trouble. Her mind would start wandering away from the threat behind slashed tires, which she could handle if it came down to a fight, and into waters even more treacherous. She hadn't a plan for Val, and little strength to resist her.

One thing came through loud and clear after spending time with her—the first real personal interactions they'd ever had. She'd never really known her, only the persona that everyone cloaked themselves in when trying to figure out exactly who they were. Donning armor of a sort, disguised as leather jackets or suggestive clothes and attitude. She'd had the attitude, for sure, choosing to stand outside the bright circle of the chosen crowd, assuming an air of disinterest. Maybe Val had done the same thing, only her facade had been the superiority and sexuality that created a shield of another type. Who Val was now, who *they* were now, either of them, might have been born from those early masquerades, but time and experience molded a different reality.

Val had risked stepping beyond the safety of concealment, had asked for Brody to make a connection. Braver than she'd ever been.

Braver than she was now.

The phone sat an arm's length away, daring her to take off her armor.

❖

Val sat on the tiny second-story porch off the bedroom of the apartment she'd rented. The spacious upper floor of a two-hundred-year-old farmhouse was a decent compromise in terms of her commute—close to the county line, a five-minute drive from where she'd grown up, and twenty minutes in either direction from the clinic or out into the countryside. Best of all, she'd secured the privacy and the sanity she wouldn't have had if she'd given in to her mother's insistence she move back into her old room. The owner, Flora Eddy, had the first floor and was a friendly, unobtrusive landlady, and the view couldn't be beat. The yellow-clapboard country home sat on a knoll above the river, surrounded by fields tended by a younger generation of farmers now that Flora's family had died off, moved away, or decided farming was just too damn hard. Flora, though, like many born to the land, would never leave. Val was as surprised as anyone when she looked forward each night to the quiet, the serenity, and the simple beauty of a sunset over the fields. And a nice glass of wine.

Val sipped her wine and watched moonbeams flicker off the water. Her phone rested on the arm of the Adirondack chair, silent. Brody must have been home for at least fifteen minutes, and no word. No need to worry, not when there was a much simpler explanation. Brody was fine, why wouldn't she be. She just had decided not to text.

"You were pushing it, you know." Val muttered the words and sighed. Not like her at all, to intrude on someone else's privacy like that. She'd been scared, that was all. The shock of seeing that damaged truck, the willful hate in it, had struck her hard. Her city sensibilities ought to have inured her to man's inhumanity to man, but for some reason she hadn't expected it here. Naive of her, really. The city did not have a monopoly on anger and hatred.

But why Brody?

Val sighed, an irrational kernel of frustration wearing at her.

Whatever Brody didn't want to talk about, whatever reason for the attack she wanted to keep secret, stood like a wall around her. Maybe that's why Val had pushed so hard—that wall bothered her. The barrier hadn't been there earlier, when they'd walked through the fair, talking about long-ago times, sharing a meal, and enjoying the present. But that blockade had been tall and strong and nearly visible in the parking lot. No way Brody didn't have some idea of who had vandalized her truck. Or at least an inkling of what might be behind it. Val usually didn't demand others share their secrets. Most of the time, she wasn't even interested in knowing them. She sipped her wine.

She was not herself. Or maybe she was and hadn't realized it.

She'd barely registered Brody a dozen years before, when Flann had eclipsed almost everyone else for her attention. Not that she would've admitted it or had been all that obvious about chasing her. She hoped. Courtney apparently had known, probably a lot of other people too. Probably even Brody. She flushed at that realization. Brody had always been around Flann when Val had been teasing and unsuccessfully attempting to seduce her. She'd probably witnessed the whole campaign. Wonderful. That was embarrassing now. She'd only seen Flann a handful of times since she'd been back, and one of those times was at her wedding. Flann was still as charming and attractive as ever, but they were different people now and Flann was very obviously in love with her new wife. And as attractive as she was, Val found she liked the quiet intensity of a woman like Brody more.

Her phone rang. *Rang.* Not pinged a text notification. And she wasn't on call. And her mother rarely called. It rang again. She grabbed it, saw Brody's name come up, and swiped hard enough to leave track marks.

"Hello."

"So, I just thought I'd call instead of text. If that's okay."

"Of course. Yes." Val sounded a little breathless to herself and felt her heart pounding much faster than it should be. Deep breath. Deep breath. Better. "Everything is good there?"

"All's quiet. I didn't wake you, did I?"

"No, I was waiting…" Val rolled her eyes. Obvious much? "I was just having that glass of wine I was telling you about."

Brody laughed. "I noticed you didn't drink much of the vodka tonic."

"The idea was more appealing than the reality. And I had to drive."

"White or red?"

"Red. I prefer the little bit of bite. Whites tend to be too sweet." What was she babbling about wine for? "Are you a wine drinker?"

"Not so you'd notice."

Brody still sounded like she was smiling. Val pictured the grin, the energy in her sharp gaze. Her breath hitched again. "Beer, then."

"We got wine on base. Pretty terrible wine, really. So yeah, it's beer for me."

"Do you miss it?" Val asked.

"The beer or the service?"

Val's pulse galloped. Brody shied away from questions, and she didn't want that to happen. But she wanted to know. Everything. "The service."

"No," Brody said without hesitation. "I certainly don't miss the war or the stupid senseless loss on every side."

"Of course. I was thinking more of the lifestyle."

"I know what you meant," Brody said. "There's a certain security in it, the safety of knowing where you fit. But what I cared about most was the work, and whatever little I could do to make a difference for the ones getting chewed up out there."

"And you're doing it still."

"Yeah, and that's what I care about most."

"I'm glad—"

Her call waiting dinged. The answering service. She wasn't on call. For a heartbeat she considered not answering, but maybe Joe needed her.

"Brody—I've got a call. Can you hang on just a second?"

She's going to hang up. Why would she wait?

"Sure."

Val let out a breath and switched the calls. "Dr. Valentine."

"Sorry, Doctor—I've got a Henry Turner on the line who says he needs to speak to you. I told him you weren't on call."

"I'll take it, thanks."

"Doc Valentine?" A gruff male voice, tight with tension.

"Hi, Hank. It's Val."

"I wouldn't have asked for you, but something got after my sheep and one of my sheepdogs got a big old hole in his side and I'm afraid to move him. Bleeding pretty good. I know Joe's covering, but the dog's way up the top of the hill and I thought—"

"I'll be there as soon as I can. Is it Buzz?"

"Yeah." His voice hitched.

"Okay. Keep pressure on the wound and keep him warm. I'll be there."

"Thanks."

Val quickly switched back. "Brody"—she hurried inside and grabbed her keys—"I have to get out to Eagle Bridge for an injured dog out in the fields."

"You need help? You're going right by me. I can wait on the highway—won't take you any time to pick me up. I'm a passable field medic."

That had to be an understatement. Val ran outside and started her SUV. Her equipment was all loaded. She always made sure of that. "If I have to do more than stabilize him, I could use a pair of knowledgeable hands. You sure? It's late."

"I don't sleep much. I'll be waiting."

"On my way." Val tossed the phone on the passenger seat. The night was clear and the roads empty. She pushed the pedal to the floor.

Chapter Fifteen

Sorry, Honch." Brody grabbed a light denim jacket from a peg by the door. "You can't come on this trip."

Honcho gave her a serious look, then turned and went back outside through the hatch.

Brody closed the inside door, made sure the screen caught, and jogged through the darkened trailer park to the road. The nearest houses were a good half mile away. The trailer park, backing up to an upland stand of pines and apple trees, had been carved out of what had once been fertile fields. Some farmer had needed the money and sold off part of his land. That happened a lot around there. The road fronting the property, not even close to being anything that could be considered a highway, mostly saw traffic first thing in the morning with people going to work in the neighboring towns, laborers heading off to a job site, and farmers out checking their fields. By five in the evening, most everyone was back home again.

Now, a little after eleven p.m., the road was just a silent shadow stretching off in either direction, illuminated only by the moon and stars. The night was completely clear and cooler by a good twenty degrees than the day had been. Still, August nights were sultry. She kept her jacket unbuttoned over the T-shirt she'd pulled on when she'd stripped out of her uniform earlier. She couldn't quite believe she was standing in the dark waiting for Val to pick her up. She couldn't say even now why she'd called her instead of texting, except a text seemed too impersonal, too brief, and not at all what she wanted. What she'd really wanted was to hear Val's voice again.

Val sounded different than in her memory, and that was just proof of how memory distorted the good and the bad. She doubted Val's voice had changed all that much. Her low soprano, smooth and light, reminded her a little of sunlight in the morning. She liked the little bit of tease that crept into Val's voice sometimes too, and the way she'd pretty much drawn a line in the sand back there in the parking lot when she'd said she'd call the law if Brody didn't. Not challenging, just deliberate and sure, steel beneath the satin tones.

That was different, the way Val had stepped in, the subtle command in her voice. Brody was accustomed to orders from her superior officers and, maybe, a strong demand from Jane now and then. But Jane and Val were nothing alike. Jane was her friend, her buddy, her comrade, and someone she would gladly risk anything for. Val was something else altogether, and she wasn't sure what name to put to it. Val was a presence in her mind that didn't seem to let go, had never really let go, and now, every time she slowed down just a little, Val was there. Hearing her voice was the least of what she wanted, so she'd grabbed her phone and hit Call before she could ask herself why.

She looked up the road as headlights lit up the trees coming toward her like soldiers marching in formation, there and gone in a flicker of shadow. Ten minutes. Val hadn't wasted any time. Brody held out an arm and, when Val pulled over opposite her, tugged the passenger side door open and climbed in.

"Hi," Brody said.

"Hi." Val pulled out immediately, her eyes on the road, both hands on the wheel, keeping the speedometer at a steady fifty-five. The trees and scrub along the sides of the twisting ribbon of road flashed by in kaleidoscopic fragments.

Brody wasn't worried. The posted speed limit was forty-five, but when you'd driven these roads your whole life, you could take them a lot faster than that. The only thing to look out for at that time of night was deer. She scanned both sides of the road ahead of the headlights looking for them.

"I ought to feel guilty dragging you out," Val said without looking over at her. "But I'm glad for the company."

Brody stretched her legs under the dash and rested an arm along the window. She probably should feel awkward but registered strange contentment instead. Sitting beside Val, who piloted her vehicle with the same sure-handedness as Jane swept their helicopter through the skies, heading out into the countryside in the dead of night on an uncertain mission, was exactly what she wanted to be doing.

"I was just sitting around. Probably wouldn't have been asleep for hours anyhow."

"Were you worried about what happened back at the bar?"

"Not really. More like teed off."

"I imagine so. I certainly was."

"Thanks." Brody shifted with her back to the door so she could watch Val drive. The moonlight coming through the driver's window lit her up. Her pale yellow T-shirt tucked into jeans and work boots weren't at all the kind of things she'd worn in high school. Neither were the casual preppy clothes she'd been wearing that morning. She looked great in all of them. "I don't usually cave in so easily, you know."

Val smiled, her eyes front still. "Is that what you did?"

Brody chuckled. "You kind of backed me into a corner there."

"Did you mind?"

Brody pictured Val leaning against her in the dark somewhere, somewhere the past, the future, all dissolved into the moment. When now was all that mattered. Heat surged from her middle into her chest. She'd walk willingly into that ambush, put up no resistance. "Nope."

"Good. I'm not usually so aggressive about sticking my two cents in when I haven't been asked."

"Like I said, I didn't mind." Brody's throat was tight, and her control sounded as thin as the tether she had on it. "Consider it a standing invitation."

"Sure you know what you're doing with that offer?" Val shot her a quick look—piercing, searching. "I might turn into a nuisance."

"Positive. And I doubt it."

"Will you let me know if the police turn up anything?"

"Sure."

"Thank you."

Brody settled back, enjoying the way the moonlight alternately sharpened and then blurred the angles of Val's face. "You know, you've got a lot of different looks."

Val's mouth tilted into a smile. "I'm not sure how to interpret that."

"I was just thinking you look good in your farm clothes."

"Oh, I'm sure." Val shook her head and chuckled. "I'm going to take that as a compliment."

"It was meant that way. I mean, you look great, no matter what…" Brody let out a breath. "I should probably just stop there."

"I don't know why—I'm enjoying it. I think I can hear you breaking out into a sweat."

"Not possible," Brody said. "I'm totally serious. You're beautiful."

Val jerked, her lips parting as if her breath had just rushed out. "Why did I never notice you were such a charmer?"

"Me?" Brody snorted. "Definitely not in high school. And I'm not any different now. Just noting a fact."

"Well, I disagree, but thank you." Val shook her head. "I have a feeling I missed out on a lot back then."

"We were different."

"We were." Val laughed. "And of course, we just met tonight at the fair."

"That's right," Brody said, remembering their joking introductions earlier. "Clean slate, fresh start."

"I already feel as if we're at the beginning," Val said softly. "Memories and all notwithstanding."

The words punched through Brody like a fist. "You know, I used to dream about riding around on a summer night with you—only usually I was driving."

"Did you?" Val's voice was soft, wondering, sensual.

"Yep."

"Why don't I know that?"

"I never said."

Val looked at her, a brief flicker that shot bolts of electricity down Brody's spine.

Val's eyebrow rose. "Because…"

"Lot of reasons." Brody shrugged. No point in ignoring the obvious. "Flann was a big one."

"Ah, Flann." Val pressed her lips together, huffed. "I suppose I did have tunnel vision." She spared Brody another quick glance, one that burned. "My mistake."

"We're here now."

Val sighed. "We are. Right now. And we've got a wounded dog to deal with."

Brody straightened, checked out the window as Val turned into a lane leading to the farm. Val had covered the ten miles to the farm east of town in eight minutes. "What do you need from me?"

"I'm not really sure yet. Let's see what we've got. Best-case scenario, we can field dress and bring him back to the clinic where we can take care of things under controlled circumstances."

"And worst-case?"

"Worst-case is he's too badly injured to move and we'll have to do whatever we can in the field, or…" Val pulled around in front of a big barn where halogen spots shone up under the eaves. Lights burned in the farmhouse itself, smaller than the barn, but she suspected almost everyone was awake and outside somewhere. "Emergency vet care is expensive, and they might decide they can't afford it."

Brody winced. "That has got to be so hard."

"It is," Val said, "but being a vet, part of the responsibility is understanding the owner's needs as much as the animal's."

Val shut off the engine and Brody followed her out of the vehicle. Val opened the back and tugged out a big emergency case like those Brody used in the helos.

"Here, I'll take that one." Brody grabbed the oversized tackle box.

"Thanks." Val pulled out another one as a woman in jeans, a baby-blue hooded sweatshirt, and muck boots jogged toward them.

"Val, thanks so much for coming," the woman said, her long ponytail flying straight out behind her. "Hank is up on the ridge with Buzz. I've got an ATV over here for you."

"Thanks, Penny. This is Brody, she's going to give me a hand."

Penny shot Brody a brief look and hurried away, too preoccupied to be curious or just used to helpers showing up.

"Penny used to be Penny Wilbur," Val murmured as they hurried after her. "A year ahead of us. I think they got married right out of high school."

"I remember now," Brody said. "She was a friend of yours, right?"

"More or less." Val saw no point in mentioning there might have been a guy Penny had a thing for who was more interested in her than Penny. And Val hadn't been interested, not really, but she hadn't let him know that for a while. Not one of her favorite memories. Things seemed to have worked out well for Penny, though.

Two ATVs stood idling by the side of the barn, Penny astride one, waiting.

Val placed her case in the rack on the back of Penny's and Brody slotted the other on the second ATV. Val glanced at Brody. "I guess you should ride behind me."

Brody smiled and shook her head. "I guess it's the night for it."

Val climbed on and Brody slid into the tight space behind her on the four-wheeler. She had to wrap an arm around Val's middle to keep from getting bounced off. As they started up the steep incline behind the barn toward the ridge of the rolling pasture framed by woodland, Val's hair blew in her face, the strands soft and smelling of lavender. If she leaned just a little closer, her cheek would touch the side of Val's neck. She spread her palm against Val's middle. As they hit a bump, Val's muscles tensed beneath her fingers. Val settled her palm over Brody's hand and squeezed.

"Sorry for the bumps," Val called back to her, zigzagging across a field choppy with stalks. A faint glow flickered just over the ridge ahead.

"I'm good," Brody yelled, leaning against Val's back to steady herself and not overbalance the ATV. Val's fingers momentarily slipped between hers. An accident, had to be, but Brody's heart pounded and her stomach clenched all the same. Heat stirred between her thighs. She'd never been this close to Val in her life, except in her imaginings. Like memory, her imaginings were only a weak imitation of reality.

They bumped over uneven furrows and shot toward the top of the steep pasture.

"Hold on. Don't want to lose you," Val said.

Brody pressed her free hand on the crest of Val's hip. Her cheek brushed Val's ear and her chest pressed into Val's back. Fire kindled and flame flared deep within her. She twitched and tightened her grip.

"Okay?" Val asked.

"Yeah. Good." Brody forced herself to lean a little bit away. She needed to concentrate, and she wasn't going to be able to do that if her entire body was on fire.

"Here we go," Val said and slowed the ATV.

The light Brody'd seen from below grew brighter, and she made out another pair of ATVs, these idling with their headlights illuminating two figures crouched on the ground. Val pulled the ATV to a stop next to Penny's, and for a second, Brody felt Val lean back into her. Then Val swung her leg over and the moment dissolved.

Brody climbed off and hefted the equipment case as Val crossed into the circle of light. Her legs quivered. Bumpy ride, that was all. She hurried after Val and saw the big white dog immobile on the ground in a swath of crimson, a man kneeling above the animal, bloody hands pressed to the dog's flank. As always happened in moments like this, pain and fear and uncertainty receded, and every sense sharpened.

"On your six, Doc," Brody murmured.

Val registered the words as she hurried toward Hank. The words might have been automatic, even routine for Brody, but they struck a chord she hadn't expected. She liked the idea of Brody being there for her. Of course Brody just meant out here in the field, assisting her, but her mind, her body even, translated that into something much different. Something that stirred longing and excitement in equal measure. The strange, enticing mixture simmered somewhere in the recesses of her consciousness as she knelt next to Hank.

"Let me see what we've got here, Hank," Val murmured. When he didn't move, barely seemed to register her presence, she gripped his wrist. "Hank, let me take over for you."

"'Fraid he's gonna bleed out," he mumbled, his voice ragged.

"Brody," Val said as she gently slid her gloved hands under Hank's. Blood seeped steadily beneath her fingers. The dog was breathing, but shocky, his pulse weak and thready. "Set up an IV for me? It's in the gray—"

"I've got it," Brody said. "Sixteen-gauge intracath?"

"He's a big boy—he can handle that. Don't suppose you've ever—"

Brody knelt next to her, a rubber band tourniquet in her hand. "Once or twice. Our dogs got hit now and then. If I had time."

"Good. Give it a shot. I'm going to see if I can find this bleeder."

Brody picked up the dog's front leg and set to work. Val looked over her shoulder. Penny and two kids, a boy and a girl, stood nearby. "Penny, bring that other ATV around. We're gonna need more light."

Penny turned to the girl. "Beth—do what the doc says."

Beth hurried to move one of the Grizzlys.

"Brody?" Val asked.

"I think I…" Brody plugged in the IV line. "Yep, got it. You were right, nice big vein."

"Open it up and then dig out the instrument pack from the red case. Then give him a cc from the syringe with the morphine."

Brody swiveled around and came back with the plastic-wrapped tray. She opened it on the ground next to Val. "I'll push the meds. One second."

"Hank," Val said firmly, "I need you to move back now."

Penny gripped her husband's shoulder. "Come on, honey. Let Val work."

Val freed up one hand and gripped a hemostat. Brody leaned in close, a large sponge in one hand and a flashlight in the other.

"We're going to get one shot at this," Val whispered.

"Yep," Brody said, shining the light on top of Val's hand.

"Don't sponge unless I tell you to." Val moved her hand, a bright red arc of blood shot up, and she focused on the stream, following it back to the torn muscle on the dog's chest. She clamped the base of the stream blindly. "Gently, just clear the field."

Brody sponged. The bleeding slowed, stopped.

Val let out a breath. "This dog tangled with a big cat." She supported the hemostat in one hand. "Can you load me up a big silk suture? They're in—"

"I saw them," Brody said. "Hey, Hank…can you hold this light for the doc?"

"Yeah. Yeah, I can." Hank's voice was hoarse but steady.

"Here you go," Brody said a minute later.

Val stitched the bleeder closed and removed the clamp. The big gash stayed dry. She finally took a deep breath and her pulse climbed back down out of the stratosphere. "Okay. We'll close this up, give him some antibiotics and some more fluid. He's current on his rabies. I did that last month."

"Is he going to be okay?" Hank asked.

"I think so—do you have a kennel or a stall you can put him in? He won't be running anytime soon."

"We'll put him in the mudroom where we can watch him," Hank said.

"I'll check him tomorrow. You'll need to be careful he doesn't get bumped around on the way down."

"I'll hold him. Penny can drive us down in the side-by-side."

"Good." Val stood, eased the kinks in her back. She stood next to Brody as Hank lifted the dog. "That was a nasty one. I'm not sure I could have handled that without you."

"You would have. Nice job, Doc."

"Thanks." Val settled onto the ATV and waited for Brody. Brody climbed on behind her and slid an arm around her waist. A flood of anticipation curled in Val's middle. "I think I'm going to owe you another beer."

"I'll remind you," Brody murmured, her breath warm against Val's ear. Her fingers splayed over Val's middle, and Val trembled.

Chapter Sixteen

Brody packed the emergency kits in the back of Val's car and waited in the front seat while Val went over the instructions with the Turners. Hank had already taken the dog into the house, but Penny and Beth listened attentively, exchanged cell phone numbers with Val, and hurried away.

Val climbed in, settled behind the wheel, and leaned back. With her eyes nearly closed, she clasped the wheel loosely with both hands. "Well, that was something else."

Brody put her back to the door and stretched her arm out until her fingertips touched Val's shoulder. She made the move so naturally it took her a second to recognize what she'd done. A couple of ATV rides that left her whole body on alert weren't really a good reason to assume Val welcomed the contact. Val didn't pull away, and maybe she wasn't even aware of the touch. Brody moved her hand just to be safe. "Some fun, huh?"

Val snorted. "Which part—the ass-breaking ride through a cornfield, the surgery by headlight, or the pee-your-pants terror of not finding the damn bleeder?"

Brody laughed. "All of the above?"

"You're a sad case, Brody Clark."

Val's voice held a hint of teasing, more than enough to make Brody want to touch her again. She kept both palms firmly planted on her thighs. "First time for a big field operation?"

"I've done plenty of castrations and minor surgeries for infection, that kind of thing, out in the field, but never a major trauma. Not like that."

"Pretty awesome," Brody said.

"Yeah, it was. We were good together."

Val tilted her head on the seat and looked Brody's way, her body mostly in shadows. The barn lights slanted into the front seat and illuminated her face. In the muted glow, she looked triumphant. She'd crash later when the adrenaline wore off, but right now, she was high on the excitement of going to battle and winning. Brody knew the feeling. Her heart raced and every sense was heightened. Life was good when you beat the odds.

Brody's fingers trembled to trace the curve of Val's jaw, to find the pulse beating in her throat. The warning bells rang and she backed toward solid ground. "If you were nervous, I couldn't tell. More importantly, neither could the Turners."

"You sure were a rock," Val said.

Brody shrugged. "I've had my share of field action, waiting for a safe window to transport an injured troop to the helicopter. It never gets easier, but you learn to work despite the fear. We weren't under fire up there on the hilltop, but a life hung in the balance, and more than just the life of that dog. That family would have suffered if we'd failed."

"We didn't, though, did we." Val's smile shone like a banner in the moonlight.

"Nope. We didn't, and now, you've been baptized under fire. Everything else will be easier."

Val laughed. "Well, I hope you're right, and I hope I don't have to find out for quite a while." She shook her head, her hair flying around her shoulders and settling against her cheeks as she leaned forward to key the ignition. The move was automatic and effortless and the sexiest thing Brody had ever seen.

Brody's throat clamped down on a moan.

Val turned the vehicle around and headed out the dirt lane toward the road. "I don't even know what time it is."

"Believe it or not, it's only zero-one twenty."

"It feels like it ought to be dawn." Val hit the gas and they hurtled down the empty highway. As was custom during the hours from dusk to dawn, she drove in the middle of the road, staying away from the invisible shoulders, not worrying much about oncoming traffic at this time of night.

"You're not going to get much sleep tonight," Val said, "if you're planning on getting your truck looked at first thing in the morning."

"Like I said," Brody said, "I've got a lot of practice catching rack time at odd hours. I wouldn't have gotten much sleep tonight anyhow."

"Are you on call tomorrow?" Val asked.

"Not until tomorrow night. The regional air mobile unit is taking call with us for now, and"—she chuckled—"I've got fair duty tomorrow, midmorning."

Val glanced over at her. "Funny, me too."

Brody grinned. "So I don't exactly have to be super rested for that."

"Oh, you might be surprised." Val slowed as she reached the town limits, keeping close to the posted speeds until they emerged on the other side. "You're going to get plenty of curious people coming around tomorrow."

"Well, I guess that's the point. PR and all." The village disappeared behind them and disappointment dampened Brody's high as Val turned into the main gate leading to the mobile home park.

"Oh, not just about the sexy helicopter, but about you. Folks are going to want to know all about you."

"Nothing to know," Brody said quietly and gestured to her right. "Down that way. We're in the back corner."

"You're wrong about that, you know. You're fascinating, and not just because you're a hometown girl who turned out to be a hero." Val drove slowly, carefully avoiding the errant tricycle left in the middle of the lane, a stray dog prowling around here and there, and the inevitable opossums and other night creatures searching for food.

Brody gritted her teeth. Val might change her mind if she knew that the secrets she kept made her more of a coward than a hero. "That's it there in the back corner."

"You don't see that, do you?"

"'Fraid not." Brody laughed and hoped Val would let it go.

"Take my word for it. I find you to be a most fascinating woman, among other things." Val stopped in front of a surprisingly large modern-looking recreational vehicle with a chain-link fence extending from one corner and running off into the dark where she couldn't see. But she had no trouble making out the bright eyes of an animal, standing close to the fence. "I notice you've got the hunter working."

"She pretty much always stays outside if I'm not here, and half the time when I am. She's the suspicious sort."

Val shut down the car. "I can see why she would be, after what she must have experienced. Maybe the two of you are a little alike that way."

Brody let out a breath. "Val, you don't—"

"Yes, I know. I don't know you. You're right, but I know some things about you, and I like all of them. So if you're suspicious, I'll assume you have good reason, just like Honcho."

"Thanks."

"How worried are you about what happened with the truck?"

Brody shrugged. "I'd be an idiot not to be a little worried, but I'm not going to be paranoid."

"All right then, I'll try not to worry either."

Brody's fingers moved softly over Val's arm and along the peak of her shoulder. "I appreciate it, but I don't think you need to."

"I know it probably seems odd, ridiculous to you even, that I should worry." Val edged closer, leaned in to Brody's touch. "I know we don't know each other at all, and you're perfectly capable—"

"We know enough for this," Brody murmured, and kissed her.

Val's mind went blissfully and instantly blank. But far from numb. Her nerve endings lit up like Times Square on New Year's Eve, bright and noisy and chaotic. Her lips blossomed, hot and full. The tip of Brody's tongue slid over the seam of her mouth, warm and wet and unbelievably confident. Brody kissed the way she liked to be kissed, not as an appetizer, but as an entrée. Like kissing was the only meal she ever needed, and one she intended to savor, to sate herself on. Val opened for her and invited her to feast, instantly alight with the swept-away force of Brody's hunger. She moaned, slipped a hand behind Brody's head, spread her fingers through Brody's hair. The dark strands she pictured behind her closed lids were softer than she imagined, the muscles in Brody's shoulders as hard as she expected. She caressed Brody's neck and Brody leaned closer, got an arm around her waist, managed to turn her until their chests touched. Her breasts tingled, nipples tightening beneath the maddening confines of clothes. Why was she wearing clothes? And why was the damn gearshift between their thighs, preventing their hips from touching? The throbbing between her legs let her know how much she wanted that and a lot more.

Val dug her fingers into Brody's shoulders, backed her off an inch. "I'm too damn old to neck in my car." She dragged Brody's lower lip between her teeth for an instant, just a little nip. But God, she wanted to make her as crazy as she was feeling right now.

Brody groaned and the sound shot through her, electrifying and molten.

"Is that a no?" Brody asked, husky and a bit desperate.

"Hell no," Val murmured, wanting what she wanted, wanting Brody to reach in, reach everywhere, and put out the flames before she was nothing but cinder. Not giving a damn about wise or unwise or reasonable or any other thing except the taste of Brody's mouth and the way Brody's breath hitched and the low growl of lust in Brody's throat. "That's your cue to invite me in."

Brody's hands ran over her shoulders, fingers firm and possessive and promising more. "My quarters might be a little cramped, but if you don't mind…"

"You've got a bed, don't you?"

Brody kissed her throat, put her hot mouth against Val's ear. "I do."

"That should suffice, then." Val shivered, needing to cry or scream or start shredding the T-shirt she'd gripped in her fist. When was the last time…ever…never… "We need to do this now. God, I'm…"

Val pushed her away and reached behind her with the other arm to open the door. She climbed out on numb legs and heard the door slam. Brody was around the front of the car in the time it took her to almost finish wondering if she was doing something crazy. The thought was barely formed when Brody took her hand and pulled her toward the trailer. Brody's fingers were hot, her grip like iron sheathed in velvet. Oh yes—exactly that, exactly right. She could already feel her inside.

"Is there anything you want to know?" Brody pulled open the screen and banged open the inside door.

"No." Val climbed the stairs and stepped across the threshold. "Wait."

Brody turned, her eyes glinting in the faint light coming from a small light over a kitchen counter, sharp and feral, a wolf in the night.

"You're single, right?"

"Completely."

"Good." Val grabbed the bottom of Brody's T-shirt and yanked it out of her pants. She kissed her, sliding her hand under Brody's shirt, pressing her palm against her abdomen. Brody took a step back and Val followed, a dance she joined without conscious thought, body following body, need answering need, want calling to want. Val hooked her fingers inside Brody's waistband and the muscles against the back of her fingers tensed.

"Mm, nice," Val murmured against Brody's mouth.

Brody's fingers closed around her wrist. "Far enough."

Val tossed her head back, laughed. "Says who."

"Mercy," whispered Brody. "Or I'll embarrass myself."

"Oh no, you won't." Val licked Brody's lower lip, circled lower beneath her pants—but not quite low enough—to do her in. "I won't let you. Not until I'm ready."

Brody groaned. Something thumped behind her, then a sound she knew well. A dog panting a welcome.

"She won't bother us." Brody turned a shallow corner and pulled Val with her toward a good-sized bed tucked into the far corner of the RV.

"Not worried." Val let Brody go and pulled off her T-shirt, taking the silk bra underneath with it, dropping them behind her. Brody went still as a statue, and Val's breasts tingled.

Moonlight came through a square window opposite the bed, and the stark hunger on Brody's face was easy to read. Val's nipples tightened, and the primitive, feminine animal within her reared its head and sang out in triumph. "Something wrong?"

Brody shuddered. "No. Just can't breathe."

Val laughed, unbuttoned her jeans, and slid the zipper down. She watched Brody watch her, followed the flash of lust cross her face, went hot and wet inside. Soon. Had to be soon now. "That might be a problem."

She pushed her jeans down, unlaced her boots as the denim pooled over the tops, and kicked everything free until she was naked. A wonderfully wild rush of power tore through her, making her want to howl with the pure freedom to feel…everything. She tightened between her thighs, her belly tensed. Her breasts felt swollen and ripe, exquisitely sensitive. Brody still hadn't moved, still had her clothes on, and Val pressed close against her. She moaned as her skin electrified. Brody's heart pounded against hers, and she swayed against the rigid column of Brody's body. "You can touch me now."

"Val," Brody whispered, her fingertips barely brushing Val's hips, "if you want slow, I'm not going to be able to do it."

"Is that why you're afraid to touch me?"

Brody gripped her, spun her around, and pushed her down onto the bed. She was on top of her in a heartbeat, the rough denim of her thigh between Val's legs tormenting her swollen, exposed clit.

"No," Brody growled, her mouth, her teeth against Val's throat. "This is." She caught both of Val's wrists in her hands and held them against the bed, as if Val might disappear. Her mouth roamed Val's throat, her chest, the rise of her breasts, the taut peaks of her nipples. Teeth grazed the center of her abdomen and lower, and Val whimpered. For all Brody's fearless possession, she was infinitely gentle. When Brody pushed off the bed and knelt between her thighs, Val reached for her, found her head, pressed close to her mouth.

"Please," Val whispered. "Please don't wait."

Savage, exquisite tenderness engulfed her, teased her and taunted her and honed her to an edge she'd never reached before. Her body arched, blood pounded in her clit, and she came in a blinding torrent. A scream, a curse, a prayer tore from her throat, until she was thrashing and bucking and laughing at the end.

Brody's cheek pillowed against the inside of her thigh, and Val traced the arch of Brody's brow, over her cheek and along the angle of her jaw. "Why would I ever want you to take your time doing that."

Brody chuckled. "Good thing you didn't want me to. Had to have you."

Val managed to push herself up onto her elbows and looked down at Brody's supremely satisfied face. "Did you now?"

"So bad."

Val smiled. "Good. Because there's going to be more."

Brody pressed both palms to the inside of Val's thighs and bent to kiss her. Val's head fell back, and she almost gave in to the sweeping tide of need that instantly swamped her. She managed to get a hand under Brody's chin and pulled away. "But not right now."

Brody growled and crawled up onto the bed, straddling Val's body, her strong jeans-clad thighs on either side of Val's hips. "Why not?"

"Because," Val said, twisting her hand in Brody's shirt, "you still have all your clothes on, and unless there's something very, very wrong with me, you need to come."

Brody shuddered and the arms that bracketed Val's shoulders quivered.

"I can wait."

Val unbuttoned Brody's jeans, unzipped with one hand and slid her other one in at the same time. She found what she was looking for and Brody twitched. She smiled, satisfied. "I don't think so. Get your clothes off." She stroked the length of Brody's clit.

Brody moaned, and Val whispered, "That's an order."

Brody stripped. "Now what?"

"On the bed, on your back," Val said.

Brody stared at the ceiling, eyes blind, a death grip on the sheets twisted in her fists, her muscles screaming. No air. Couldn't breathe. Pressure pounding in the depths of her stomach. Val's mouth skimmed and teased.

"I'm going to come." Her voice strange and flat.

Val's mouth moved a fraction of an inch. "Not yet."

The breath Brody needed so badly gushed out, her lungs still burning. She might've sobbed. "Please."

Val pressed her cheek against the inside of Brody's thigh and circled her fingertip over the base of Brody's clit. "Not quite there yet."

Brody's jaw locked painfully. Her thighs trembled. Her head pounded, explosions of glaring white light bombarding her eyelids. She made a sound, halfway between a whimper and a moan. "I'm going to die."

"Mm. No. I won't let you." Val pushed her way up until her body rested against Brody's, her breasts against Brody's chest, her thigh edged onto Brody's pelvis. She stroked her breasts, her belly, feathered her fingers at the apex of her thighs. Brody trembled.

"I know you're close." Val kissed her softly. Kissed her again, harder, deeper, pulling Brody away from the razor's edge.

"No more, no way." Brody grasped Val's hips, shifted on top of her, and groaned when Val's leg came between hers.

Val laughed. "What do you think you're doing?"

"Fuck, you feel good," Brody gasped.

Val quivered, her fingers tightening on Brody's shoulders. "You like?"

Brody found Val's gaze, locked onto her. Her vision was hazy, but she could make out the haze of desire in Val's eyes, the seductive curl of her lips. "More than like. More than anything. I want to come. So bad."

Val choked in a breath. "God, you look good. I love teasing you."

"I'm fried. You're killing me."

Val circled her hips, rolled her thigh over Brody's center. "You're not quite…"

"Bullshit," Brody gasped. "Do that again, and I'll come all over you."

Val swallowed a whimper, but her eyes glazed and her hips bucked. Brody tightened her grasp on Val's hips and rose to meet her. One thrust, two, and she broke, the floodwaters cascading over the brink, carrying her away.

"Oh yeah. Yeah."

Val pressed her face to Brody's neck, her hips twisting as Brody came hard and long. Val's breath rasped in her ear and Brody stroked her back.

"Did you just come again?" Brody murmured.

Val weakly nodded her head. "You're so unbelievably sexy—you just pushed me over. God. I can't move."

Brody wrapped an arm around her shoulders, tugged the sheet up over them with the other hand. "Good. No reason to."

"I want to do that all night," Val slurred, barely finding the energy to speak.

Brody chuckled. "Be my guest. If you can move."

"In a minute," Val mumbled, and then her steady breathing evened out into the cadence of sleep.

Brody held Val, her muscles loose, her blood still pounding through her pelvis, her heart galloping erratically. She hadn't been with a woman in a long time, and never like this. Never with such blinding hunger, such unfettered need. She felt as vulnerable and exposed as if her skin had been flayed off, and still she wanted more. She wanted to hear Val's gasping cry of release, wanted Val's hands and mouth on her again. She wanted Val. Just like always and never like this.

She heard a thump beside the bed and whispered, “Good dog. You’re a good dog.”

Honcho nosed her arm and settled down to sleep. Brody stroked Val’s bare shoulder and closed her eyes.

CHAPTER SEVENTEEN

Brody's eyes shot open. Honcho stood in the doorway to the narrow hall that ran back to the living area. She growled low in her chest.

Hold position. Instant sit rep. Full dark outside. Her internal clock said she'd been asleep a couple of hours. At least an hour to go before dawn.

She sat up, pushed back the sheet tangled about her hips, and eased Val's head off her shoulder.

"Brody?" Val murmured softly, her arm tightening around Brody's waist. "Honcho heard something."

"I know. I'll go look," Brody said softly. "Go back to sleep."

"Are you sure?" Val sat up. "Wait, I'll come with you."

Brody turned, kissed her. "It could be anything—probably a raccoon or possum rattling around a garbage can somewhere close by. It'll just take me a second."

"I should—"

"Here." Brody grabbed Val's phone from the shelf above the bed and handed it to her. "If I'm not back in ten minutes, call 9-1-1."

"Put your pants on at least."

"Plan to." Brody chuckled, already half dressed. She knew exactly where her clothes were, even if she had undressed in a haze. In seconds she pushed her bare feet into her boots and picked up the baseball bat she kept in a corner, the only weapon she still had. She grabbed the Maglite from the charger on the shelf by the bedroom door and stuffed it in her back pocket.

Honcho rumbled again.

"Let's go see," Brody said, and Honcho trotted down the hall on point.

Brody disappeared soundlessly, and Val lay back in the dark. Her heart thundered too hard for her to even close her eyes. She stared at the unfamiliar ceiling, nerves gnawing at her insides. Honcho was a war dog. She didn't spook, and she didn't alert for scavenging animals or falling leaves. She alerted to the enemy, which in her dog brain meant any intruders in her territory, any living thing that didn't belong, or dangerous foreign objects that smelled wrong and carried the threat of imminent death. Brody knew that as well as she did. And of course Brody would go out to investigate.

Of course Brody would *insist* on going out alone. Everything about her, from her military training to her choice of profession, was geared toward protecting others. Val admired her for that, found it incredibly sexy even—except not just now. Right now she struggled with a choking fear of whatever might be outside in the night, fear for Brody and for Honcho, and recognizing it for what it was—mindless, atavistic reflex—didn't help all that much. She was still a bundle of anxiety. If she hadn't thought she'd be in the way and that she could do more good inside with the phone ready to call for backup, she would have insisted on going with Brody.

Still, she hadn't promised to stay in bed, and she wasn't going to cower in the dark any longer. She quietly got up and gathered her clothes.

❖

Brody slipped rapidly through the darkened RV, careful not to brush against any of the light switches in the narrow hall. When she reached the main room, she edged up to the window beside the door and, keeping her cheek flush against the wall, peered out. Her eyes had adjusted to the dark, but in the absence of anything other than moonlight, she couldn't see more than fifteen feet. She watched a few more seconds, searching for shadows that moved in the wrong place, waited for Honcho to signal she'd spotted something. Honcho halted by the door, head cocked, listening.

Brody whispered without turning, "I thought you were staying inside."

Val let out a breath. "I am inside. I thought I was being quiet."

Brody grinned. "Not too bad, really. Wait here, okay?"

"I will."

"Okay, Honch, let's have a look." She eased the door open and let Honcho glide out. She followed, the baseball bat held loosely in one hand, and, bending low, sprinted toward the cover of Val's car. She couldn't see Honcho, but she wasn't worried. Honcho understood the rules of engagement and would seek cover in the shadows and scrub as she reconnoitered. If she encountered anyone, she'd give a warning and Brody could light them up with her Mag. Honcho wouldn't attack unless on command or if someone managed to get to Brody.

Brody skirted around the front of Val's SUV and scanned the area immediately around her RV. No sign of anything suspicious. No movement other than the softly shifting branches of the pines in Honcho's run. But an engine rumbled somewhere close, growing steadily fainter. A stab of light, so quick she would have missed it if she hadn't been looking toward the road, flickered through the trees and disappeared. A vehicle leaving the trailer park, or possibly just passing on the road. She couldn't be sure. She watched a few more seconds, saw no sign of any other vehicles, and walked as far as the next RV. Nothing, not even a stray pet. Honcho reappeared and fell in beside her.

"Nothing?"

Honcho trotted along, ears up, her posture alert but calm. She hadn't found anything. Brody dropped a hand to the back of her neck and squeezed. "Good job."

As Brody entered the RV, Val said, "Anything?"

"Nope." Brody locked the RV door behind her and took Val's hand. "Nothing. Probably just an animal. Let's go back to bed."

Val followed as Honcho went out the dog door into the run. "Does Honcho usually growl at raccoons?"

Brody put the baseball bat back in the corner and the Maglite on its charger. "If there's something in her territory, she'll let me know." She sat on the bed and pulled Val toward her. When she got Val snug between her spread legs, she unbuttoned Val's pants and slid the zipper down.

"Has it happened before?" Val asked.

Brody tugged Val's pants down, and Val toed off her boots. "She spends a good part of her time outside, even at night, so I can't be sure. I think because you're here, she's a little bit more on guard."

"So you're not worried?" Val ran her fingers through Brody's hair. Her voice had dropped, gotten a little husky.

"I'm careful." Goose bumps popped out on Brody's arms. She hadn't been this amped even when she'd been outside in the dark hunting for a potential intruder. She lifted Val's shirt, kissed her stomach. "But I'm not worrying."

Hell, she was barely thinking.

"Good." Val stroked Brody's arm. "I know it's probably nothing, but all the same." She leaned into Brody, rubbing her middle slowly across Brody's mouth. "I know you're doing that to distract me, you know."

"I'm doing it because I want you. Bad." Brody circled the soft skin below Val's navel, kissed a bit lower. Val hadn't bothered with underwear when she'd gotten out of bed, and she was half naked. Brody clasped her backside, pulled her against her mouth, and lowered her head.

"Uh-huh." Val stepped back and shed her shirt. "If you want me in bed, take off your clothes."

Now Val was totally naked, bathed in a shaft of moonlight, every curve and angle glinting silver. An apparition worthy of an art gallery. Brody's stomach tied itself into a knot. A big, tight, aching tangle of need and want and wonder. "It'll be dawn in less than an hour."

"More than enough time. If you hurry."

Val held her ground, refusing to climb into bed, and Brody laughed.

Helpless. She was totally helpless.

The adrenaline from the hunt instantly morphed into lust, and Brody stripped in half the time it had taken her to dress. She lunged for Val, caught her hand, and dragged Val down on the bed. Val landed on her back and caught Brody's arm.

"I want you on top," Val whispered.

Need eating her alive, Brody obeyed. Val wrapped a leg around the back of her calf and pressed into her. She was already warm and wet. Val moaned and slid up and down Brody's thigh—quick, demanding strokes that left a trail of heat behind.

Brody's breath whooshed out and the knot in her middle tripled in size, threatening to choke her. Her whole body ached, she wanted her so bad. She was ready to be inside her right then. Cripes—she couldn't just keep jumping her every time she got within inches of her, but she had no control. None at all. She tried to put on the brakes and braced her arms, opening up a few inches of space between them. "I'm not sure I managed to tell you how hot you are, how beautiful."

"You didn't have to, but it's nice to hear." Val's fingers speared through her hair, a hand sweeping over her shoulders, down her back. Val rocked against her thigh. Her breath came hard and fast. "Right now, you can show me." Val bit the muscle at the angle of Brody's neck, slowly and just short of too hard. "If you want."

"Oh, I want." Brody shifted just enough to get her hand between their bodies, slid through the welcome between Val's thighs and inside her in one long, sweeping caress.

"God." Val sounded stunned. Her hips jerked and she pushed down hard, taking Brody deeper. "That's right. Just. Exactly. Right."

Val's last words were swallowed on a low, tortured moan, and Brody smiled, a tight tense smile as every atom in her being focused on Val. She homed in on her breathing, on the pounding of her heart against Brody's chest, on the rise of her hips and the twist of her thighs. All she wanted, all she needed, was to give Val exactly what she needed.

"I want to come," Val muttered, her head thrashing. "Baby. Baby, make me come."

Val's hips rose and fell as Brody thrust. Brody kept pace with her, deeper when Val pushed up to take more, faster when her hips rocked, slowing as Val's body tensed and arched. Val's belly tightened, her hips jerked, short desperate spasms.

"Oh yes," Val cried, grasping Brody's arm so hard as she came there'd be fingerprints.

Brody lost her breath. Lost a little bit of her mind and little bit of her heart at the same time. She stayed exactly where she was, buried deep, as Val slowly relaxed and let out a long shuddering breath.

"Okay. That was…something else."

Grinning, Brody settled beside her, leaning on her elbow so she could watch the sunlight chase away the silvery moonlight and slowly paint her in gold. "Morning."

"Mm." Val turned into her, burrowed her face in Brody's neck, and flopped an arm across her middle.

"You're amazing." Brody kissed her. "And that's way lame and not half of what I wanted to say. It's just…I don't have words for what you do to me."

"Those words are working just fine." Slowly Val turned her head, blinked through the haze of pleasure, and focused on Brody's intent features. She'd never been one to quantify or qualify orgasms, but good God almighty, that had been off-the-charts, mind-blowing, awesomely good. She throbbed in places she hadn't even been aware of having before, and her clit, as wrung out as it was after that cataclysmic explosion, pulsed and jumped like a race horse at the gate. And she couldn't possibly, not again. Not just yet, at least. "You're awfully good at that."

"I'm glad you think so."

"Oh, I think so. Give me a few minutes, and I'll show you exactly what I think. I intend to take your head off—figuratively, of course."

"The way I feel right now, it could be literal and I wouldn't notice." Brody kissed her again and took her time with it. The monster that demanded more and more and more whenever she looked at Val was mercifully sated for a minute, and she wanted to taste her. She wanted to drink her down. She wanted to wander off into her scent and heat and never come back. She heard a sound come out of her throat that sounded a lot like a sob and clamped down on it.

"You okay, baby?" Val murmured, stroking her as if she was fragile, or precious, or maybe both. "Let me touch you. I know what you need."

Brody sucked in a breath, forced her words out slow and even. "I'll have to take a rain check on that. I mean, if you want to some other ti—"

"Yes, I want. Are you crazy?" Val sat up. "Why?"

"Sun's up."

Val closed her eyes and groaned. "Has it occurred to you that we've been on a schedule since we met? Met again, I mean. Maybe we should just disappear for a day—or twenty."

Brody laughed. "They'd probably find us."

"Hmm. Jane would, I bet." Val raised a brow. "Is she an ex? Or a sometime present?"

"You mean sex?" Brody looked astonished. "No. Never. Why?"

"She seems awfully fond of you. And protective."

Brody shook her head. "It's a buddy thing. We're friends."

"Of course, sorry." Val wasn't the jealous type. Correction. She hadn't *been* the jealous type before this. She just didn't want to think of Jane taking care of anything Brody needed. "I can make it quick. If you tell me you're not turned on, I'll suffer a crisis of confidence."

"Oh. No need to worry. I'm locked and loaded." Brody kissed her until she was sure Val got the message. "I also feel fabulous. And I can wait."

"I know," Val said softly. "Was this worth the wait at all?"

Brody frowned. "First of all, every second I've spent with you, in bed or out, has been incredible. And the sex was beyond incredible—you're gorgeous and passionate and so hot I'm still burning up inside."

Val blushed. Blushed! She could feel it, and she never did that. "All right, stop."

"*And*," Brody went on, her gaze fierce, her palm where it cupped Val's cheek meltingly gentle, "I haven't been waiting. Not the way you think—I dreamed about a girl who once was you, for quite a long time." Brody's grin was wistful. "Maybe right up until the first time I saw you again. But this wasn't about her, or the dream, or the memories. This was all about you—and we just met, remember?"

Val blinked and held back the moisture threatening to spill with sheer willpower. "Yes, all right." She cleared her throat. Tried again. "I just…I don't know. You remembered me, and I…"

"Didn't remember me?" Brody's tone was gentle, teasing.

Val groaned. "Can we just forget this whole conversation?"

"Sure." Brody settled her back against the pillows and pulled Val against her. She kissed her temple. "As long as you know none of that matters. We're not them—at least not completely. If I was me from back then? Hell, I probably wouldn't have had the nerve to kiss you in the car."

Val pulled back, stared. "Why not?"

"You were so far beyond my reach—popular, beautiful, smart, rich—no wonder you didn't notice me."

"Oh God." Val sighed. "I was unhappy, angry, snobby, and trying to solve all my problems by getting the attention of…well, whoever I could. Count yourself lucky you weren't one of them."

"I'm counting myself lucky now," Brody said.

Val kissed her. "So am I."

"So we're good?" Brody tilted her chin with a finger and kissed her.

"Just as long as you remember I want mine," Val murmured against her mouth.

Brody grinned. "I guarantee I won't forget."

Val sighed. "I guess we should get on with it. Is there a shower in this thing?"

"Yep. There's only room for one, though."

"You go first, and I might be able to move by the time you're done. I'm coming with you to look at your truck."

"You don't have to."

"Maybe not, but we're both going to need coffee, and you're going to be busy. And…" Val pushed herself up and kissed Brody, firmly, long enough to be certain she had Brody's full and undivided attention. "I want to."

Chapter Eighteen

Flann slid the coffeepot onto the machine and pushed Brew. She kept the kitchen lights off except for the one over the stove and tried to be as quiet as possible. Her plan was to wake Abby with coffee half an hour before Abby needed to be up. With their schedules, she just never knew when they'd be in the bedroom at the same time again. Sneaking off into an on-call room was tempting, but now that she was an attending, she tried to act like it. And Abby would probably say no anyhow. She'd have to ask her if she'd had any on-call interludes during her residency days. She pictured Abby sneaking off with some unknown fellow resident, rushed and urgent, and heat shot straight between her legs. She glared at the slowly dripping coffee. "Come already, will you?"

The footsteps behind her that were not Abby's put a damper on the fire, and she watched her plans for morning sex go out the window.

"Morning," Blake mumbled, already at the refrigerator. He foraged around for a second and came out with orange juice.

"You're up early." Flann handed him a glass.

"You too."

"I had a case about three. Donnie Winslow managed to put his truck in a ditch and got roughed up."

"He okay?"

"Yeah." Flann pulled cream from the fridge and hit her coffee with a splash. "Broken arm, dislocated ankle, and bruised up pretty good."

"So you didn't have to operate on him?"

"He's got a splenic hematoma I'm watching, but it's stable so far."

"So how come you're just getting home?"

Flann shrugged. "I was there, so I helped one of the ER residents close up Donnie's facial lacerations."

Blake drank down the orange juice and pulled a package of English muffins out of the circa 1950 green breadbox with painted-on daisies and some other flowers that were probably lilies that Abby had found at a yard sale.

"What's your excuse?" Flann said.

Blake jumped. "Sorry?"

"For being awake so early. You have farm call today?"

"No, Margie and I were supposed to be in the ER the rest of the week, but we have the fair."

Flann laughed. "Tough duty."

"Yeah. I have to bring Roo over today and get him registered."

"You think Roo can beat out the rest of them in the crowing competition?"

"I know he can."

"Attaboy. You gotta have faith in your fighters."

Blake grinned, but his usual enthusiasm wasn't behind it.

"So." Flann leaned against the counter and sipped her coffee. "What's bothering you?"

With anyone else, she would have expected the usual *nothing*, because, hey, she'd been sixteen once and that would've been her answer, especially if one of her parents had asked. Really, who wanted to get into deep thinking when they were a teenager and life was ruled by hormones and adrenaline. She still wasn't all that big on introspection. But Blake was not a typical teen. He was one of the most self-aware kids she'd ever known. He'd proven that by recognizing who he really was and standing up for himself. What he'd been through had been tough and scary, but he'd been sure and strong and brave the whole time.

"Can I ask you a question?" Blake said.

"Sure."

"How do you know if you like somebody as a friend or…you know, more than a friend."

A chasm opened up at Flann's feet and she couldn't see the bottom. If she took a wrong step—hell, *any* step—she had a feeling she might disappear down that dark hole forever. Oh boy. She could call Abby, but he wasn't asking Abby, was he. He was asking her. Okay—approach it like a surgical emergency—get all the facts, don't jump to conclusions. Exam and labs first.

"Well, what's it feel like to have a friend?" Flann asked.

Blake looked surprised, as if he hadn't expected that question. That was a good thing—hopefully. He gave it some thought, which was totally like him.

"It feels good," he said slowly. "Like I can say anything, and it will be okay. Like I don't have to pretend about anything, I can be honest. And safe. Like I can have fun and be myself and not have to worry if I do something dorky or even do something stupid and maybe not nice."

"Sounds like you got that nailed."

"Do you feel that way about Mom?"

Flann's stomach did a very respectable backflip, several, as a matter fact. "Yeah, I do. I can be a jerk, and she'll still love me. And I can be uncertain or scared even, and I know she'll be there."

"But you don't think of her like a friend." Blake said it like he already knew the answer.

Flann let out a breath. "No, I don't. We're friends, sure. But I've never thought of her that way. This is probably going to make you feel weird…"

"It's not like I don't know you guys have sex. A lot."

"Thanks for that," Flann said dryly. "So you know what I mean. I think your mom is the most beautiful, talented, strong, amazing woman in the universe. And she's also the sexiest. And you know, from the minute I saw her, I wan—"

Blake's hand came up. "Yep, I got that."

"Right. You get my point. This hypothetical friend of yours," Flann said, "do you get any of those other feelings I'm talking about?"

Blake fished his English muffin out of the toaster and made a show of buttering it. Flann topped off her coffee and waited.

"Sometimes, I think about kissing them."

Flann registered the pronoun. Did that mean the kid Blake was talking about was gender fluid? Or did it mean Blake didn't want her to know who it was? Because the obvious suspect was her sister. No point avoiding the obvious. "Is it Margie?"

Blake cut her a look. "Sorta, yeah, but not always."

"Okay," Flann said. "This is getting interesting."

Blake laughed, and a little of the tension went out of his shoulders. "I'm not really sure you know, but there's this guy I like a lot too. Dave Kincaid?"

Oh boy. Flann schooled her expression to the reveal-nothing-to-the-patient except supreme confidence and certainty look. "The quarterback?"

Blake nodded. "Yeah, he's part of our squad, you know. We all kinda hang out together sometimes."

"Right. And you kinda think about kissing him."

"Maybe, sometimes. He's really funny and really nice and sometimes I think he's watching me."

"He might be, sure. You like him as a friend, then?"

"Not as much as Margie. I don't know him as well…it's more…"

"Physical," Flann said.

Blake nodded. "Yeah, but I'm not so sure that's a good idea, you know? Just the physical thing."

"I think maybe you might be overthinking this too much."

"What do you mean?"

"Well…" Flann climbed up out of the chasm where she'd been dangling by her fingertips. She had this, mostly. "What do you and your friends do if a couple of you are interested in something more than being friends—that happens, right?"

"Sure, yeah. I guess."

"You guys don't do everything in a group, do you? Do you date, or what? Do you even call it dating?" Maybe she didn't have it quite yet. How could a dozen years or so put her so out of touch?

Blake grinned, looking a little like he felt sorry for her and a little like he thought she was funny. "Well, if people want to hook up, then sure, they do things just the two of them, but first they'll text or post something privately, you know—talk. See where it goes."

"So maybe you should try that with one or both of them. If they're interested and you're interested, then you can meet up." Flann took a mental step back from the edge. She knew her sister. "And Margie—she'll for sure let you know one way or the other. She never waffles."

"Oh, I know." Blake cocked his head, and the humor left his eyes. "Are you going to be mad, if me and Margie, you know, turn out to be more than just friends?"

"Why would I?"

"I don't know," Blake said, staring at his bare feet. He never did that. He never got uneasy or embarrassed.

"Hey," Flann said, "where is that coming from?"

"If we did, you know, get together, it might not be so easy for her."

"Why not?" Flann wanted him to get it out. This wasn't just about Margie or dating or whatever it was called these days.

Blake shrugged. "You know why not."

"Because you're trans?"

Blake nodded.

Okay, slow and easy. This was the listening part. "Has anything come up recently?"

"No, but...do you think everybody knows?"

"Oh, man, I don't know." Flann grimaced. "Probably not everybody, but you know nothing's private around here. So I imagine a lot of kids in school are going to know. Not just the ones you hang with."

"Yeah, and the ones who don't like me might give my friends a hard time."

"There's always that possibility. If anything happens, you know you need to speak up, right?"

"Yeah, but maybe it's not fair to, you know, to get somebody else involved."

"Like Margie or this Dave guy."

"Yeah." Blake looked and sounded miserable.

Flann clamped down on the urge to strangle someone. That was not going to help. But how the hell had Abby coped with all this bullshit Blake had faced for years and still remained so calm and steady? She knew how—Abby kept her head for Blake, so she'd have to manage it somehow. If the heartburn didn't kill her. "Okay, I get where you're coming from. And I know you don't want people you care about to have a hard time. But you're not doing anything wrong. You know that, right?"

"I know."

"And sometimes, Blake," Flann said gently, "you have to trust other people to know what they want, and you need to trust them to be honest with themselves. You can't make decisions for other people. I know Margie, and you can count on her to be straight up front with herself and you. This Dave, I don't know."

"If we end up talking, I guess I'll find out."

"Good place to start."

"So, do you think this makes me bi?"

And just like that, the edge of the cliff started crumbling again. "I don't know. Does it matter? Isn't what matters how you feel about the people in your life, the ones you care about, the ones who really matter? And if you're attracted to someone, and it feels good and it's something you both want, does it matter what you call yourself…or them?"

"I guess it doesn't." Blake grinned, and his smile looked a little stronger, a little like his old self. "I think it's enough I got the trans part down."

"You sure do." Flann slung an arm around his shoulder and pulled him into a hug. She thought the kid might resist, but he didn't. For an instant, he rested his cheek against Flann's shoulder. Flann kissed his temple. "And you know, anytime you want to talk things over, with me or your mom, we're here."

"Do you mind if I don't, you know, tell you everything?"

Flann ruffled his hair. "Hell no. As long as you're keeping your pants on."

Blake laughed. "Okay."

"Listen," Flann said, "I'm driving out to the homestead in a bit. You want a lift out there to meet up with Margie?"

"Yeah, that would help. I want to go get Roo on the way to the fair. Margie won't have to come into town to get me first."

"Good enough. Let me bring your mom some coffee, and we'll head over."

Blake headed off to get dressed, and Flann pulled down another cup from the cabinet. That had gone pretty well. Now if her conversation with her mother only went half as well.

Flann tiptoed into the bedroom and set the steaming cup of coffee on the bedside table. She leaned down to kiss Abby good-bye.

"Everything okay?" Abby said quietly.

Flann sat on the edge of the bed and caressed Abby's hip. "Yeah. You been awake for a while?"

"Not very long. I could hear you two talking, but I didn't catch the details. Sounded a little serious."

"You want a replay?"

Abby clasped Flann's hand. "Not necessarily. If he talked to you, he wanted to hear what you had to say. But it's all good?"

Flann let out a breath. "I think it is. Just teenager stuff." She ran a hand through her hair. "Although, you know, the kind of teenager stuff we'd rather he didn't think about for ten years."

"It's that time, like it or not." Abby chuckled. "I had one of those with him not that long ago too. He's probably comparing notes."

"Oh, man, I hope not. Because I'm pretty sure I would've failed."

Abby sat up, slid an arm around Flann's waist, and kissed her. "I know that's not true. I'm sorry you didn't get much sleep last night."

"I'm good. I got what I wanted before I got called in."

"Oh, is that right."

Flann kissed her back. "Yup."

"Well, if you're very, very good, you might get more of that tonight."

"I'll be good, and ready."

Abby laughed.

Flann stood before she changed her mind about the rest of her plans. Abby needed to get to work and she still had some thinking to do. "I'm gonna run Blake out to the homestead. You free anytime later?"

"I've blocked out a working lunch to catch up on budget stuff. Want to join me?"

"I'll try."

Abby rose, threaded her arms around Flann's waist. "You okay?"

"Yeah." Flann held her, breathed her in. "I'm good."

"All right, baby. I love you." Abby squeezed her butt and let her go. "I'll see you later."

Blake was waiting outside by the Jeep, looking like his usual bright-eyed self. He chatted excitedly about the fair, and Flann made agreeing sounds in the right places as she drove. When she pulled down the lane to the homestead and parked behind Margie's truck, the sun was just coming up.

"I hope I'm not too early," Blake said.

Flann laughed. "No way. You know my mother's been up cooking for an hour, and Margie wakes up like a baby bird with her mouth open, looking for food. You'll be just in time for breakfast."

"That's good, because I'm starving."

"Said another baby bird."

Blake grinned.

The back door was open as always, and the smells drifting out made Flann's stomach rumble. Her mother, spatula in hand, stood at the stove and Margie watched from the table with a cup of coffee.

Ida turned. "Hello, you two. You're just in time."

Blake smiled shyly. "Good morning."

"Hey," Margie said.

Blake sat down beside her, and Ida gave Flann a raised eyebrow. "I didn't expect to see you on a weekday morning. Have you been up all night?"

Flann shook her head. "About half."

"Then you should eat. It'll get you refueled for the rest of the day."

"Dad here?"

"Up and gone. Said he wanted to make rounds early and talk to Harper about one of the medical residents." Ida poured pancake batter onto a sizzling cast iron skillet. "Problem?"

"Not exactly, but…" Flann glanced at Margie and Blake. "You guys think you can give us a minute?"

Margie picked up her coffee. "Sure. As long as you're done before the pancakes get cold." She led the way outside and Blake followed.

Flann joined her mother at the stove as Ida flipped pancakes. Her stomach growled again.

"So?" Ida asked.

"I had a case in the middle of the night, nothing serious, but while I was there, I heard that Brody had some trouble last night."

"Brody told you?"

Flann snorted. "Hardly. One of the OR techs who'd been over at Bottoms Up before their shift."

"Is Brody all right?"

"Yeah, but someone vandalized her truck while it was parked in the lot over there. Got to all four tires."

Ida expertly plated the pancakes and poured another batch from the ceramic bowl with a big red rooster on the side. "Intentional?"

"I don't know. Seems odd, don't you think? Her just being back and all?"

Ida gave Flann a long look. "Flannery, don't you think *everything* about Brody leaving *or* being back is a little odd?"

"I guess I just didn't want to think about it very much. I was too pissed off."

"And hurt," Ida murmured.

Flann ground her teeth. "So if you thought something was wrong besides Brody being an ass…hat, why didn't you ever say anything?"

"Because it wouldn't have made any difference. Brody had left, and by the time we knew it, she'd enlisted. Then she was doing a hard job in a dangerous place, and dragging up the past, when nothing could be changed, didn't seem like a good idea."

"So what are we going to do now?"

Ida smiled and flipped the next round of pancakes. "What do you want to do, Flann?"

"I want to kick somebody's ass. I thought I'd start with Brody."

"Mm. How did that work out for you when you were teenagers?"

"About fifty-fifty, me versus her."

"Seeing as you're both older, although probably not any wiser, I'd rather neither of you damages the other. What's your backup plan?"

"I thought I could talk to her."

"That one sounds a little safer. Why don't you start there."

"Yeah, all right."

Ida patted her cheek. "You know, baby, you wouldn't be half as angry if you didn't care so much. Just remember that."

Flann sighed and kissed her mother's cheek. "Right. I knew you'd say that."

Ida laughed. "And that's why you came."

Chapter Nineteen

Val pulled in to the parking lot next to Bottoms Up five minutes after six. These early mornings were turning into a routine, but at least this morning the reason was a more than pleasant one. Waking up to Brody Clark at any hour would be just fine, and if she could squeeze in another hour of the kind of fabulous sex they'd just had…then, sure, waking up before the sun was no problem at all. Brody's truck was the only vehicle still there. She put her SUV in park and kept the engine running. Anything to prolong the just-two-of-them time, before she had to move on into her day. And how weird was that—wanting to linger with a woman well beyond the I-had-a-great-night and thanks-again stage. "I don't mind staying until you get this sorted out. You might need a ride somewhere."

Brody pushed the car door open but made no move to get out. "This is going to take a while, and I know you've got things to do."

Val grasped Brody's arm. "I don't mind."

Brody leaned across the front seat and kissed her. "Thanks. I'll be fine. If I get stuck, I'll call Jane to come get me."

Jane, huh? Val managed not to snarl. Brody said they were just friends, and she totally believed her, but all the same. She didn't want to drive away and let some other woman step right in. She almost laughed. Really, would she be peeing a circle around Brody and her truck next? She really *needed* to leave so she could regain a little perspective here. They'd just had a great night and super sex, but it was just one night. Then why did it feel like so much more? "I'm at least going to get you coffee. How do you take it?"

"If you're going to the café, I'll take a redeye."

Val smiled. "Woman after my own heart."

Brody almost said she might be, but caught it back. The words might be a little too close to the truth, and it was too damn early in the morning to think about that. She hopped down, holding the door open with one arm as she looked back into the passenger compartment. Now that she had a little distance, she didn't want it. What she wanted was to touch her again. Just for another minute. "Last night was terrific."

"It was." Val smiled, and Brody's heart felt a little lighter. That smile was almost as good as a touch. Something she could hold on to for a while.

"I'll be a few minutes," Val said. "Want something to eat with the coffee?"

"Surprise me."

Val laughed. "I intend to."

Brody closed the door and watched until Val turned the corner toward Main Street. Holy hell. She'd just spent the night with Sydney Valentine. Never in her wildest dreams. She almost chuckled. They had been wild dreams too, some of them, but nothing that could touch the reality. Everything about being with Val was better than she'd imagined, and the sex went beyond incredible. Terrifying might be a better word for it. She'd never wanted a woman with such consuming hunger before, never given herself without restraint. Felt so much, so damn right. Scary stuff.

Maybe all the good stuff was.

Even looking at her sagging truck and ruined tires didn't completely demolish her good spirits. She took three-hundred-sixty-degree photos with her phone and looked up the number for Stan's Auto Repair.

Stan picked up, sounding completely awake at six ten in the morning. "You got Stan. What can I do for you?"

"Stan, you might not remember me. Brody Clark—"

"Brody! Where you calling from, man?"

"About a quarter mile away at Bottoms Up in the parking lot."

"No kidding. You're back in town?"

"I am, and I've got a bit of a problem."

"What, you crash another motorcycle?" He laughed, as only an old biker could. Who hadn't dropped at least one bike on the highway somewhere?

Brody stomach churned, but she tried to match his tone. "Nope, gave them up. Just four wheels for me now."

"Getting old before your time, Clark. So what do you need?"

"My truck is sitting over here with four slashed tires. I was hoping you might have some used ones I could get on it so I can get it moving again. I'd rather not tow it, but if I have to…"

"Slashed tires, you say," he said slowly.

"Yeah. I think they're pretty well done in, but if you think there's anything to salvage, I'd be happy for you to try."

"Who did it?"

"No idea." She looked over her shoulder as a sheriff's cruiser pulled into the lot. Now what? "Listen, Stan, I know it's really early, but—"

"Hey, no problem. What's the make and model of your truck? I'll see if I've got something that will work for now."

"Thanks, Stan. I appreciate it." She gave him the specs, pocketed her phone, and walked over to the cruiser just as Tom Kincaid got out. "I thought you were off duty this morning?"

"I will be as soon as I check in at the station, but I'm in no rush." He tipped his uniform hat back a little and, hands clasped around his gun belt, surveyed the truck. "Doesn't look any better this morning than it did last night."

"Nope. Looks worse."

"So, did a little sleep give you any new ideas about who might have done this?" He regarded her steadily, his appraisal frank but not accusatory.

"Even if I had an idea," she said slowly, suspecting he knew she had a pretty good one, "you and I both know there's no proof. There's no money in pointing fingers."

"There is if it gives me someone to keep an eye on."

"And if I'm wrong, it'll just cause hard feelings."

"You see," he went on as if she hadn't just tried to close the conversation, "we don't see a lot of random vandalism around here. Oh, once in a while some guys will use mailboxes for batting practice, but nothing that looks personal, you know? And this…it kind of looks like your truck was targeted."

"No real reason to think that," Brody said.

"I heard Lloyd had words with you last night."

Brody sighed. "Lloyd and me exchanged a few words, true—but there was nothing to it."

"Uh-huh. Well, I was wondering—" Tom cut off as Val parked her SUV next to Brody's truck and got out. He glanced at Brody and waited silently as Val carried two cups of coffee and a white waxed bakery bag over to them. She held one cup out to Brody. "I added cream. Hope that's okay."

"Perfect." Even if she hadn't taken cream, which she did, she'd probably have said the same thing. Val bringing her coffee was about the sexiest thing she could think of, short of being in the bedroom with her again. "Thanks."

She passed over the bakery bag next. "You didn't look like a scone kind of woman to me. But they had cinnamon rolls."

"Nailed it in one." Brody peered into the bag and glanced at Tom. "Want one? We've got enough for a platoon in here."

He shook his head. "I'm having breakfast with my wife as soon as I get home. If I don't show up hungry, she'll be unhappy. Then I'll be looking at a whole day of chores."

Brody laughed.

"What's the plan here?" Tom asked.

"Stan Smith is on his way."

"I'll let you get on with what you're doing, then." Tom turned toward his patrol car, took a few steps, and turned back as if he'd forgotten something. "Say, when you get a chance, I'd like to talk to you about the accident."

"The accident," Brody said coolly. "That's ancient history. You were probably, what, twelve?"

Tom grinned. "Thirteen, but we keep good records. It wasn't hard to find."

"Like I said, ancient history."

"I'm sure you're right. All the same." He held out his card. "Call me."

He climbed into his cruiser, backed out, and disappeared.

Val looked at Brody. "What was that all about?"

"Absolutely nothing. He's just an eager young officer with not enough to do. He's probably overqualified for his job."

"Uh-huh." She popped the lid on her coffee and took a sip. "I'll take one of those cinnamon rolls."

Brody leaned against the hood of the truck and set the bag between them. Val reached in for a cinnamon roll, and Brody took one herself.

"I don't remember an accident." Val took a healthy bite of the gooey cinnamon bun, somehow managing not to get a single drop of icing on her. How did she do that?

"It wasn't exactly big news," Brody said, chasing her first bite of cinnamon roll with coffee. She thumbed icing off her lip. "You wouldn't have heard about it."

"Why does he think it's important?"

Casual question, but they'd been circling this for a while now. Maybe not the details, but the bit of her past that just wouldn't stay buried. Brody knee-jerk answered, "Like I said, he doesn't have enough to do."

Val cocked her head. Studied her the way Brody imagined she studied an interesting X-ray. She sure felt transparent just then.

"You know," Val said, "you're really obvious when you're being evasive. And I'm not the least bit subtle when I'm being intrusive, am I?"

"Not really, no." Brody let out a breath. They'd slept together the night before. She liked Val, a lot. And Val wasn't asking about anything that wasn't public knowledge, or at least that half the people in the town wouldn't remember. She had no reason not to tell her, at least as much as she knew for sure. "I was a really restless sleeper when I was a kid, and I was usually awake before the sunrise. I had a broken-down Triumph motorcycle I'd put back together myself from spare parts I hunted up around the county, and I'd ride early in the morning when the roads were empty. I'd just turned eighteen, and I went out early one day like usual. The roads were wet, or maybe there was an oil spill I didn't see, but I went off the road and crashed my bike pretty good. I managed to bang myself up too. Fortunately, nothing major was broken except my bike."

Val's gaze darkened. "It must've been a pretty spectacular accident if it generated a police report."

"Patrol car found me. I was a little confused, and I didn't have a phone with me. Come to think of it, I didn't even have a phone back then. Anyhow, they made out a report, I guess. That's all there was to it."

"That must've been shortly before you left, then, right?" Val's tone was quiet, thoughtful.

"Couple of weeks."

"Why do you think he's interested now?"

"No idea," Brody said, and she wasn't lying. Tom Kincaid had been just a teenager at the time and probably hadn't even heard about her accident. If he had, he wouldn't have known her. Why he'd bothered to check her out now, she didn't know. Maybe he'd been looking for a criminal record, but she couldn't see why, unless he'd heard something about her going to live with the Riverses. But that was even older news than her accident, and she hadn't been the one in trouble. He had no reason to put that accident together with anything else. Hell, *she* wasn't even sure.

"But you suspect something." Val made it a statement, not a question.

Brody sighed. "Nothing for sure."

"You're saying that a lot lately. I know you don't have any reason to trust me—"

"Whoa! Hold it right there." Brody grabbed her hand. "That's absolutely not true. I don't have a single reason to distrust you."

Val smiled. "That is not exactly the same thing." She poked Brody gently in the center of the chest. "You are an expert at guarding your secrets. If I was the kind of woman who was bothered by that, I might be a little crazy by now."

A shard of ice shot straight through Brody's heart. She was fucking this up. This needed fixing right now.

Brody lifted Val's hand, kissed her knuckles. "I'm not trying to be secretive. I just would rather leave the past in the past."

"Oh, believe me, I get that. So would I. But sometimes, the past comes after us. We're both here now, and apparently so is a little bit of the past."

"A little bit, maybe. But we agreed, just met, right?" Brody's heart pounded while she waited. Every second clocked in at an hour. Maybe a year.

"True, and I'm sticking to it," Val said. "I'm enjoying the getting-to-know-you part. But I'm not the world's most patient woman. I'm not going to push just yet. Let's see what happens first."

"What happens?" Brody's head swirled. She wished to hell she'd brought Honcho. Honcho knew how to guide her through a minefield. She could use a little guidance right now.

Val slid closer and kissed her. "You know, with us."

The blood drained from Brody's head and pooled instantly in the pit of her stomach. "Yeah. That sounds like a really good idea. I really like the us part."

Val tapped her chin. "So do I."

"So…uh, when can I see you again?"

Val smiled. "When are you free?"

"I have to wait here to find out about the tires. I'm due at the fair late morning. Maybe I could…I don't know where you live."

Val laughed. "I like the way you think—and you're absolutely invited to stop by. *But* I have to go home, change my clothes, and get over to the fair to take care of crates full of orphan animals this morning. I will be thinking about last night, though."

Brody's thighs trembled. She'd never felt so much at the mercy of a woman in her life. "You're killing me."

"Delighted to hear it. Come find me when you get to the fairgrounds." Val leaned in to kiss her again.

Another car pulled into the lot and Val broke away with a tiny chuckle. "My, this is a busy place this morning."

Brody gathered her wits together, expecting Stan. She stiffened when it wasn't Stan who got out of the Jeep.

Flann strode toward them, surveying the truck. "Wow, you weren't kidding, Val. That's a mess."

Brody glanced at Val.

Val shrugged. "Flann was getting coffee when I was in the café, and she asked me what I was doing there at the crack of dawn."

"I think I said ass-crack," Flann said, grinning. "I'd already heard about your tires, though, from one of the OR techs who was here last night."

"Some things never change," Brody said.

Flann gave her a long look. "Maybe they should."

Val squeezed Brody's forearm. "I'll see you later at the fair. Don't forget we're going to set Honcho up with the vest today."

"Right, I'll find you."

Val smiled and nodded toward Flann. "See you later, Flann."

"Yeah, Val. Have a good one." Flann didn't look in Val's direction as Val strode to her car, climbed in, and drove away. "Honcho?"

"My dog. I brought her back with me."

"War dog?"

"Yeah." Brody felt Flann watching her. "So? What else?"

"So? So you're home, what, a couple of days? And somebody decides to slash all four of your tires. That's weird."

"Bad luck."

"Or bullshit," Flann said. "What's going on here, Brode?"

"Noth—"

"You're a lousy liar. Always were."

Brody clenched her jaws. She did that a lot when Flann was around. "What are you doing here, Flann?"

"For starters, I'm pissed off that somebody went after your truck. I'm pissed off that maybe the next time, they're gonna go after you. And I'm mostly pissed off because I think you must know why, and for some reason, you're not saying."

"Thanks, I appreciate you worrying…"

Flann snorted.

"I mean it," Brody said. "I appreciate it, but there's no reason to."

"That worked, at least with my mother, when you disappeared. But now you're back, and it doesn't work as well."

"I'm sorry you're pissed at me." Brody closed her eyes, took a breath. She met Flann's hot gaze. "No, wait. I'm sorry I pissed you off. I'm sorry that I hurt any of you. I can't change the past."

"You're right, you can't. I'm getting a little tired of being pissed off at you, though." Flann pointed to the bakery bag. "Are there any more of those cinnamon buns Val was buying in there?"

Brody tossed her the bag. Flann fished one out, took a big bite, and put her butt against the front of Brody's truck, so they were leaning almost shoulder to shoulder.

They stood there silently, watching the scant traffic go by while Flann polished off the pastry.

Flann dusted her hands off on her jeans. "You kinda made a mess of things, Brody, and you need to clean it up. For my mother and father, and for all of us."

"I'm working on how to do that," Brody said.

"Fair enough. You can start by coming to dinner on Sunday."

Brody's chest tightened. Sunday dinner was a Rivers tradition. The family always got together on Sunday. "I don't know, maybe it's too soon."

"No, it's way too late. Bring Valentine with you."

Brody's shoulders tightened. "What?"

Flann laughed. "Oh, come on. I saw the kiss, it looked…hot. She's hot."

"Shut up."

Flann chuckled. "Seriously. Come to dinner, bring Val. Nothing heavy."

"Did your mother put you up to this?"

"No. Well, not exactly. She said it would probably be better if I talked to you instead of thumping on you."

Brody frowned. "But why? I thought you wanted me gone."

"No, Brody," Flann said quietly. "That's just it. I never wanted you gone."

Chapter Twenty

"I'll get a check out to you this afternoon, Stan," Brody said. "You saved my butt coming out here now."

"Hey," Stan said as he tossed the last tire into the back of his truck. "Not a problem. I was just sitting around listening to the news." He shook his head. "Not that I really wanted to hear any of it. Besides…" He grinned. "You took these four old tires off my hands. I been wondering who I could palm them off on."

Brody chuckled. The tires were practically new, and she'd had a struggle just to get him to let her pay for them, let alone his time and labor. "Yeah, some things never change."

He gave her a long look. "I dunno, Brody. Sometimes they do. I have to say, I didn't expect to see you back, but I'm glad you're here."

"Yeah, me too." She surprised herself as soon as she said it. The last thing she expected to feel about being back was glad, but she was. She was glad to see that the town had not changed all that much. Sure, some of the stores along Main Street had closed or changed their names, but plenty of them still remained just as she remembered them. The café hadn't been called a café before, but it still occupied the old bank building on the corner, and the menu might've been updated a little bit with espresso drinks and an array of breakfast pastries, but the staples of bacon and eggs and pancakes hadn't changed either. She was glad to see the hospital not only still open, when so many across the country had closed, but being reborn, bringing new blood and new hope to the community. She was glad to see people like Stan, who she'd pretended she hadn't missed, but she had. And Flann, and Ida, Margie, Harper, and the other Riverses she hadn't seen yet. Seeing them again went beyond glad. A hole in her heart she'd tried hard to ignore was filling again.

She grinned to herself. And then there was Val.

Glad, happy—hell, over the moon out of her mind—didn't begin to describe what she felt about meeting Val, not again, but truly for the first time. On equal ground, as adults, with a little more awareness and a lot of other things she hadn't imagined she could feel. She let out a breath. "Yeah, I guess I am glad to be back."

He nodded as if he approved. "Well, if you decide to get back on the road on an appropriate vehicle, you let me know. I've got a Harley I've been working on that you might find suits you. Come around and tinker with her a little when you get the chance."

"I'll do that, Stan. Thanks."

He gave her a wave, hopped into his big Ram 4x4, and backed out of the parking lot. Her phone rang as she slid behind the wheel of her truck.

"Morning, Jane," Brody said after checking the caller ID.

"Hey, you over with the truck?" Jane sounded half asleep, her husky voice slow and lazy. If she hadn't given Brody a ride home the night before, she'd think Jane had closed out the bar.

"All fixed up. I was just heading home."

"So I was wondering," Jane said in that same faintly sluggish tone, "if you could do me a solid and hold down the fort over at the fair for a couple hours this morning."

"Sure. You okay?"

"Mm, yeah. I got to thinking about the new rig last night after I dropped you off and took a quick trip up to the hospital. I just wanted to check her out again, you know? Make sure everything was tidy."

"What, did you work last night?" Brody frowned.

Jane chuckled. "I don't think you could call it work."

The light went on and Brody laughed. "I get it. You've got company."

"That I do. And it appears we've passed all our required flight examinations in one try, so she'll be leaving town on a one p.m. flight. I'm gonna, you know, spend a little quality time with her before then."

"Devi."

"Got it in one."

"What happened to what's his name—Jake?" Brody didn't bother keeping track of Jane's bedmates, not that there were all that many, until Jane mentioned seeing them more than once. She'd thought Jake might have rated a second look, but maybe not.

"That was Ohio, and that was then. We parted friendly. This is very much now."

"Right. Okay. You…enjoy yourself. I'll handle the fair stuff."

"Thanks, buddy."

Brody slid the phone into the console, turned on the engine, and considered her next move. Honcho needed a run after the excitement of the night before, especially since she'd be surrounded by strangers all day at the fair. Working off a little excess adrenaline would be good for both of them. Plenty of time for that before she was due at the tent. She glanced at her phone, a few inches from her right hand. Val ought to be home by now. Too early for her to be at the fair either. Maybe she had an hour or so free. Maybe Brody could catch her before the day got busy, get her naked and in bed again.

Brody's heart hammered in her chest and an insistent pressure pounded out a beat between her thighs. And maybe she needed to put the brakes on her libido and take things a little slower before she scared Val off. She drummed her fingers on the wheel, lust and reason waging a battle for her willpower.

"Right." She knew just the thing to settle her down.

Brody headed for the hospital.

Ten minutes later, she pulled into the lot, parked in what she already thought of as her spot, and jogged over to the ER entrance. The bright lights, air of expectation, and bustling staff gave her a jolt of energy. She wasn't due on shift until that night, but she wanted to find out how the crew from the regional air mobile unit had done on their shift. That crew took call from their own base and flew their own birds, but Matt would still have oversight over any calls coming in to the Rivers. She found him on the first try, in the break room with a cup of coffee and a doughnut.

"Morning," she said.

He looked freshly shaven and wide-awake, like he always did.

"Didn't expect to see you today. Don't you have fair duty?"

He grinned and polished off his doughnut.

"Ha," she said, pouring herself a cup of coffee. "Yes, as you know, but I don't need to be there for a while."

"So why are you here?"

She sat down beside him. "How did things go last night with the Saratoga crew?"

"Quiet. Air mobile responded to a house fire up north." His expression grew somber. "Turned out to be a coroner's case, so no transport was needed."

"That's tough," Brody said. Nobody liked to have a call end with a DOA, even if the individual was deceased before any intervention could be instituted. They all flew to save lives.

"So what's the matter, bored with the entertainment choices around here?" Matt teased.

Brody flushed, very glad he wasn't a mind reader. She didn't think it was a good idea to tell him she was mostly amped up from really good sex and an insistent desire to repeat it. She wasn't sure working would actually take her mind off anything, but it was better than sitting around replaying every touch, every glimpse, and every sound until she made herself nuts. More nuts than she already was, at least.

She smiled. "Yeah, that's it. Nothing much on cable at seven a.m."

"Uh-huh. You're on tonight, so don't let me hear about you trying to sneak in a few calls before then."

Brody shook her head. "No, sir. I'll work on the training schedule a bit and head right on over to the fair."

Matt snorted. "You do that."

Grinning, Brody left him to finish off another doughnut and grabbed a seat at the intake station. She liked having the hum of the ER for company as she familiarized herself with the experience and work hours of the staff who wanted a spot on the flight rotation. Forty-five minutes later she'd made decent progress and was just packing up when Courtney Valentine leaned over the counter.

"Are you doing the flight schedule?"

"Yep." Brody smiled. "It's mostly done. I'll email everyone sometime tomorrow with the rotation."

"Great." Courtney hesitated and looked around as if to see if anyone was in hearing range. "So, I hope, you know, anything you might've heard doesn't have anything to do with this."

Brody tilted her head, gave Courtney a look. "I do my best to make my decisions based on what people do, not what other people say about them. It's something you might give some thought to."

Courtney straightened, her brows rising. After a second, she said quietly, "Yeah, maybe you're right."

Brody closed her tablet and slid it into her bag as Courtney hurried away. She picked up her phone and saw the message icon blinking. She swiped to open, saw Val's name, and her stomach flipped.

Just wanted to say hi. Everything okay with truck?

Brody hesitated. Val just being friendly? Possibly. How to answer? She could play it cool, play it safe, but what would be the point. She was already way past friend stage. She didn't sleep with just-friends. Hopefully, Val didn't either. *A-ok. You've been on my mind.*

Same here, came back instantly. Then: *I have an hour. Are you free?*

Brody's hands actually trembled as she replied. *Yes. Where are you?*

Home. The Eddy place, second floor.

Have to get Honcho. Be there in ten.

:) *C u.*

She called a quick good-bye to Matt, who was chatting with one of the PAs, and made it home in five minutes. She hadn't even pulled the truck all the way in to the narrow strip of gravel that served as a driveway before she knew something was wrong. Honcho would have heard the truck, and usually she'd be standing at the fence, alert and watchful, waiting for Brody to enter the trailer. Now she sat ten feet inside the fence, ears up, quivering, and intently focused on something in her run.

Brody jumped out of the truck and quickly scanned the area, looking for whatever had caused Honcho to alert. When Honcho went out on patrol in a war zone, if she smelled or sensed danger, she sat to alert her handlers. Out here, the choices were limited. An animal predator of some kind—big cats had been sighted although rarely; bears, but they were usually too afraid to approach even domestic animals; and coyotes, who would rarely venture into a dog's territory unless they were starving. But a rabid animal would be fearless.

The other possibility was a human interloper, and this time she didn't even have a baseball bat.

"I'm on my way, Honcho," she murmured. Honcho's ear flicked to signal she'd heard.

Brody eased her way inside the run and made sure the gate was closed but not latched in case she needed a quick exit. The twenty-by-forty-foot fenced-in space looked empty except for the two of them. She stopped beside Honcho and followed her line of sight. "Good girl, Honcho. Show me."

Honcho trotted forward and Brody kept pace, checking left and right. Honcho would not lead her over a path of danger. Close to the far end of the run, about five feet from the fence in the shade of the big tree, Honcho stopped and sat again. Brody studied the steak lying on the ground. It looked reasonably fresh, about two inches thick with the bone still attached.

Fury burned in her chest. She buried her fingers in the ruff on Honcho's neck. "Good dog. Good job. Come."

She spun on her heel and strode back to the trailer, letting herself in through the back door with Honcho on her heels. She grabbed a dog bone from the jar on the counter for Honcho's reward. "Good girl."

Honcho took the bone but headed for the front door. She wanted a bigger reward, and she'd earned it.

"I know—we'll run later, I promise." Brody found a big freezer bag, went back outside, and retrieved a spade from a utility compartment on the side of the trailer. As she walked back to collect the steak, she checked the nearby trailers for signs of a strange vehicle, not that she would necessarily recognize one. She didn't know all her neighbors, but if someone was sitting in a vehicle or just getting ready to drive away, she could get a license plate.

The only vehicle in sight was a dusty Kia parked at the unit across from hers. Empty. Somewhere a baby cried, somewhere a television was turned up loudly, and somewhere a motorcycle revved. But nothing nearby looked suspicious. She shoveled the steak into the bag, being careful not to touch it. Once it was bagged, some of the tension but none of the anger faded. She shoveled dirt and gravel over the spot where the steak had rested and tamped it down with the blade. Honcho wouldn't dig it up, but she felt better having buried whatever had been on that meat. Because something had been.

The ground outside the kennel fence was strewn with leaves and rocks and hard-packed earth, leaving no chance for any kind of footprints. She doubted anyone would even consider searching for them. When she was satisfied she'd done all she could to secure the run, she left the shovel standing against the back of the trailer until she could douse it with Clorox, and went back inside to call Val.

Val picked up on the second ring. "Brody, hi. Something come up?"

"Yeah, listen, I'm sorry I'm late."

"No," Val said quickly. "I'm sure you've got a lot to do. I probably should have waited—"

"No, you shouldn't. I want to see you, but I ran into a problem at home."

"What? What's wrong? Did something happen? Are you hurt?"

"No, no. Nothing like that." She took a breath, the rage still simmering. "I think someone tried to poison Honcho."

"What! Where is she? Does she have any symptoms?"

"No, she's way too smart to eat something she finds. She recognized the steak as something that didn't belong in her territory. She won't eat anything that I don't approve."

"Thank God. Do you have it?"

"Oh yeah. I was wondering—"

"I'll meet you at the clinic, and we'll get some samples sent off for tox."

"I'm sorry about this, Val. I know you need to be at the fair."

"Don't be ridiculous," Val said, her tone stony and cold. "I'll have someone cover for me from the shelter if we're delayed. We need to find out who did this and string them up by their gonads."

"I was thinking of something a little more painful."

Val laughed and gave her the address for the clinic. "I'll see you there. And Brody…be careful, all right?"

"I plan to. I'll be there in twenty minutes."

"I'll be waiting."

Brody disconnected and opened the door. "Come on, Honcho. Let's go see Val."

Honcho bounded down the stairs to the truck, her tail wagging. She was almost as happy as Brody at the idea of seeing Val.

Chapter Twenty-one

Brody jumped into her flight uniform before heading over to Val's clinic so she'd be ready for the fair—maybe she'd get there almost on time—and clipped the short leash to Honcho's recreational collar. That collar signaled she was going out to have fun and wouldn't be working. When Brody passed the turnoff to the river running path, Honcho gave her a wounded look designed to make her feel guilty.

"I know I promised you a run, and you're going to get it, but you'll have to wait until we finish fair duty. Yeah, I said that already too, but we *are* going to see Val."

Twenty-five minutes later, Brody pulled into the parking lot in front of the Saratoga Animal Hospital and Surgery. The single-story brick and stucco building adorned with wide front windows on either side of a columned entryway looked more like a suburban home than a professional building, in keeping with the upscale neighborhood and wealthy clientele. The lot held Range Rover, Mercedes, and Porsche SUVs—all of which spelled money and a little absurdity, although the rigs did look sleek and slick. Brody smiled to herself. Bet Val didn't get chicken poop on her face when seeing clients here.

When she walked around and let Honcho out, Honcho gave a long-suffering sigh but trotted along beside her side with her tail up, nose quivering, taking in the new atmosphere. Every new environment was exciting to her, offering the possibility she'd get a reward if she found something of interest to her handler. Brody hadn't been her handler in the service, but Honcho's training and instincts didn't disappear with retirement, any more than Brody's had. And all good war dogs, whether trained for SAR, explosives, or security, worked for reward. Some purists felt praise was enough of a reward, but Brody'd known IED guys who carried a squeaky toy and dog biscuits in their flak jackets to praise and reward their dogs when they spotted lethal explosives. Honcho was happy with dog biscuits, and even though Honcho wasn't on patrol any longer, Brody rarely went anywhere without one in her pocket. The clinic waiting area was empty except for a woman in a silk shirt, skinny black pants, and heels with a cat in a carrier, and a preppy-looking guy with a French bulldog who barked at Honcho.

The woman looked at Honcho with suspicious eyes and said testily, "I hope you've got a good hold of that dog."

"She's safe and sound, ma'am, guaranteed."

The woman sniffed.

A sixtyish man of average height, with a full head of close-cropped curly dark hair and a noticeably casual wardrobe of faded jeans and a green polo, stood up as Brody approached the sign-in counter. He grinned at Brody and extended a hand. "You must be Brody Clark. I'm Joe Finnici, the other vet here. Val said you'd be coming along. She's in the back getting set up."

"Good to meet you, sir." Brody shook his hand, found his grip warm and firm. Brody felt a little bit like she was meeting Val's family. The tie between her and this man must have been exceptional for her to give up the professional and personal life she'd established and come back here because he needed her.

"That's a beauty of a dog you got there. Ex-military?"

"Yes."

"How's she adjusting to civilian life?"

"She gets a little bored now and then, but overall she's good."

Joe laughed. "I remember the feeling. I was Navy, long time back."

"Sorry to hear that, sir," Brody said with a straight face.

Joe laughed again. "Army, huh?"

Brody nodded. "Flight medic."

"Well, come on back. Let's get this one checked out."

Brody detected a limp as she followed him through a door and down a hall with closed doors on either side and one on the far end. Val came through the far door and stopped when she saw them coming. She'd changed into a maroon-and-white-striped fitted shirt, tapered gray pants, and low-heeled black boots. She also wore a white lab coat with her name embroidered over the left chest pocket. Brody chose to believe Val's electric smile was reserved just for her, especially since she knew hers was so wide she had to have totally abandoned all hopes of being cool.

"Hi," Brody said, and her voice cracked just a little. Oh yeah, completely not cool.

"Hi. You made good time." She knelt down to Honcho's level and studied her intently. "Hi there, Honcho." She held out a hand, still watching the dog. "How's she doing? Any odd behavior? Excessive salivation, increased thirst, confusion, or abnormal gait?"

"No, nothing. Totally normal. I can guarantee she didn't touch that steak." Brody unclipped Honcho's lead. "Okay, girl."

Released, Honcho trotted over to Val and put her muzzle against Val's extended hand. Val smiled and ran a hand down her body. "She certainly looks good."

"She's fine," Brody said.

"You have the steak?"

"Yeah. In the truck. I didn't want to walk around in here with it."

Joe said. "You can use the side door on your left there and bring it in that way."

"Thanks."

"If it's okay with you," Joe said, "I'll take this beauty into the exam room over here and just give her a quick look over. She won't mind that, will she?"

"No. She's used to getting examined. Just tell her what you're doing first."

"Always do," Joe said with total seriousness.

"Honcho, come," Brody said and let the dog into an exam room. "I'll be right back. Stay."

Joe closed the exam room door.

Val said, "I'll be in the lab back here. Do we have to worry about documenting custody? What did the police say?"

"Nothing." At Val's raised brows, Brody hurried on. "It's a steak. Nothing distinguishing about it. Anyone could have purchased it at any of a dozen places around my place. It could have been lying out there for five minutes or five hours. I didn't see anything unusual, so what is there to report?"

Val's gaze narrowed. "Do you think whoever dropped the steak over the fence is the same someone Honcho reacted to in the middle of the night?"

"Possibly. Again—no witnesses, no evidence."

"Yes, well, let's see the steak. Maybe we'll have something to work with after this."

We? Val wasn't the type to sit on the sidelines—she'd already made that clear. But Brody didn't want her anywhere near what was going on—whatever the hell that turned out to be. She supposed it could be someone who objected to her getting special consideration at the trailer park to fence off a run, or someone who didn't like veterans, or dogs, or who knew what motivated people to take violent issue so easily these days. Or it could be someone letting her know the past was not forgotten. Whatever it was, she didn't want Val tangled up in it.

"Right. I'll get it," Brody said abruptly and strode outside.

She retrieved the bag from the floor of the back seat, checked to see nothing had leaked, and brought it back.

Val waited in a good-sized room that ran the width of the building, a row of windows in the far wall looking out on a narrow strip of grass and trees. The main space hosted an impressive array of equipment—an X-ray machine, a portable ultrasound, a centrifuge, and an incubation chamber.

"Right over here." Val led her through an aisle to a long lab bench against the wall where she'd arranged an array of test tubes, culture plates, and specimen containers.

"Nice setup," Brody said.

"We find the more diagnostics we can do here, the better chance that clients will let us perform more extensive workups on the animals that need it. As soon as we utter the words *specialist* or *referral*, the compliance rate falls and we're relegated to treating with half measures."

"Must drive you nuts."

Val shrugged. "It does."

"You have much cause to see poisoning?"

"Unfortunately, yes." Val grimaced. "It's a prevalent problem, especially in some of the rural areas but right here in town too. Rat poison is usually the biggest culprit, but we've seen pesticide poisoning, contaminated feed lots, even natural toxins as by-products from bad mulch or hay."

As she talked, Val pulled on gloves, took the steak out of the bag, and slid it onto a sterile towel on the countertop. She snipped bits of meat away from multiple areas and dropped them into test tubes and containers filled with various colored solutions. She swabbed the surface with a sterile Q-tip, rolled the liquid over the surfaces of several culture plates, and slipped them onto a rack in the incubator.

"Looks like you can check for most everything right here," Brody said.

"We'll see what grows out on the petri dishes, but I expect that to be normal surface bacteria, considering the meat's been sitting outside. The rest we'll send out for chemical analysis. My money is on rat poison. See here?" She pointed to several areas of mottled black and gray discoloration interspersed over the maroon surface of the steak. "That's not decomposition. The steak is still reasonably fresh. That's something smeared over the surface of the meat causing a chemical breakdown. Some kind of poison. That's the easiest thing to get without anyone asking any questions."

"And if it was?"

"Depends on the dosage, how much of it is on there, and how much an animal ingests. But it's difficult to treat. It's often fatal."

"I'm gonna kill somebody," Brody muttered.

"I imagine you want to. I'm feeling a little homicidal myself."

"You'll contact me as soon as you know something?"

"Of course. We should have prelim results within twenty-four hours." Val pulled off her gloves, checked boxes on a lab form, and put the pen down. "I'll call myself to let them know that we need a rush on this."

"Thanks. I don't know how to thank you."

Val leaned against the counter and speared Brody with her gaze. "You could start by telling me what the hell is going on."

Brody slid her hands into the pockets of her navy-blue work pants. She'd pretty well run out of vague answers, and Val was too smart to keep letting her slide. The better part of valor was to shut up and hope.

"And don't," Val said sharply, "tell me that you don't know, because you've got to have a good idea."

Back to the wall, she said out loud what she was hoping not to be true. "I'd say someone's really unhappy that I'm back."

"Who?"

Brody sighed. A direct question and not one she could really avoid answering. "I honestly don't know for sure."

"Oh, screw that," Val snapped. "You have a really good idea, so we'll do this the hard way. You can start by telling me why you haven't called Tom Kincaid."

Brody let out a breath. "And tell him what? That I *think* someone tossed bad meat to my dog, but I don't have any idea who or when or even *if* the damn meat was poisoned?"

"And the person who woke us up?"

"Who I never saw or found any sign of?" Brody ran a hand through her hair. "Believe me, I want to find out who the hell is doing this. They went after my *dog*, for fuck's sake."

"Your dog," Val said quietly, shaking her head. "Of course that would matter more to you than yourself."

"Come on, Val. You know what I mean."

"What are you going to do then, because I know you're going to do something."

She'd been thinking about that since the minute she'd seen the steak lying on the ground. She wasn't a personally violent individual. She'd defend herself if attacked, and she'd kill if confronted with a lethal threat to her fellow troops or friends or family. Honcho was her family. She didn't have a gun, even though she had fantasies of wanting to shoot someone, and even if she did believe in personal firearms, she wouldn't go looking for trouble while carrying one. That wasn't just beyond the law, but downright stupid. But she wasn't afraid of up-close in-your-face confrontation, and someone needed talking to. Besides, anyone who would sneak around slashing tires and poisoning dogs was a coward, and in her experience, cowards usually ran.

Val shook her head. "Your silence tells me you plan on handling this yourself, somehow, and it seems to me that that's a mistake. Whoever is behind this has made some pretty pointed and pretty dangerous threats."

"I know, and believe me, the last thing I want is to put anyone else in danger."

"I'm sorry?" Val's brows drew down. "Are we talking about the same thing here?"

"Look." Brody stepped closer and caught Val's hand. Val didn't pull away, but tension radiated from the stiff muscles in her neck and shoulders. "I don't want you caught up in this thing. I'll understand—in fact, it would probably be a good idea—if I got this sorted out before, you know, anything else."

"Let me get this straight," Val said coolly, withdrawing her hand. "I tell you I'm worried that someone is out to hurt you, and that you might be on the verge of making a really stupid decision to confront them on your own, possibly leading to harm and injury, and your answer is you don't want to see me anymore?"

Brody winced. "I don't think I said that exactly."

"Well, that's what I'm hearing." Val folded her arms over her chest, her expression glacial. "I understand you're the kind of person that runs toward a fight, who runs into danger to save others. I am as impressed as hell by that and respect you tremendously for what you've done on the battlefield and what you do here every day, but this? This is reckless and selfish and more kinds of unacceptable than I can think of."

Brody sucked in a breath. "I—"

"And you know what, Brody," Val said, steamrolling over anything else she might've wanted to say, "I get why Flann is pissed off at you if this is what you did the last time you ran into trouble. Because shutting out the people who care about you is exactly the wrong thing to do."

"I'm sorry you feel that way," Brody said quietly. She turned at the sound of footsteps behind her.

Joe stood in the doorway, Honcho by his side.

Brody cleared her throat. "All good?"

"A-OK. I'd give a lot for a dog like her."

"Yeah," Brody said. "I'm lucky to have her." She glanced back at Val. "Thanks for everything."

Val nodded, her gaze dark and angry. Brody clipped Honcho's leash and took her out to the truck. She couldn't believe she was wrong to want to protect the people she loved. Only why did it always come down to losing them?

Chapter Twenty-two

Val spun back to the lab bench and hid her embarrassment by making a show out of organizing the forms she'd already filled out. Great. Joe must have heard most of that perfectly ineffectual and infuriating exchange. Way to drag her personal business into the middle of the clinic and parade her tenuous control on her temper around too. Why had she let Brody get to her that way? Other women she slept with never had that kind of power. But then, none of them got to her the way Brody had—deep down where she wanted to be touched. Damn her anyhow.

Val shook her head, shook off the remnants of the sinking feeling in her stomach that had followed the closing of the door as Brody'd walked out. "I'll just get these copied for the records and call transport to make a special trip out to pick these specimens up."

Joe cleared his throat. "Ah, sorry if I interrupted something."

"No," Val said quickly, hoping she sounded casual and unconcerned. She was anything but. She was furious and, worst of all, hurt. Hurt that Brody could think so little of herself and of *her* to think trying to confront some lunatic was a good plan. How could Brody not know how terrifying that was for the people who lo…cared about her. And that was, of course, completely ridiculous. Brody had no reason to consider her feelings. Why would she? They were strangers, hadn't they agreed to that?

"Hogwash," she muttered. That had never been true and was even less so now that they'd…done what they'd done.

"Haven't heard that one in a while," Joe said.

She looked over her shoulder. "You're still here."

He slipped his hands into his pockets. "Yeah."

"Why?"

"I don't know, I thought you might want to talk."

"Don't we have a waiting room full of patients?"

"Mary should be here by now. She can keep them company for a few minutes." He shrugged. "Plus, all we've got out there are an emergency flea consult and an overanxious daddy worried that his five-month-old bulldog has only one testicle."

Val rolled her eyes. "God, you'd think it was his own."

"Now, now, you know how sensitive us boys can get about those kind of things."

"Exactly."

"So—you think the poison attempt is for real?"

Val grimaced. "I think so. Probably rat poison. There's no way that's an accident, and there's no way to mistake who was targeted. Brody has a dog run built off the back of her trailer. She's the only one with anything like it in the entire trailer park."

"She's living in a trailer park?"

"Why does that seem so odd? I thought it was odd too, but why should it be? It's perfectly legitimate. And her place is nice inside—like an efficiency apartment."

Joe could draw whatever conclusions he wanted from her knowing what Brody's living arrangements were like. Since he wasn't blind and deaf, considering the conversation he'd walked in on, most likely the obvious one. Not that she minded the sexuality part—that wasn't a secret between them—but the sex part she'd prefer remained private.

"You know what it is," Joe said musingly. "It's a CHU."

"I'm sorry?"

"A CHU—containerized housing unit. Have you ever seen pictures of a forward operating base over there? It's a series of containers, just like a trailer only without wheels, and not as many rooms inside. So it's familiar, I should think."

"Oh," Val said softly. So many little things she didn't know about her. So much she wanted to know. "You think?"

"Maybe. But why not? Economical too, and mobile. Easy in, easy out."

"Yes," Val said. "Easy out."

Joe tilted his head. "So is that what has you all fired up? She's a runner?"

"Ah…"

"It's not just about the dog, is it? I kind of got the impression there was…more…going on."

"This is weird, you know that, right? Talking about this kind of thing."

He smiled. "Is it? I've known you since you were seventeen years old. You've been gone for quite a while, but there were the occasional phone calls, especially when you were dealing with a tricky diagnosis or just when you were bored and missed real veterinary medicine."

Val rolled her eyes. "More than occasional, and not just when I'd had enough of the fast lane. I missed you too."

She was stalling. Joe knew her as well as anyone in the world, certainly better than her mother and most of the friends she'd left behind. She had a social circle, people she liked, whose company she enjoyed, but she'd never really had confidants. She'd never actually had a best friend other than Joe. Maybe because she was always competing with the other girls when younger, and too busy when she got older. But Joe, he was constant. Why hadn't she come back sooner—everything that mattered to her had been here. Now, even more.

She took a breath. "I'm upset because I care about her, and I'm worried about her, and she's stubborn and hardheaded and has a hero complex."

Joe nodded. "Yup, I could see that."

"Which part?" Val said grumpily. She was used to being the one in charge in a relationship, and she did not enjoy wondering if she'd seen the last of Brody. Even if she had rather pushed her out the door.

"All of it. Looked like there was a connection there, in both directions."

"Yes, well, it's hard to be connected when one of you insists on playing Lone Ranger."

He smiled, rocking back and forth on his heels, his expression thoughtful. "She's been gone awhile too, right? After her mother died?"

"What?" Val frowned. "I don't think so. She joined the Army out of high school. We were in the same class."

"Oh, that's right. She lived with the Riverses for a while there. It was easier to do that sort of thing back then. A girl with no close relatives, a family willing to take her in and provide a home before she could get swept up and lost in the system. Probably couldn't do that today."

"I never really knew the family circumstances—we weren't… close, back then. I haven't asked about it now—it seems like a painful topic."

"It's hard for anyone to lose a parent, I don't need to tell you that," Joe said, "but maybe especially hard when someone's young, and when it's a violent or tragic death."

"How so?" Val asked quietly. She didn't really feel like she was prying, not when apparently the details were public knowledge. And if she could just find a few pieces of the puzzle that was Brody, maybe she'd understand. Maybe she wouldn't want to shake her until her gorgeous head rattled off her equally gorgeous shoulders.

"As I recall, it was a teen mother kind of situation, so Brody's mother wouldn't have been much out of her twenties, if that. Drugs, I think. Yes, an overdose. And there'd been talk—" He shrugged. "Well. There's always talk. Let's just say it was a hard situation for everyone."

Val sighed, sick to her stomach. She hated to think of Brody, or anyone really, suffering through that at any age, but as a teenager—no wonder she didn't want to talk about it.

"I can't imagine how any of that is related to this," Val said, "but something happened sometime and it's not finished, I know it."

"She'll come around. She'll talk to you," Joe said. "Just be patient."

Val snorted. "I wish I was as sure of that as you are."

"The dog trusts you. And you know why? Because she can tell that Brody does too."

"I hope so," Val whispered, and then, too quietly for Joe to hear, "because it's already too late for me." Too late to turn back.

❖

Brody pulled into the exhibitors' parking area half an hour before the official opening of the fair, and a line of cars with eager fairgoers already waited at the entrance for admission. She'd stopped on the way to give Honcho her much promised and much delayed run and herself a chance to walk off some of the confusion and bleak emptiness that lingered after her conversation with Val. Somehow she'd managed to screw things up with Val and she couldn't even pretend she didn't know why. Secrets had almost destroyed her life once, and she'd managed to build something despite having left everything that mattered to her behind. She'd probably been crazy to think she could just start over again, again, and with the woman of her dreams at that. What Val wanted wasn't unreasonable. Brody just had no idea how to give it to her.

As she wended her way between trucks, vans, and trailers toward the hospital tent, standing out from the other exhibitor tents like a beacon with its high peaked white roof and big red cross, she could almost imagine she was back at the FOB. Adrenaline coursed through her and she automatically reached to tighten the camo vest she wasn't wearing. Honcho felt it too, radiating alert awareness as she usually did when she investigated a new area for possible threats.

"You shouldn't have much work to do here today," Brody murmured, "but you're going to be getting a lot of attention. Better you than me."

Across the lane from the medical tent, Blake, Margie, and a bunch of other kids hustled around at the vet tent, as Brody thought of it. Barking dogs and perturbed felines occupied three long rows of stacked crates. The kids moved down the rows, filling water dishes and food bowls and attaching them to the crates. Two harried-looking adults walked around with clipboards, directing the action.

A thirtyish Latinx with a shaved head and a bulky build that stretched the fabric of his black security uniform sat in a canvas folding chair inside the hospital tent, reading a paperback book. His wide black utility belt held the array of equipment she'd expect—Maglite, radio, short flexible baton, pepper spray. No firearm. He looked up as Brody walked in. "Morning."

"Hey," Brody said. "Sorry, did we have a meeting scheduled?"

"Nope, but I thought I'd catch you before things got crazy. I wanted to go over the LZ out back." He rose, shoved the book, which from what she could see of the man and woman in a clinch on the cover, was a romance novel, into his back pocket. He held out his hand. "Paul Sanchez."

"Brody Clark. The pilot's not here yet, but I can go over things with you."

"That works."

"Just give me a second to get these brochures and whatnot set up in case someone comes by while we're out."

"No problem. Shouldn't take more than a minute or so." He looked down at Honcho, who sat by Brody's side. "Great looking dog. ED?"

"SAR," Brody replied.

"Army?" he said.

"Yes," Brody said, figuring she'd be having this conversation about a thousand times before the week was out. "Both of us. Flight medic."

"Supply," he said.

With that, they'd established more of what they had in common than an hour's worth of casual conversation could have accomplished, and he waited silently while she set out the promo materials she fervently hoped she would not have to discuss. She weighted them down with coffee cups embossed with the hospital logo. "Let's do it."

She followed Paul around behind the tent and surveyed an area about twice the size of the rooftop of the hospital. Orange cones, moveable waist-high aluminum barricades, and yellow tape marked *Do Not Cross* designated the landing zone directly behind the tent.

"Plenty of space," Brody said, scanning overhead. "No power lines or visual obstructions. What kind of staff will you have to keep people away from the bird when it's on the ground?"

"We can put someone on the gate around the clock."

"We'll be on active call part of the time, which means we'll be in and out."

"Not a problem. You let me know when you're inbound or ready to dust off, and we'll clear the area."

"Good enough." She'd fill Jane in when she arrived.

"I'll drop off a radio for you this afternoon."

"Thanks."

"That covers it for now," Paul said.

Brody and Honcho headed back to their station as Paul went the other way. Brody expected Val to show up soon. She wanted to see her, even though she knew it was going to hurt. This time, she didn't mistake the blonde sorting through the material at the table for Val. How she ever had, she didn't know. "Hi, Courtney. Are you visiting, or…?"

Courtney blushed. "I, uh, volunteered to help out."

"Okay, great." Brody put Honcho on a down stay. Courtney was probably hoping to get a leg up on her colleagues for a spot on the flight roster. Couldn't fault her for ambition, that was for sure. "I'll be right back."

"Sure," Courtney said.

Brody ambled over to the vet tent and waved to Blake. "How's it going?"

"Great. We've got a lot of really cute animals looking for a home. Want another one?"

She laughed. "Forget it."

Margie joined them. "Hi, Brody. Flann said you'd be coming to dinner soon."

"Uh, yeah," Brody said. That was the last thing she wanted to think about right now.

"Cool," Margie said. "Hey, have you seen Val?"

Brody stiffened. "No, why?"

"Oh, no reason, I just thought—" Her smile widened. "Never mind. Here she comes."

Brody steeled herself and turned. Val hurried toward them, a leather bag slung over her shoulder. The wind caught her hair and Brody recalled running her fingers through those strands as Val leaned down over her. Her stomach tightened. Yep, it was awesome to see her, and yeah, it hurt. "Well, I'm going to let you all get to work."

"See you later," Blake called.

"Bye," Margie echoed.

Brody cut a diagonal across the lane toward her tent, where several people already perused the brochures and chatted with Courtney. When she reached the tent and turned around, Val was looking her way. She nodded, and for an instant, she thought Val was going to come over and talk to her. Her heart leapt, but then Val gave her a brief wave and turned away. Hope, she discovered, was a hard thing to kill.

Chapter Twenty-three

Just before noon, Jane called.

"You back online?" Brody asked.

"Yup, just checking out the bird. I'll be setting down over there, ETA fifteen minutes."

"Good enough, I'll alert security to clear the LZ."

"What's it look like?"

"Early morning, first day kind of crowd. Mostly seniors, not too many kids yet." Brody'd been talking up the new air mobile unit, explaining what they did and how that benefited patients and the medical center. A few yet-to-be-convinced individuals grilled her on how much all of this fancy stuff was going to cost them in taxes. Since she figured she wasn't getting paid enough to take that on, she suggested they talk to the town board or the mayor's office. Mostly, though, everyone who stopped by was happy about all the new activity in town.

"Working hard?" Jane asked.

"It's been steady. I imagine we'll pick up once you get here. Nothing like a pilot to get people excited."

"That's what I hear." Jane sounded pleased with herself.

Brody mentally rolled her eyes. "Uh-huh. That's what I hear too, at least from you."

Jane laughed. "I'll radio when we dust off."

"Roger that."

Brody radioed Sanchez on the frequency he'd given her and advised him of Jane's ETA. While she waited for his people to arrive, she glanced across to the vet tent, which had drawn a big crowd of spectators. The kids, half a dozen of them, moved between the cages, taking out animals for visitors to see. In the midst of it all, Val. Talking to first one potential adopter, then another, bending down to pet some of the animals, handing out brochures. Not looking in Brody's direction. Could be she was just busy—or could be she really wasn't thinking about Brody at all. Or wanted to forget her.

Seeing her so close and being excluded from her universe was a million times tougher than it had been back when Val was more a dream than a reality. She'd touched her now, held her, been touched by her. This was a pain that threatened to hollow her out until she cracked. Brody forced herself to look away, and when she did, the world grayed a little.

The sound of the approaching bird jolted her back on course, and leaving Courtney to entertain the few people who weren't headed toward the sound of the approaching helicopter, she hurried around to the LZ. A crowd lined the barricades, and a security guard stood in front of the closed gate. The bird descended, and Jane set her down in the center of the LZ amidst a small cloud of dust. The engine quieted, the rotors slowed, and Jane jogged across to the gate. The instant she was through, people surrounded her, most of them wanting to know if they could look at the bird.

"We'll post a schedule of times when you can tour her," Jane told those questioners. "I'll give you a little walk around and you can see what she looks like inside. In the meantime, we've got some brochures at the tent on the specs of the bird as well as what we do."

And just like that, the crowd flowed away, following after Jane like the Pied Piper. Brody joined the parade, shaking her head. Jane was like that. She'd never met anyone she didn't want to talk to and could charm the pants off...well, just about anyone. Giving Jane a shot at entertaining for a while, Brody hung back at the far edge of the gathering. Across the way, Blake came out of the vet tent carrying a crate under one arm with a bird inside. As she made her way over to take a look at his rooster, two teenage guys in camo caps and shirts, jeans, and army boots stepped into Blake's path. One was taller than Brody and husky, the other string-bean thin and a head shorter than either of them.

Brody was close enough to hear the bigger one growl, "Will you look at this. Two freaks at once. Where you going with that freak bird, boy? Or maybe I should say girl?"

Blake shifted the crate under his arm, moving the caged rooster farther away. His head came up and he met the gaze of the taller, bigger teen.

"Hi, Yancy. Kevin, isn't it?" He looked from one to the other. "Having only one leg doesn't slow him down at all. His name is Roo, by the way."

They both looked surprised. The big one, Yancy, took a step closer. "How about you? You're missing more than a leg, aren't you?"

Brody was just behind the pair when Margie, along with a muscular dark-haired guy in a high school football jersey and another girl, appeared behind Blake. The girl, a small redhead in a tank top and jeans shorts, gold bracelets jangling and her bright red nail polish glittering, planted her hands on her hips. "You two need to disappear. Like, yesterday."

Yancy snorted. "Yeah? And who's gonna make me, you?"

She smirked. "I didn't have that much trouble getting rid of you when you tried jumping me on our first and"—she tossed her head, long hair swirling around her face—"only date, did I?"

Yancy flushed and his hands fisted. The boy with him, Kevin apparently, laughed.

The good-looking boy in the football jersey set his hand on Blake's shoulder. "You guys need to take off. We're busy here."

Yancy tried to stare him down and finally averted his gaze, muttering, "Never figured you for a queer lover, Kincaid."

"You know what," Blake said, his expression still friendly, "we have a lot of cleanup to do in between showing the animals. You guys can stay and help if you want to."

For a second, Brody thought the two boys might actually take him up on it. Then Yancy snorted.

"Yeah, right. You're all just a bunch of mutts."

He spun on his heel and marched away, his sidekick scurrying in his tracks.

Margie said, "Come on, Blake, let's take Roo down to the chicken barn so we can get him registered."

Kincaid said, "You want the rest of us to go with?"

Margie shook her head. "No, we got this."

Blake smiled at him. "Thanks though, appreciate it."

"Forget about those jerks. See you when you get back." Kincaid and the redhead rejoined the crowd milling around the crates.

Brody watched Blake and Margie disappear in the opposite direction with the rooster in the crate and tracked them out of sight. The two asshats did not reappear. When she glanced back at the vet tent, Val was watching her. When Val didn't immediately look away, she strode over to her.

"I thought for a minute there we were headed for trouble," Brody said.

Val grimaced. "Sometimes I know exactly why I prefer animals to people."

"Yeah. That took about everything I had not to get in the middle of that," Brody said.

"I know, it's really hard to let them handle things themselves, but they do and it makes them all stronger for it." Val hesitated. "Well, I better get back."

Brody sucked in a breath. "I guess I should give Jane and Courtney a hand."

Val glanced over at the tent and smiled. "I don't know, Jane looks like she can handle almost anything, and then some."

"Well, it takes a certain something to fly those birds into combat, and whatever it is, she's got it all."

"Mm, I imagine that's true." She smiled at Brody, a nice, just-friends smile. "Oh, I've got the vest for Honcho. There's nothing to do except put it on her. Should I get it?"

"Sure."

Val hurried into the tent, rummaged in the bag she'd been carrying earlier, and returned with an army green vest with Velcro straps and a small battery pack on the side. She held it up. "I thought this color might look familiar to her."

"It does to me," Brody said.

"Just put it on, snug but with a little room for her to move naturally, and turn on the battery pack here." Val pointed to a small switch. "The sensors are on either side of her spine. She won't feel them."

"How will you get the trace?" Brody asked.

"Telemetry download."

"Fancy."

"That's us." Val laughed. "Leave it on overnight. I'll let you know what we see."

"Okay. Thanks." Brody couldn't come up with anything to keep Val there, even though Val seemed to be waiting for something. "I'll, uh, check with you on it later, then."

"Great." Val watched her go, biting back the invitation to have lunch with her later, or dinner, or just about anything. She'd told herself all day she wouldn't do that. She'd pretty much made herself clear as to where she stood on her and Brody, or at least she hoped she had. She wasn't getting involved with Brody if Brody's approach to everything in life was to go it alone. She'd just recently realized she'd already been alone most of her life. She'd been alone in high school despite being surrounded by people who acted like they were her friends, but who really just wanted to be seen as part of the in-crowd. Whatever that might really be. Then she'd been too busy gathering the courage to let her family know she wasn't going to follow the path they wanted, and when she'd finally taken a stand, their disapproval and disappointment had left her alone again. She was done being alone, especially with those she cared about. And she already cared way too much for Brody Clark.

She kept reminding herself not to look Brody's way while she tried to find suitable homes for the animals who'd been abandoned or abused or were simply unwanted. Fortunately, plenty of people were interested, and while she showed animals and interviewed potential new owners, she hoped all that activity would make it easier not to think about Brody Clark, for a minute anyway.

❖

The rest of Brody's afternoon passed in a flurry of questions about flight medics, helicopter demos, and show-and-tell with Honcho. Without a doubt, the helicopter and the dog were the big attractions. People weren't nearly as interested in the new air mobile unit as what kinds of things Honcho was used for. Honcho was on her best behavior and didn't seem to take any notice of the vest. Maybe she felt more at home in it—like she was working again. Brody appreciated the feeling.

At five the night shift arrived—a couple of members of the

regional air mobile unit and an intern from the hospital who looked none too happy to have been volunteered. Brody took Honcho home, checked that all was secure around the place, showered and changed, and headed to the hospital for her shift. Jane found her in the break room nursing a cup of coffee.

Jane dropped into a chair next to her with a can of Coke in her hand. "Well, that was fun, huh?"

Brody snorted. "I've had worse details."

Jane eased back and stretched her legs out, crossing her booted feet at the ankles. "Yeah, me too. Can't wait till tomorrow, and we can do it again."

"At least we pulled the night shift tomorrow." Brody grimaced. "We'll be switching out the seniors for the teenagers."

"I noticed that little dustup over at the vet tent this morning. I thought for a second you were going to get in the middle of things."

Brody sipped her coffee, which had somehow gotten cold when her mind was wandering. She couldn't help thinking back to her early morning conversation with Val, and the cold distance between them all day. They'd both been really busy, but she hadn't imagined it—Val was avoiding her. That bothered her just as much as Val pretty much telling her to shape up or march. Val had a way of looking into her eyes, when they talked, when they were anywhere near each other, and every time she did, Brody felt seen in a way she'd forgotten she needed. Val reminded her what it was like to be connected to anyone, only with Val, the connection ran so much deeper.

"Earth to Brody?" Jane said softly.

Brody jumped. "Oh. Those guys. Just a couple of jerks, hassling Blake."

"It looks like Blake and the other kids handled it okay."

"Yeah, he's got some good friends and—" Brody shook her head. "I don't know, things seem a little different than I remember, but maybe it was me and not everybody else."

"What do you mean?"

"Those kids, they're not afraid to speak up for themselves, and each other."

"I wouldn't imagine much scared the Rivers kids, and you lived with them, didn't you?"

"Yeah, for a while."

"Can't imagine them not sticking up for you, or you them."

Brody stared, not seeing the brightly lit break room, but a dim, predawn road in a misty valley. "Yeah. I guess you're right. Maybe it was me after all."

Jane punched her lightly in the forearm. "You're awfully morose tonight. I wasn't being critical. All of us would request do-overs of some time in our lives if we could. So what's really bugging you?"

"Did you ever have the feeling you were screwing things up, and you weren't quite sure how to fix it?"

Jane laughed. "All the time. What is it you're screwing up? I know it's not work, since I've never known you not to be on top of everything in that regard. So that leaves us with…" She paused and raised her brows. "Women. Or should I say, a particular woman?"

Brody shot her a look. "That's part of it." She blew out a breath. "Okay, maybe a big part of it."

"The lovely Dr. Valentine?"

Brody sighed. "Yeah."

Jane studied her through narrowed eyes. "Just how deep does this go already?"

"I think as deep as it gets."

Jane took a slow breath. "Well, okay then. What exactly have you done?"

Brody stared at her coffee. "That's the problem, nothing."

"Must be something." Jane tapped her Coke can. "Let me guess. She wants serious and you don't."

"Good guess, but…no. Not exactly."

"She wants sex and you don't."

Brody laughed. "Come on, Jane."

"You do, and she doesn't?"

"Jane."

"Oho. It's not sex. This sounds serious—"

Matt's voice came over their radios. "We got a call for urgent transport from Tupper Lake Community Hospital."

Jane pointed a finger at Brody. "Later on this."

"Where is Tupper Lake?" Brody radioed as she dumped her coffee cup in the wastebasket.

"A hundred and fourteen miles up north. Programming the flight route now."

Brody glanced at Jane and replied, "Isn't that out of our—"

"We're the closest available bird," Matt said, "and they've got a pregnant female MVA victim in labor. Let's roll."

"Right." Relieved to leave her quandary behind, Brody jogged into the ER and called out, "Mari, you're up on rotation for air mobile. Want to ride?"

The PA's face lit up. "Absolutely." She turned to one of the other PAs. "Charlie, can you take the patient in five, waiting on X-rays, probable humerus fracture?"

Charlie waved. "Got it, go."

"I owe you one," Mari called as she raced after Brody.

The flight to Tupper Lake took fifty minutes. From the air the hospital looked like a mini-mart—it was that small. They landed in the parking lot outside the emergency room. A blonde in pale blue scrubs and a young-looking guy in a rumpled white lab coat hurried out to meet them.

"Air mobile from the Rivers," Brody said as she and Mari hoisted their stretcher down from the bird. "What have we got?"

The blonde whose name tag identified her as an ER nurse spoke up. "We've got a thirty-seven-year-old gravida one female, thirty-one weeks, front seat passenger in an MVA. Restrained. Premature labor started at the scene. Fire rescue brought her here, but we don't have a neonatal unit, and with her high risk, we need to transfer."

"Vital signs?" Mari asked as they pushed the stretcher down the hall after the ER staff.

"Pressure's borderline low," the male resident said, "pulse 118, contractions every nine minutes."

"Have you gotten a transvaginal ultrasound to check the cervix?"

"Uh." The resident looked at the nurse. "I wasn't comfortable doing that with no OB in house."

"Right," Brody said, shooting Mari a glance. They needed to get this woman to a tertiary care center right now. "So let's get her loaded up. Is there another parent or family member here?"

"The father's in the waiting area." The resident sounded anxious. They obviously didn't get too many acute traumas here. "He wasn't in the car with her. What should he do?"

"Talk to him, tell them where we're taking her, and make sure we have contact info in the paperwork."

"We do," the nurse said. "I filled it out myself."

"Great," Brody said, glad that someone with experience was around. "I'll call him as soon as we get her to the Rivers. Tell him to wait until we contact him. Also, make sure he has some support, if possible, so he's not driving down alone."

"Right," the nurse said. "We'll take care of it. Thanks for coming."

Brody said, "Anytime."

Brody introduced herself and Mari to the anxious mother, explained what they were going to do, and had her transferred to a gurney and on the way back to the Rivers in two minutes. As senior flight medic, Brody liaised with the hospital by radio and managed the in-flight care while Mari took vital signs and charted. The patient remained alert and stable, and Jane piloted them back smoothly and quickly. The bird set down on the rooftop two and a half hours after takeoff.

"I've got to refuel," Jane radioed as Brody and Mari handed the stretcher out to the ER team. An OB resident and several of the ER staff whisked her away. "I'll restock her for you."

"Thanks." Brody and Mari took the next elevator down.

"What do you think?" Brody said.

Mari's eyes glittered. "That was totally awesome. Who do I have to bribe to do that again?"

Brody laughed. "I'm not immune to pastries from the Breadbasket, but even without them, you'll be in rotation again."

"And what if I want to do that full-time?"

"There's a flight medic certification program for PAs. Give it some thought and let me know. I can go over it with you."

"Thanks."

Once Brody was sure the mother was stabilized and they'd moved her up to maternity, she called the father and filled him in on the details. "There's a chance OB will be able to prevent early delivery, but even if she does go tonight, it's going to be at least three to four hours. You've got plenty of time to get down here. The most important thing you can do for her is to get here safely. You have someone who can ride down with you?"

"My mother's coming," he said.

"All right then. Are you good to drive?"

"Yeah," he said, sounding a little less panicked. "Yeah, I'm good. And hey, man, thanks."

"Don't mention it."

Brody waited until Jane returned, checked the bird, and headed to the on-call room. When she stretched out in the dark on the bottom bunk, she thought about Val. That was definitely going to keep her up. She rolled over and punched her pillow. When she closed her eyes, she pictured the guys bullying Blake and the way his friends gathered around him in support. She flipped over on her back. Damn it. Why did she ask herself *now* what might've happened if she'd trusted the people she'd cared about as much as Blake did? She knew why. Val had accused her of being a Lone Ranger. Maybe Val was right, but all she felt right now was lonely.

❖

Just after four a.m. Brody's radio sounded, and she shot up on the bunk. Jane groaned as her legs appeared over the side of the top bunk. Jane jumped down as Brody rolled out and into her boots.

"MVA," Matt reported. "Twenty miles out, two dead at the scene, two to transport."

Brody thumbed her radio. "On our way."

Courtney was in the ER and Brody tagged her on the way through.

They were up and airborne in under five, and at the scene nine minutes later. The clear black sky, punctuated with pinpoints of starlight, gave way to a false dawn as they drew closer. Jane set them down just outside the ring of first response vehicles, and a uniformed sheriff cleared the way for them. Two white-shrouded forms lay on the blacktop road amidst shattered headlight glass and fragments of vehicles. A small compact car so crumpled Brody couldn't make out the model angled into a ditch on one side of the road, and an SUV, its front crushed and driver's side door crumpled, faced the wrong way in the middle of a country road. A woman in fire rescue turnout gear trotted to meet them.

"We've got them ready to go," she said. "Eighteen-year-old male driver, crush injury to the chest, unstable BP, probable facial fractures. Female passenger, sixteen, maybe. We haven't found her ID yet. Closed head injury, loss of consciousness, questionable neck injury. IVs running on both, collars in place. Both unrestrained, open alcohol containers in the vehicle."

"Courtney," Brody said, pointing toward the female patient, "you take her. I've got the guy."

With the help of the ground paramedics, they got the two patients loaded in and secured, and Jane took off when they were stable. Two minutes into the flight, the male's pressure bottomed out.

"Get me a line to the ER," Brody said to Jane as she began CPR. "Courtney, you handle the meds and keep a watch on the other patient."

"Right," Courtney said breathlessly, opening the crash cart box.

"This is Remy, go ahead," Abby Remy radioed back.

"I've got an eighteen-year-old male with a crushing chest injury in cardiac arrest," Brody said. She kept Abby updated on the vitals as they continued resuscitation. Jane had them down in eight minutes, and Brody still didn't have a rhythm or a pulse. When she pushed open the doors, the ER team surged forward.

"He's been down for nine minutes," she said to Glenn as she shifted the stretcher out. "I've got nothing. Second patient unconscious but stable."

"You two take the second one," Glenn said. "I'll take over the compressions. Let's go, people."

Brody and Courtney transported the female patient down as the ER team preceded them.

Brody handed her off to Mari and Abby and hurried over to the team working on the boy. Five minutes later, Glenn called time of death. Brody stood at the foot of the stretcher, looking at the boy's pale, smooth face. She'd seen many deaths before, and every one made her feel like a failure. She let out a long breath. "Damn it."

Glenn gripped her shoulder. "We got a chest tube into him. Massive blood loss. Probably transected aorta. Nothing would've made any difference."

Brody knew it was true, but it didn't change the heavy feeling in her chest.

"How's the other one?" Glenn asked.

"She's stable and headed down for a head CT," Brody said.

"So that's a save."

"Yeah," Brody said quietly.

She didn't finish all the paperwork until after eight and the sun was high. She needed a cup of coffee but she just didn't have the energy to go get one. Instead, she showered, pulled on clean scrubs, and headed home, weary in body and soul.

Her fatigue dropped away as she pulled up to her trailer and parked beside Val's SUV.

Chapter Twenty-four

Val almost changed her mind and drove away half a dozen times in the half hour she'd been sitting there. When Brody hadn't shown up by seven thirty, she wondered if Brody wasn't coming home at all. The hospital was only a ten-minute drive away. Immediately she started conjuring up all the reasons Brody wasn't coming, and why she was out of her mind to be sitting there. Maybe Brody was having breakfast in town with someone. Jane? Oh God, not Courtney. No, better idea. Maybe she was sleeping at the hospital after a long night. Alone, right? Yes, right. Better picture. Maybe Brody was anywhere of half a dozen places with almost anyone doing whatever she damned well pleased, and if she sat there very much longer wondering about it, she'd likely make herself crazy.

She needed a…deadline. That was it. She'd give herself until eight o'clock. If Brody wasn't there by then, she wasn't coming home. At eight, she extended it by five minutes, and again every five minutes after that. She wasn't even sure she could say why. But if she drove away, she'd spend the day feeling unfinished. As if some vital piece of the puzzle that was her life had been dropped, kicked aside, and needed to be rediscovered before it vanished completely, leaving her with a hole in the center of her existence where no other piece would fit so precisely.

When Brody pulled in next to her, rolled down the window on the passenger side, and stared across the front seat at her as if she were a wondrous apparition, she knew why she'd waited. She'd waited to see the look in Brody's eyes, the one she'd begun to count on, the one that said she was something special. She probably wouldn't admit it to anyone, it was hard enough to admit it to herself, just how much that mattered. To know that to this one woman and none other, she was special. Worth waiting for. Worth fighting for.

She hoped.

She was glad too that she'd waited, because Brody was special to her, and she needed her to know it. Brody looked worn out, and more tired than she'd ever seen her. The neat black row of sutures on her forehead stood out in stark contrast to her pale skin. She'd seen her without sleep, she'd seen her angry, and she'd seen her worried, but she'd never seen her look the slightest bit defeated, and that was the only word she could put to it right now. That look scared her.

"I got you coffee," Val said, "but I think it's cold by now."

Brody cleared her throat and seemed to make an effort to speak. "You could give me iced coffee right now, and I'd be happy."

Her voice was gravelly and rough, matching the hollow, drawn look on her face.

Val picked up the cardboard carry container with the two cups of coffee, hers half finished and the one she'd gotten for Brody on the chance she might want one. The excuse, really—one of several she'd convinced herself were plausible reasons for her to be there. She climbed out of the SUV and waited while Brody got out of her truck and came around the front of the cab to meet her. Val held out the coffee.

"Here you go. Oh, yours is the one on the right."

Brody took the coffee and a long sip. She half closed her eyes and let out a long sigh. "I can't tell you how much I needed that."

Val took a step back and leaned against the side of her SUV, freeing her own cup and setting the cardboard carry tray on the hood. "Rough night?"

"Some good, some bad," Brody said.

Val knew what that translated into. Brody'd lost someone. "I'm sorry for the bad."

"Thanks." Brody took a long swallow of coffee. "What's going on?"

"Oh," Val said. Right, of course. After everything she'd said the day before, Brody must find this strange, her being there, unexpected, and certainly uninvited. "Ah, I have the readings from Honch's vest and…" She checked her watch. "I should be able to get the chemistries this morning, right about now, from the lab."

Val hoped Brody wouldn't ask her why she hadn't just called, since the only answer she had was that she wanted to see her. Needed to see her. Had spent a restless night, waking every few hours, thinking of her, and telling herself not to. That hadn't done any good at all. She missed her. And she wanted her. That was new and, despite everything, delicious.

She loved the feel of Brody's naked body against hers. Her skin was sleek, hot, tantalizing. And her hands, God. When Brody touched her—why hadn't she known how amazing it could be, why hadn't she noticed what she'd been missing? Brody caressed her with sure, possessive strokes, alternately gentle and devouring. And when she took Brody in return? Commanding all that power and beauty and unvarnished need? When she made her come? Val's heart fluttered, and she reminded herself those thoughts were likely to leave her frustrated if not foolish.

Fortunately, Brody didn't question her, not when Honcho was the subject. "Is she okay?"

Val laughed, reining in her runaway sex thoughts. A mighty feat when she was this close to Brody. "She's about as good as she could be. She's not anxious—she's focused. I noted down a few times yesterday when she was particularly alert to the crowd and correlated it to her stats. No signs of stress. She's just doing what she was trained to do."

"I could tell she liked to work, but I wasn't sure what to make of her restlessness. Dogs can get PTSD too."

"I'm not seeing that, in her behavior or her tests. My guess is she'd be happier if she had more to do."

"Maybe I'll see about the two of us doing some volunteering with local law," Brody mused.

Val's heart leapt again. Did that mean she was staying? "I'll call the lab and see what they've found from the steak, let you know."

Brody said quickly, "Would you like to come in? You can call from here. I don't have anything to eat, but—wait, English muffins. I have English muffins."

Val laughed. "Do they have raisins in them?"

For just a second, the clouds lifted from Brody's face. "Of course. Are there any other kind?"

"Sold." Val pushed away from the SUV.

Brody held out her hand, seemed to think better of it, and ran it through her hair. "Right, then."

Brody led the way, unlocked the screen door, and held it open for Val. The early morning sun angled in through the windows at either end and above the sofa. The effect was hazy, nearly dreamlike. Brody turned almost in slow motion and put her coffee cup down. "Val."

Her voice was hoarse, needy.

"Brody."

Moving fast, Brody took Val's coffee cup, put it somewhere, and backed Val up against the door. Her hands skimmed Val's sides, teased over her breasts. Val gasped.

"I want to kiss you," Brody muttered.

"Then you'd better," Val said, her desperation so raw even she could hear it.

She might've said something else, might've even moaned, but Brody's mouth was covering hers, hard and hurried and hungry, and she lost track of everything except desire. Val closed her eyes, gripped Brody's shoulders, and dug into the hard muscles that cascaded down her back. This, *this* was exactly why she'd come. To imagine anything else would've been self-deluding, and she was done lying to herself. She was done settling.

She yanked Brody's scrub shirt out of her pants and dragged her nails up Brody's back. Brody hissed and buried her face in Val's neck, her teeth a light torment against her skin. Val dropped her head against the wall, bared her throat, submitting with all the power she possessed. Brody pressed closer, all hard angles and hot, gorgeous flesh.

"I can't—" Brody gasped. "I want you so much. Can't. Stop."

"Then don't," Val said. "Just take me to bed."

Brody tugged her down the short narrow hall into the bedroom at the back, shedding shoes and shirt along the way. When they reached the bed, they were half naked, Brody in just her scrub pants, Val with her shirt open, her pants unzipped and one kick away from being off.

"Take off the rest," Val ordered, managing not to trip as she stripped and dropped onto the bed. A second later Brody followed her down, and they were gloriously naked with Brody's thigh between her legs. The sudden pressure against her way-too-ready clit made her cry out.

Val arched, opened, welcomed the slick glide of Brody's flesh over hers.

"I am going to make you come so hard," Brody gasped.

"Then now would be the time for you to fuck me," Val said and, somewhere through the distant haze of need, heard Brody laugh.

Sight, sound, awareness dimmed. She was achingly full, electrifyingly taut, strung to the breaking point. With the first stroke, she grabbed Brody's arm, felt the steel muscles ripple.

"More," she said, needing to break, to overflow, and wanting so badly to hold on.

Brody knelt between her thighs, deep inside her, steady and strong and deeper with each stroke, sensing her, guiding her, following her every tremor with a teasing whisper of her fingertips. Just there. Just so incredibly beautiful.

Brody caught her breath, needing nothing more than Val. Not air, not even a heartbeat, but only to be poised on the edge of Val's pleasure. She could live there, die there, and nothing else would matter.

Val tightened around her, her legs straining, her belly clenched, her back bowed. And then a single cry, piercing in its sweetness, and Val came around her in pulsing torrents. Brody groaned and lowered her head until her forehead rested between Val's breasts.

"I love you," she whispered.

She didn't move, couldn't make her muscles work, and a long time later, Val stroked her hair.

"I can't seem to get enough of you," Val whispered.

Brody rolled onto her side, guided Val's head against her shoulder, and kissed her. "I'll never stop."

Val smiled wistfully. "You have no idea how much I want to believe that."

"I can tell you and tell you, but if you let me, I'll prove it, every day."

"I think that's how it's supposed to work."

"I don't know about other people, but I know that's the way it will work for me." Brody hesitated. "If that's what you want."

"Are you sure you're not just in love with the girl you remember?"

Brody smiled. "I was never in love with her. Obsessed, yes."

"Mm, not such a terrible idea."

Brody laughed.

Val slid her leg over Brody's and caressed the faint dip in the center of her abdomen, down her middle, and between her thighs. Brody hissed and her legs tensed. Val smiled. Oh, how she loved having that beautiful body to tease and taunt and satisfy. Featherlight, she circled and stroked.

"You have amazing control," Val murmured, pressing a sensitive spot with a fingertip. Brody jerked and Val clenched inside. "I would have come twice by now."

"I don't want it to end."

Laughing, Val picked up the pace. She wanted to make her explode. She needed to take her, needed to know she could break that glorious control. Brody sucked in a breath, her hips lifting to meet Val's hand. Val kissed her, bit down on her lower lip.

Brody stopped breathing for a long quivering moment and collapsed with an anguished moan. "Fuck."

Val's head spun. "God, you make me so hot. You are so sexy I can't stand it."

Brody turned her head, her eyes hazy and dazed. "That was… excellent."

"Thank you so much." Val grinned.

Brody laughed weakly. "You know exactly what I need."

"I wish I did," Val said softly. "I don't know everything about you, and I probably never will, but give me a chance, and I'll work on it."

"Take all the time you want." Brody kissed her. "I haven't been very fair, have I. I'm sorry. There were things I should have told you."

Val tilted her head, tried to read her eyes. "Don't make me guess."

Brody let out a long breath and pushed herself up on the pillows. Something between them held in the balance.

Val moved away enough so they were still touching but gave Brody some distance. Brody's hand moved to her thigh and Val clasped it, intertwined their fingers. "Tell me?"

Brody stared straight ahead, her palm icy cold. "My mother had me when she was just barely sixteen. Her parents threw her out. They were religious. She went to live with her father's brother, who believed in practicing a different kind of religion, I guess. He had a bunch of kids, one boy a little older than her who already had a kid of his own. Her uncle was strict, like her parents, and his kids were pretty rebellious. My mother never said much, but I think something went on between her and the older cousin because, as soon as she could, she moved out with me. I was about two. We lived in a trailer park, not this one, but one a lot like it."

Out of the corner of her eye Val caught Brody's small, sad smile. She tried to imagine what Brody's life had been like, what her mother's had been like. She couldn't, not really. Her experience growing up had been so different, so blissfully unaware and narrow. She could only be grateful she was hearing this now, when maybe she'd outgrown some of her youthful self-centeredness enough to appreciate how much trust it took to share this. When Brody fell silent, Val said softly, "She kept you, and she took you out of a bad place. That was brave."

"She did the best she could." Brody's voice had strengthened, and her sensual mouth tightened. "I didn't get all of this at the time, not until I was old enough to put the pieces together. But by the time I was ten, she was using, entertaining for money, and the cousin was coming around again. I'll never know if she wanted him around or if it was because he was the one that was bringing her the drugs. Maybe the two were the same thing."

"Bastard," Val muttered.

"Yeah, anyhow. When I was fourteen, just about, Duane, that was his name, had delivered something, heroin I think now, and my mother OD'd. I turned him in, they busted him with enough of the stuff to charge him with distribution, and he went to jail."

"And your mother?"

Brody shook her head.

"I'm so sorry."

"Yeah, me too." Brody let out a long breath. "But Duane died in prison. He got shanked. I have to say, I was glad. His son Lloyd—you met him the other night at Bottoms Up…"

"The jerk who hassled you," Val murmured, her stomach curdling.

"Yeah, that's him. He blamed me for his father. At first it was just your normal kind of bullying, verbal mostly, a shove here or there, but the older he got, the more he hated."

"Did anyone know?"

Brody shook her head. "No, I was living with the Riverses by then—Flann and I'd gotten to be friends." She laughed. "Believe it or not, we were in the chess club together. I have a knack for it, and I used to beat Flann's ass regularly. That really bothered her."

Val lifted Brody's hand and kissed the back of her knuckles. Anger warred with a helpless urge to reach back and change the past. Of course she couldn't, and Brody didn't need her to. She kept her tone teasing. "So naturally you two became friends."

"Yeah." Brody gave her an appreciative smile, some of the shadows leaving her eyes. "What good are friends if you can't compete and make each other better?"

Val pretended to roll her eyes. "Well, you two certainly did a good job."

Brody settled back a little more into the pillows, resting their clasped hands on Val's thigh. The taut lines of her body relaxed. "Anyhow, when I ended up pretty much homeless after my mother died, Flann's family took me in. I don't know why I didn't tell anyone about Lloyd. Guess I just figured he'd get tired of it eventually."

"And you're stubborn and like to take care of things yourself." Val kissed her cheek. "Not a criticism, by the way."

Brody snorted. "Probably not the best call at the time. Lloyd had a crew that hung with him, and things kinda escalated until one morning when I was out riding my motorcycle alone. He ran me off the road with his truck."

"My God, Brody!" Val had never been very confrontational, certainly not physically, but she had a sudden, intense desire to hunt that man down and hurt him. The impulse came from somewhere deep inside, some primitive place that drove animals to protect their mates. She shivered, the fury an inferno turning her blood to ice. "That goes a little beyond bullying. He tried to kill you."

"Maybe," Brody said with infuriating nonchalance. "It's hard to know. Maybe he got carried away in the moment, maybe didn't even mean to force me off the road, but when I walked out of the emergency room pretty battered and with a concussion, he was waiting in the emergency room parking lot. He told me next time it wouldn't be me. It might be Flann or Margie or someone else I cared about."

"Did you tell anyone?"

"No," Brody said. "I waited until I recovered a little bit, kept my head down, and when I could, I packed my bags and joined the Army."

"Why? Why keep it a secret?"

"Because I couldn't prove anything. Because it would've been my word against his, and he had plenty of friends who would've said he was somewhere else, and because I believed him." Brody shifted, took Val's other hand. "He hated me enough to kill someone I cared about or at least hurt them, and I couldn't let that happen."

"So they don't know, Flann and the others."

"No."

Val nodded, let the past and her fury go. Brody had made a choice, one that made sense to her at the time. What mattered now was the present. Their present. "You think it's him, with the tires and the dog?"

"I can't think of anyone else. Maybe it's not him but one of his friends, one of his old crew."

"You can't let him do this."

"I know." Brody rubbed her eyes. "I'm not sure exactly what to do about it."

"Well, for starters, you need to talk to Tom Kincaid."

"I don't have any proof."

"No, maybe not, but it's still the right place to start. And, Brody…" Val searched for the right words. Brody needed to make her own decisions, but she had a stake in this too. If anyone hurt Honcho or Brody, she didn't know what she'd do.

"I know." Brody smiled wryly. "I need to talk to Flann and the others. Better late than never, right?"

"She's family. They all are."

Brody cupped Val's face, leaned close, her gaze impossibly dark, inescapably intense. "I don't know how dangerous this situation could be. Maybe it's nothing, just a little leftover anger and he'll be finished now. But I don't want you—"

Val pressed her fingers to Brody's mouth. "Did you mean what you said a little while ago, about loving me? Or was that just sex talking?"

Brody gently moved Val's fingers, kissed each one. "It was definitely sex talking."

Val laughed and Brody grinned.

"Nice," Val murmured, her body quickening at the memory.

"It was that," Brody said thickly, "*and* I meant it more than I've ever meant anything in my life. I swear."

"Then you don't get to decide for me or for us. If there's going to *be* an us, I'm not going anywhere."

"Do you want there to be an us?" Brody asked, her voice tight with trepidation and hope.

"Why do you think I'm here?" Val framed Brody's face, kissed her. "As far as I'm concerned, there already is."

Brody pulled her close, kissed her until Val pushed her down and straddled her.

"You think you can distract me that way?" Val asked breathlessly.

"Thought I'd try." Brody grinned.

"You're going to talk to them? Kincaid and the Riverses?"

"I will. Soon."

Val nodded. "Soon is good. Right now, though, you have other things to take care of."

Brody swept her hands down Val's back, settled her legs between Val's thighs. "I'll get right to it."

Chapter Twenty-five

Between Val's regular client schedule, the fair demands, and her on-call shifts, Brody only managed to find Val alone a few times during the next few days. Every time she did, the sun came out a little more, her heart felt a little lighter, and the world righted itself.

On Sunday, when neither of them had anything on the schedule, Val pulled up in front of the trailer and Brody came out with Honcho by her side. Val rolled down the window. She was dressed for a casual day in gray linen pants and a short-sleeved navy silk shirt. "Hi."

"Hi." Brody leaned down and kissed her. She hadn't done that for almost twenty-four hours. She hungered for it, the way she would have if she'd gone without a meal for a couple of days.

Make that more than a couple of days. A couple of weeks, maybe.

Val put her arm out the window and caressed the back of Brody's neck, holding her in place while she kissed her back, thoroughly and with an urgency to match Brody's.

"Okay then," Val said breathlessly. "It is a *very* good morning."

"That makes up for about a tenth of what I'm in need of."

Val laughed. "Is that right?"

"Yep." Brody was pretty damned content just standing there looking at her. Happier than she'd ever been in her life. But after a few seconds, the urge to put her hands on her came roaring back. "Maybe we could find some excuse—"

Val shook her head. "Oh no. We are going. Get in."

"Yeah, you're right." Brody opened the back door, Honcho hopped in, and she got in the passenger's side. She needed to do this, she knew. She wanted to do it, *had* wanted to do it for years. Probably since the day she'd left. Looking back, she saw now she'd had other choices—better choices—but she forgave herself for not having the best judgment at the time. She knew the others would forgive her too. At least, she hoped they all would.

Val drove the four miles to the homestead and pulled in behind a jumble of trucks, 4x4s, and an SUV. She shut off the engine and turned to Brody, her fingers dancing over Brody's neck and shoulder. "It's going to be fine."

"I know." Brody took her hand, kissed the back of her knuckles. "Thank you for being here. You could have waited until the smoke cleared—assuming it does."

"No, I couldn't." Val rubbed her palm over Brody's jeans-clad thigh. "This is not the kind of thing you should do alone. And since you're not alone any longer, I'm here."

Brody sighed. "It might take me a while to get used to that."

"That's okay, we have time." Val smiled that sexy seductive smile that made Brody want to grab her and drag her into the bedroom. "And hey, I'm as nervous as you are. I'm the new girl on the scene, and… your girl. So, you know, it feels like my first time here even though I know them all."

"You're the first girl I've ever brought here." Brody traced a finger along her jaw. "And the last."

"Good," Val said with a husky finality that gave Brody a picture of endless tomorrows, of possibilities she hadn't yet plumbed but couldn't wait to explore. She leaned over and kissed Val gently on the mouth. "I love you."

Val cupped her face. "I love you too."

Brody waited until after the big family lunch, where everyone had found seats around the enormous oak table, Carson's toddler Davey balanced on his father's lap, Margie and Blake banging shoulders next to each other, Flann across from Abby, Harper opposite Presley, Edward at one end and Ida at the other. Edward and Harper and Flann falling naturally into discussion of a medical case, and Ida letting them go on for a minute or two before reminding them, "Sunday dinner."

The family. Her family. She sat on Harper's right, just like always, but now, Honcho lay stretched out next to the screen door and Val sat across from her. Val laughing, talking to Carson about some book they were both reading, Bill nodding solemnly when Brody mentioned what she did now, knowing that he knew what she had done before this, connecting in that wordless way that veterans did.

When the coffee came, Brody cleared her throat. "So there's something I wanted to tell you all."

The silence enveloped her, but she didn't feel alone. The faces that turned to hers were encouraging, accepting. All except for Flann's. Her wary gaze simmered, making the darkness in her eyes hard to read. When Brody'd nearly finished the story, Flann pushed back her chair, scraping it on the scarred oak floor, and walked out.

Watching the stiff set of Flann's shoulders as she sidestepped Honcho and shoved the screen door open, Brody let out a breath and finished what she had to say. "That's the whole of it. Except that I'm sorry."

Val reached across the table for her hand and Brody grasped it, nodding gratefully.

"You have nothing to be sorry for, Brody," Ida said. "You weren't at fault, for any part of it. And if there's ever a next time—even a possibility—you will tell us."

"Yes, ma'am."

"We're proud of everything you've accomplished," Edward said, "and very glad that you're home."

Harper nodded and leaned back in her chair. "Mama and Dad are right. You're back where you belong here, and that's what matters. Besides, Presley's got big plans for you."

Presley laughed, and so did Brody. Carson, Bill, and the teens echoed Harper, and Brody almost saw her way clear to breathe easy for the first time since she'd left home. Almost, but not just yet.

"Well, I think I'll take a walk." Brody squeezed Val's hand. "Be back soon."

Val's gaze was as warm and comforting as a caress. "No hurry. I'll be here."

"Thanks." Brody told Honcho to stay and walked out onto the porch. Everyone else got up from the table and began clearing the dishes, just like any other Sunday. She took a long breath of the hot afternoon air. One more battle left.

Flann was nowhere in sight, but Brody knew where to find her. She threaded her way down the grassy slope behind the house, scattering annoyed chickens as she went, and followed a narrow trail through the copse of tall oaks and pines that looked out over the river. The tree house looked exactly the same. Weathered rough board siding, brown tin roof, a rope ladder looped around a big horizontal branch that supported part of the cabin floor. She grabbed the rope and climbed up the way she'd done a hundred times before, swaying a little as the rope twisted, the sun on her back and the scent of earthy fields like a rich, dark cloud around her. When she shouldered the hatch, half expecting it to be locked from the inside, it opened easily on well-used hinges. They'd been coming back here still, Flann and Harper. All the times they'd huddled here, planning some adventure, came back with the sweet ache of memory, and she pushed her way up and inside.

The square room with mismatched windows and cast-off furniture hadn't changed. The view from the window, framed by leafy branches, still seemed to stretch forever over acres of gold and green.

Flann sat on a wooden camp stool by the windows, her back to the room. Brody found another one in the corner and pulled it over. Flann didn't look at her, so she waited.

"Kincaid," Flann said flatly after a while. "He's certain he can't do anything about what Lloyd did back then?"

"No. It's just my word about the accident. No witnesses, no report, and after all this time…no way to make a case. Probably wouldn't have been, even then."

Flann cursed.

Brody waited some more. "I told him what I suspected, about the truck and Honcho. He talked to Lloyd, and Lloyd came off clean on that—at least he had a good alibi for the whole night, and plenty of people said he'd been in the bar from before I showed up and never left."

"Doesn't mean he wasn't behind it," Flann growled. "Bullies never change."

"Could be, but he's been warned now, and he knows Kincaid will be watching him." Brody thought Kincaid was probably right—Lloyd wasn't likely to want law enforcement to be keeping tabs on him. "Kincaid figures it was Donnie Winslow—he's an old friend of Lloyd's, and always a follower. He either did it to impress Lloyd or maybe Lloyd gave him the idea. He was in the area that night—he ended up putting his truck in a ditch not far from my place."

Flann shook her head. "Son of a—I worked on him in the ER."

"Donnie was scared out of his pants when Kincaid questioned him," Brody said. "Chances are good it's over and done. All of it."

Flann finally swung around to face Brody, her eyes snapping. "What the hell, Brody. Why didn't you tell me what was going on back then?"

Brody shrugged. No way to make it sound any better now. "I believed Lloyd when he said he wasn't done. I believed one of them was really going to hurt someone, and you'd want to go after them. I also figured you'd get your ass kicked. If I wasn't here, that would be the end of it."

Flann gave her a long hard look. "Maybe, maybe they would've tried something. You're right—I would've gone after them. I might not have gotten my ass kicked, though."

Brody snorted.

Flann laughed and shook her head. "I feel like doing it now, but I *am* a little older and just a tiny bit wiser."

"Oh yeah, I kinda noticed that," Brody said, the coil of tension starting to ease between her shoulder blades.

"I've got a family." Flann sounded almost surprised and definitely pleased. "And a lot of other things that matter to me."

"I know what you mean."

"That includes you, you know." Flann's voice was gruff.

Brody squeezed Flann's shoulder. "I'm sorry about the time it took me to get here. I'm sorry about all the time we missed."

"Ah well. You probably would've done it anyhow. Joined up, I mean. It was the right thing for you." Flann draped an arm around Brody's shoulders, squeezed for a second, and let go. "Hell, look at you now. You're back where you belong, and that's what matters."

"So we're square?"

Flann huffed. "Well yeah, until the next time you make some boneheaded decision."

"Yeah, right." Brody grinned.

"So," Flann said as they climbed down. "Valentine, huh?"

"Yep."

Flann shot her a look. "Serious?"

"Oh yeah."

"For both of you?"

"That's what she says," Brody said.

"She looks it," Flann said. "Good for you."

"Yeah." Brody looked up toward the house where the family had gathered on the back steps, in the rocking chairs, leaning against the porch rails, talking and laughing. Val caught her eye across the distance, smiled that smile that was just for her.

"Perfect for me."

About the Author

Radclyffe has written sixty romance and romantic intrigue novels as well as a paranormal romance series, The Midnight Hunters, as L.L. Raand.

She is a three-time Lambda Literary Award winner in romance and erotica and received the Dr. James Duggins Outstanding Mid-Career Novelist Award by the Lambda Literary Foundation. A member of the Saints and Sinners Literary Hall of Fame, she is also an RWA/FF&P Prism Award winner for *Secrets in the Stone*, an RWA FTHRW Lories and RWA HODRW winner for *Firestorm*, an RWA Bean Pot winner for *Crossroads*, an RWA Laurel Wreath winner for *Blood Hunt*, and a Book Buyers Best award winner for *Price of Honor* and *Secret Hearts*. She is also a featured author in the 2015 documentary film *Love Between the Covers*, from Blueberry Hill Productions.

In 2004 she founded Bold Strokes Books, one of the world's largest independent LGBTQ publishing companies, and is the current president and publisher.

Find her at facebook.com/Radclyffe.BSB, follow her on Twitter @RadclyffeBSB, and visit her website at Radfic.com.

Books Available From Bold Strokes Books

Dangerous Curves by Larkin Rose. When love waits at the finish line, dangerous curves are a risk worth taking. (978-1-63555-353-6)

Love to the Rescue by Radclyffe. Can two people who share a past really be strangers? (978-1-62639-973-0)

Love's Portrait by Anna Larner. When museum curator Molly Goode and benefactor Georgina Wright uncover a portrait's secret, public and private truths are exposed, and their deepening love hangs in the balance. (978-1-63555-057-3)

Model Behavior by MJ Williamz. Can one woman's instability shatter a new couple's dreams of happiness? (978-1-63555-379-6)

Pretending in Paradise by M. Ullrich. When travelwisdom.com assigns PR specialist Caroline Beckett and travel blogger Emma Morgan to cover a hot new couples retreat, they're forced to fake a relationship to secure a reservation. (978-1-63555-399-4)

Recipe for Love by Aurora Rey. Hannah Little doesn't have much use for fancy chefs or fancy restaurants, but when New York City chef Drew Davis comes to town, their attraction just might be a recipe for love. (978-1-63555-367-3)

The House by Eden Darry. After a vicious assault, Sadie, Fin, and their family retreat to a house they think is the perfect place to start over, until they realize not all is as it seems. (978-1-63555-395-6)

Uninvited by Jane C. Esther. When Aerin McLeary's body becomes host for an alien intent on invading Earth, she must work with researcher Olivia Ando to uncover the truth and save humankind. (978-1-63555-282-9)

Comrade Cowgirl by Yolanda Wallace. When cattle rancher Laramie Bowman accepts a lucrative job offer far from home, will her heart end up getting lost in translation? (978-1-63555-375-8)

Double Vision by Ellie Hart. When her cell phone rings, Giselle Cutler answers it—and finds herself speaking to a dead woman. (978-1-63555-385-7)

Inheritors of Chaos by Barbara Ann Wright. As factions splinter and reunite, will anyone survive the final showdown between gods and mortals on an alien world? (978-1-63555-294-2)

Love on Lavender Lane by Karis Walsh. Accompanied by the buzz of honeybees and the scent of lavender, Paige and Kassidy must find a way to compromise on their approach to business if they want to save Lavender Lane Farm—and find a way to make room for love along the way. (978-1-63555-286-7)

Spinning Tales by Brey Willows. When the fairy tale begins to unravel and villains are on the loose, will Maggie and Kody be able to spin a new tale? (978-1-63555-314-7)

The Do-Over by Georgia Beers. Bella Hunt has made a good life for herself and put the past behind her. But when the bane of her high school existence shows up for Bella's class on conflict resolution, the last thing they expect is to fall in love. (978-1-63555-393-2)

What Happens When by Samantha Boyette. For Molly Kennan, senior year is already an epic disaster, and falling for mysterious waitress Zia is about to make life a whole lot worse. (978-1-63555-408-3)

Wooing the Farmer by Jenny Frame. When fiercely independent modern socialite Penelope Huntingdon-Stewart and traditional country farmer Sam McQuade meet, trusting their hearts is harder than it looks. (978-1-63555-381-9)

Shut Up and Kiss Me by Julie Cannon. What better way to spend two weeks of hell in paradise than in the company of a hot, sexy woman? (978-1-163555-343-7)

Spencer's Cove by Missouri Vaun. When Foster Owen and Abigail Spencer meet, they uncover a story of lives adrift, loves lost, and true love found. (978-1-163555-171-6)

Bold Strokes Books
Quality and Diversity in LGBTQ Literature